THE BI

Joanna Kavenna grew up i .... s also lived in the USA, Fran. ..... ie Baltic States. Her first book, *The Ice Museum,* ...... at travelling in the North. Her second book, a novel called *Inglorious*, won the Orange Prize for New Writers. Kavenna's writing has appeared in the *London Review of Books*, the *Guardian* and *Observer*, the *Times Literary Supplement*, the *International Herald Tribune*, the *Spectator* and the *Daily Telegraph*, among other publications. She has held writing fellowships at St Antony's College, Oxford and St John's College, Cambridge. She currently lives in Duddon Valley, Cumbria.

Further praise for *The Birth of Love*:

'A clever novel that leaves you with haunting questions about what it means to give birth – a process we simultaneously take for granted and treat with fear.' *Daily Telegraph*

'Takes readers into terrain that is still relatively virgin – the visceral, slippery business of birth, and its human intimacies . . . a heady and ultimately moving annexation of fertile terrain for fiction.' *Prospect*

'Riveting . . . She manages to pull tighter and tighter a mighty number of scientific, mythical, historical and philosophical strands, all the while holding the cerebral and the worldly in good balance . . . A compelling and original writer.' Valerie Sayers, *Washington Post*

'To surrender yourself to the revelations of . . . life and then to come back with the assertions of prose: that is the new heroism of the woman writer, and Kavenna is in the vanguard.' Rachel Cusk, *Observer*

The Birth of Love

JOANNA KAVENNA

ff

faber and faber

First published in 2010
by Faber and Faber Limited
Bloomsbury House, 74–77 Great Russell Street,
London WC1B 3DA

This paperback edition first published in 2011

Typeset by Faber and Faber Limited
Printed in England by CPI Bookmarque, Croydon

A CIP record for this book
is available from the British Library

ISBN 978–0–571–24518–5

2 4 6 8 10 9 7 5 3 1

... There is neither a here nor a beyond, but the great unity in which the beings that surpass us, the 'angels', are at home ... We of the here and now are not for a moment hedged in the time world, nor confined within it ... we are incessantly flowing over and over to those who preceded us ...

RAINER MARIA RILKE

It is blessed to behold thee – come to the one who loveth thee! Come to the one who loveth thee, oh thou who art beautiful ...

LAMENT OF ISIS

To my parents and my brother, with love . . .

The year is 1865 and Ignaz Semmelweis is dragged along the corridor though he struggles violently, kicks and shouts.

At one point he forces himself out of their arms and starts to run.

Then they seize him again, and this time they beat him, so hard he thinks they might kill him.

There is a foot stamping on him from above.

He is choking on blood.

The Vienna General Hospital will vouch for me, he is trying to tell them. I have many powerful friends in Vienna, but then he remembers no one will vouch for him.

He is alone and they have tied his arms. They throw him into a room. A room stinking of human fear and sweat and dung, with a man somewhere crying, I am the Christ. I am the Christ.

The year is 2153 and Prisoner 730004 is forced into a cell. She wonders if everyone else has been captured. Or if they are dead already. 'This is for your own protection,' says a guard, as he thumps her in the spine, so she falls to the ground. Then he locks the door against her, though she runs to the grille and begs him to release her. She hears his footsteps fading away.

The year is 2009 and Brigid feels the birthing pains deep within her and knows it has begun . . .

The Great and Amorous Sky
Curved over the Earth . . .

The Moon

Monday August 15th, 1865, Vienna

Dear Professor Wilson,

I am sorry to disturb you from your work; however, I must ask your advice about a most distressing series of meetings I had today at the asylum. As you know, I have been visiting the asylum in Lazarettgasse for some years now, examining the inmates of this accursed place, better to understand the conditions which cause the individual to discard the faculty of reason. Today I met an inmate in such a terrible and perplexing condition, as to question every notion of lunacy I have thus far elaborated. I have – with reference to the many visits I make to 'lunatics' – been developing a theory that what we call madness is often simply a rearrangement of the human personality, or an arrangement which in some way offends more ordinary sensibilities. If we were to abandon the notion of sanity as strictly distinct from madness we would save many from suffering. We would perceive that madness is a lunar condition, a condition of revelation and vision and thereby we who have allowed our perceptions to be veiled by conventional observance can sometimes learn from those we refer to as lunatics. There are many forces within the human soul which we refuse to acknowledge, many ancient presences we have turned away from, and I suspect that these often command those we call lunatic, and cause them to behave in a way we cannot understand. This is my unpopular theory; yet I discovered today a case as resistant to my theorising as to more popular theories of madness. The man is in dire need of help.

I arrived at the asylum this morning at 9.00 a.m., and rang the bell. The door was opened, as usual, by one of the burly orderlies, who ushered me into the anteroom. The room is intended to appear homely; there are some armchairs and bookshelves with innocuous books of the hour upon them, and at the centre of the room, above the fireplace, is a mediocre painting of the Alps. Everything is superficially nondescript; yet, I always think as I stand there, it is the room in which so many of the inmates are committed by their families, and are taken away wailing and pleading, in horrible fear. Herr Meyer soon arrived, who is in charge of the asylum. He is always very smart and efficient, yet over the years I have come to regard him as an unpleasant man, quite brutalised by his work, or perhaps drawn to it precisely because of the vicious elements of his nature. He smells of cruelty, and his eyes are sharp and vigilant. His manner is sly, and I generally acknowledge him with a cursory good day and proceed to my business. This morning however he was rather excited – licking his lips, even, with a thick pink tongue – and he said, 'A very interesting case, the case of Herr S. Came here two weeks ago. Consigned to our care by some friends. A violent and incontinent man.'

'What manner of lunatic is he?' I asked.

'Well spoken. Clearly once an educated man. Accuses himself of murder. And others too. He cannot give you precise names however; he finds it hard to recall specific details. This is an aspect of his madness. You should see him for yourself,' he said, nodding in his insidious conspiratorial manner.

'I should be glad to. Do you have any more information about him?'

Herr Meyer adopted his most self-important tone. 'Oh I cannot reveal the further details to you, my good man. The family has asked me to maintain the strictest secrecy around Herr S. His identity must remain obscure to outsiders such as you. You surely understand, that my first concern is the protection of my patients and their families?'

I responded with the briefest of nods, and he, smirking a little, led me through the asylum, where there were rooms furnished with the damned, and then dark corridors lined with cells. There may be worse places on earth than Vienna's public asylum but at present I cannot imagine what corner of the globe might hold them. Its corridors echo with a ragged chorus – each madman finding his own discord, some of them little more than whoops and cackles, others strident and jangling. They rail, oh how they rail against those who sent them here, and those who have not come for them, and they know – at one level I believe they know – that they have been abandoned. The ones who do not talk, they turn expressions of such despair upon you, it is hard to think that they are beyond all comprehension. As we entered the communal rooms I was briefly held back by the smell of faeces and decay – but I have long been visiting these madhouses, and have sadly grown accustomed to this noxious atmosphere and all the suffering to which it attests. (Indeed I believe these poor individuals are hastened to their ends by the severity of the atmosphere in which they exist, that it is quite impossible for any human to be cured in these conditions, and the asylums in their present state must only ever be a prison for the lunatic. I have been campaigning along these lines for a few years, but my efforts have so far been in vain). As we walked I recognised a number of the long-term residents – an age-ing man in a grimy black suit, a tattered handkerchief in his pocket, one boot off and one boot on. He would mean-der around, saying very little, and then he would stop on one leg, or he would take ten skipping steps and then two broad strides, like a child playing a game. He was hesitating in the middle of the room, until Herr Meyer pushed him roughly aside. We passed another fellow I had seen many times before, a prematurely aged man with matted blond hair, who talked incessantly, mostly of colours, as if he were the author of a meticulous system – 'And there is the red. And there is the black and the blue. And there is the pur-ple. And now the red once more . . .' and so on. I have talked several times to this man, hoping to discern his sys-tem, if one exists, but I have not yet understood it. He sounded as if he came from Salzburg, and I had been told that no one came to visit him. He, too, received the rough edge of Herr Meyer's shoulder, because he presumed to approach us, and, thus rebuffed, he turned away. 'Now the black, and then the blue . . .'

Herr Meyer kept giving me odious smiles, as if we were sharing a marvellous joke. 'I demand a hearing, I demand a hearing,' said one of them as I passed, while Meyer snorted as if this was a sublime quip and ushered me on. His absolute and abiding assumption was that these people were worthless, subhuman, simply because their reason had failed. Men such as Meyer perceive their asylums as private kingdoms, governed by their own brutal laws, and they treat the inmates like animals for the most part, as if madness has deprived them of all humanity. Despite all the reforms in our legislation this continues to be the orthodoxy in many such places. I sometimes suspect that were Herr Meyer deprived of his fiefdom, he would fall out of the realm of the 'sane' and be instantly confined himself. Indeed one must observe that it is a very debased civilisation, which allows Herr Meyer to be grand arbiter over such fragile human souls!

Water trickled down the walls, a steady drip, and I thought of those lunatics with this constant noise in their ears, and all the remorseless ways in which they were stripped of dignity and deprived of any hope of recovery. We entered an area in which the inmates were confined to cells, and everything was cast into shadow, the sounds indistinct, though no less miserable. Now Herr Meyer stopped at a cell, and, with a sardonic flourish, opened the door. A man was sitting in the corner, in chains. The cell was so dark, I could hardly distinguish his features. He seemed from what little I could discern to be blunt-featured and stocky, and he was sitting very quietly, staring into space. Herr Meyer rattled his keys, and said in his leering way, 'Herr S, there's someone to see you.' He addressed the patient as if he had no claim to any form of kindness, and Herr S refused to respond. I wondered if he could not endure the nature of his confinement, and thereby refused to acknowledge his keeper. Or if his madness took him in the catatonic way, and made him mute.

9

'Oh Herr S,' said Meyer, in a taunting tone, and I said, 'That is enough, I will speak to this man alone, thank you.'

'He's chained up and cannot trouble you,' said Herr Meyer, unabashed and still presuming to be conspiratorial. Then he removed himself, and I turned to consider the man before me.

For the first few minutes Herr S did not look up. He seemed to be deep in thought and I hesitated to disturb him. As my eyes adjusted to the gloom I perceived his hair had fallen out in clumps, and his skin was drawn tight, like that of a reptile. His hands were covered in scratches, and there was a livid bruise on his forehead, a swelling on his mouth; testifying – I imagined – to the rough treatment he had already received from Herr Meyer's attendants.

After a time I said, 'Herr S,' again, and he lifted his head. Even then he stared into space, as if he did not see me.

'Herr S, as it seems I must call you, my name is Robert von Lucius,' I said. 'From time to time I visit the occupants of this asylum, the better to understand their conditions. I do not believe that the mad are beyond redemption and must be sequestered and ruined. I believe that many of those described as mad have greater access than I to the most profound mysteries of the human spirit, if only I could understand them better. For this reason, I am regarded with suspicion by some of my contemporaries. I do not care for their good opinion, except where their censure prevents me from doing my work. I would like to talk to you, if that is acceptable.'

Once more he said nothing, and I was unsure if he had heard me or understood my words.

I said, 'Is there anything you need?'

At that, his eyes fixed on me. I must confess that I was briefly unnerved by his gaze. It expressed such hopelessness, such a terrible absence of joy. It was horribly eloquent, though all it invoked was macabre and vile. There was a chaos to his limbs which dismayed me too. It was as if his bones had been broken and had mended strangely. Everything about his posture was ugly and awkward; everything about his gaze was desperate and beseeching. He opened his mouth to speak but no sound came. He sat in this way for some time, opening and shutting his mouth, and then he grabbed his hair – I now saw one of the causes of his mottled baldness – and began pulling frantically at a clump. I was obliged to look away, feeling that he should be permitted to pass through this fit without being observed. For some time, I examined the dank wall, with its patterns of mould and grime, and when I turned towards Herr S again I saw he had slipped into his former stupor.

I said, 'I would like to ask you how you came here, if I may. Herr Meyer told me you have been here for two weeks now.' At the name of his keeper, Herr S experienced another spasm. His body convulsed, he gripped the chains and opened his mouth as if to howl. There was fear in his face, and urgent entreaty.

'Is he here?' he said, in a whisper.

'No, he is not here. He will not return while I am with you,' I said.

'How long will you be here?'

11

'I do not know.'

'Please stay as long as you can,' he said.

'Are you afraid of Herr Meyer?'

'I am very afraid,' he said to me, still in this almost inaudible tone, so I had to lean forward to understand him.

'Of what are you afraid?'

'He will kill me. Perhaps he has already. The injuries I have sustained are in themselves life-threatening. I do not think I have much time left.'

'What are the injuries you have sustained?'

'I fear I must have internal bleeding of some fatal sort,' he said. 'They beat me very badly and though I was barely conscious by the end I believe they stamped on my chest. I felt something crack and puncture, and since then I have experienced acute abdominal pain and I fear haematemesis may develop.'

'You are certain they beat you in this way?' I said.

'I am quite certain they beat me though as I said I was confused by the end and so perhaps there are omissions in my account.'

His speech surprised me. He was wretched indeed, but the rancid Herr Meyer had assessed him correctly in one matter; he was clearly a man of education and former rank. This further piqued my curiosity, and I said, 'I should discuss this with Herr Meyer, demand an explanation.'

'Oh please do not. Do not tell him I said anything,' said Herr S. He really was in fear of his life. Even in his damaged state, even with his mind hanging in tatters, he wanted to live. This has always interested me about those we define as mad, this residual life urge most of them possess. They do not regard their lives as finished. If you were to offer them a pistol they would generally refuse the opportunity to take arms against their sea of troubles. Once more, this suggests to me that these confident distinctions we forge are fundamentally useless, and that if we are ever to advance we must pay more attention to the revelations of those we currently ignore. In this instance, Herr S was evidently afraid, and had no desire to end his suffering, or to have it ended by the ministrations of Herr Meyer.

I said, 'I will say nothing to him, I solemnly swear.'

At that he became a little calmer.

'I am told you arrived here two weeks ago,' I said. He nodded faintly. 'Where did you come from?'

'I am not sure,' he said. 'Where are we now?'

'We are in Vienna.'

'Vienna? I think I know that city well. I am not sure. When they beat me I perhaps sustained an injury to the brain. Something is wrong with my memory.'

'Do you think you might have been living in Vienna?'

'I believe I was on a train. I left my home . . .' He stopped, shaking his head.

'And where is your home?' I tried again.

'I have such headaches, as if a weight is clamped to my skull. There are great gaps in my memories. I think I was on a train – I remember the noise of a station. Trains hooting, smoke rising towards a great arched roof. There were many people there; I remember I was upset by the crowds. I think I shouted at a man, "Get away from me!" He had approached too close, and I feared contagion. Then there was someone I remembered from the past, a good friend. I was so pleased to see him. I stretched out my hand to greet him. But you are here! How marvellous! How have you

13

been? I think I was wearing a suit. I was well dressed, not like this' – and he gestured to his soiled and ripped clothes. 'I was not ashamed of myself at all, as I should be now, if this friend came to see me here. I cannot remember what happened after that. There are many things I cannot remember. You say I have been here two weeks, but I have few memories of recent days. Just a grave sense of coursing regret. A feeling as if I am descending into thick black night and shall never see the dawn again.'

'You are not Viennese by birth, I assume.' I said this because the man's German, though impeccable, was Magyar in inflection and emphasis. I meant it to be a benign enquiry, yet the question seemed to anger him, because he stared suddenly towards me, and clenched his fists.

'Forgive me, but I believe you come from the Hungarian Lands?' I persisted.

'I do not know. If you say so, perhaps it is true.'

'You do not remember this either?'

'I think I do not. It is as if . . . there is a barrier standing between me and the past. A wall. A forbidding wall – grown over with ivy. I see the wall, and I note that it is high and I cannot scale it. Beyond that, I am confined.' He stopped and rubbed his forehead, frenetically. He continued this action for some minutes, until I thought I must distract him. So I said, 'Do you have any idea why you were brought here?'

'I believe I am an inconvenience to someone,' he said. 'Someone has finally tired of me. I am not sure who that is. There are many who might have grown tired of me by now.'

'Why is that?'

'Because of what I have said. Because of the charges I bring against them.'

14

'Against whom?'

'Oh, countless numbers of them. Murderers, all of them,' he said. And he leaned towards me and said, 'Because of this I have my suspicions they are trying to destroy me. They are watching me and trying to destroy me.'

In my years of studying the mad, or this category of humans we refer to thus, I have become quite accustomed to such expressions, and indeed there is a constant pattern in the pronouncements of certain sorts of more intelligent lunatics, a tendency to fashion repeated accusations against a general 'they', a gang of conspirators, assumed to be plotting against the insane individual. Frequently these accusations lack any foundation in reality; they are more symbolically representative of a sense of being cast out, or of feeling oneself beleaguered by events and powerless to control them. Naturally, were we all to dwell on the inscrutable workings of the universe, we might easily slip into this state – we are here, in an uncertain realm of death and destruction, and there is no possible way we can predict our futures, and at any moment everything we love may be taken from us, by disease, or war, or calamity of some other sort. Might we not quite reasonably propose that there is someone plotting our demise? Indeed is this not the central tenet of many of our religions, when they proclaim that there is a deity observing our every movement, listening in to our every thought, and constantly assessing us, for glory or punishment? Are not such religious men as Job repeatedly cast down by their creator, precisely to test their endurance? By the teachings of the Old Testament, Job would have been perfectly sensible in believing that a 'someone' was conspiring against him; God was indeed doing this, for His own great and all-knowing purpose, no doubt, but it was conspiracy all the same. Many such parables do not even offer glory – they entreat the believer to aim at nothing higher than the avoidance of punishment, to petition only for mercy. As our religions derive from the deepest yearnings of the human spirit, such beliefs must express an innate hope that our actions matter to someone, that some meaningful process of judgement is being applied to our lives. In childhood, we resist our parents, while needing them to observe us all the same, praise us for our good works and censure us for our bad. And once we have passed beyond the sight of our parents, we summon our divinities, to observe and assess us once more. For life without a committed observer is aimless indeed: we are alone, and no one minds what actions we take.

This is merely a theory of mine, Professor Wilson; I expect you will disagree. Nonetheless Herr S evinced a firm and – I thought at the time – generic sense that somebody was plotting his downfall, and he looked antic indeed as he informed me of his suspicions, widening his eyes and wringing his hands, as if he must cleanse them.

'These people you describe, whom have they murdered?' I said.

There was a long pause, which I allowed to develop. He sat there, hanging his head, and finally, after some minutes, he said, 'We are murderers, all of us. I am the worst of all. But they are steeped in blood too. I have murdered thousands. And they also. The difference is I admit it. I accuse myself,' and now he became a little excited, and raised his voice. 'I accuse myself of murder. Thousands of souls. I have killed thousands. Mothers and wives, laid waste.'

'The victims were all women?'

'Oh yes, the massacre was only of women. I have dreams in which I – well, it is best not to speak of them.'

'I would be most interested to hear of your dreams, if you are able to relay them,' I said. 'I believe that dreams may offer an oblique portrait of our fears and desires, because when we dream we enter a realm of ambiguity and ellipsis, and thereby much that is lost in everyday speech may be regained.'

'My dreams are all of blood.'

Herr Meyer had warned me that self-accusation formed the main theme of Herr S's conversation, and I perceived that it was inappropriate to dismiss his concerns. I find it is best in these circumstances to treat such pronouncements as fundamentally symbolic, suggestive of a state of being rather than revelatory of criminal actions, and so I felt the best course would be to allow Herr S to talk, to rail, rather, and to write down his words. With this in mind, I drew out my notebook, and this action made him all the more excited. He pointed at it and said, 'Oh yes, mark it down. Mark it down and set it all before the judge. I deserve judgement, and I will be judged if not in this life then in the next, if there is such a place.'

'I am not writing it down so that you may be judged,' I said. 'I merely want to hear what you have to say.'

'Who has sent you?' he said, suddenly, his mood changing again. He flashed a furtive glance towards me, as if I too posed a threat to his safety. 'Why do you want to know these things?'

'I am a scholar, of sorts. That is, without an attachment to a university, I make researches into those we regard as insane. This has been my interest for many years. I have published various books on the subject, and though my opinions are not at all fashionable there are some who are kind enough to consider them of importance.'

'You are a doctor?' he said. Something in his face changed. The light was so precarious, it was tantalisingly difficult to read his expressions, but I thought I discerned something more focused in his aspect. He was sporadically animated, as I said, but this was a more intent and questioning focus, as if he were truly attending to my words.

I said that I was not a doctor, merely a man of independent means who liked to conduct researches. But he was not listening at this point.

'Do you work at the hospital?' he said.

'Which hospital are you thinking of?'

'I do not know. Where is it? Nearby I think.'

'The General Hospital, here in Vienna?'

'Yes, I think so. I think that is what I mean.'

'I do not work there. I am not a doctor, as I explained before. I work mostly from home. I read and write in my study, and then I visit asylums and avail myself of any opportunity to speak with the patients. I visit this asylum roughly every two weeks. I must have made my last visit shortly before your arrival.'

'My arrival?'

'Yes, you came here two weeks ago.'

'I have been in this cell for two weeks?'

I reaffirmed that he had.

'Did you bring me here?'

'No, I did not.'

'Why am I here?' Now he was inflamed, seeking to rise from his chair, though it seemed he was too weak to move,

18

and, though he was perhaps unaware of them at that moment, his hands and feet were anyway in chains.

'I am not certain,' I said, when he had calmed himself a little. 'We were recently discussing it and you could not remember. You said you came on a train. There was a friend of yours there.'

'A friend? I did not think I had any friends left.'

'You said he was an old friend. You were pleased to see him.'

'Why are you telling me these things?'

I explained again who I was.

'Why do you keep talking about the insane? I am in prison, am I not? Surely I have been convicted, finally, of murder?' he said.

'You are not in prison,' I said. 'You have been brought to a place where you will be treated for what is perceived as your condition. I fear this treatment will do you no good at all.'

'I do not need treatment,' he said, angrily. 'I need to be punished.'

'Sadly this is indeed a punishment, nonetheless.'

'What do they propose to do to me?'

'I do not know the precise nature of your treatment. I am not an insider here. I am permitted access simply because of various friendships I have developed. I have no medical status at all.'

'But where, where did I come from? I cannot remember. My mind is full of darkness,' he said.

As we fell silent I heard – I imagine he did too – the cries of a man in a neighbouring cell. 'God God God,' the man was crying, over and over again, so it pained me to hear his incessant delivery of this word. '*GOD GOD GOD.*' This poor man, entreating a deity who had either forsaken him or had allocated him a life of suffering. For it was certain this neighbour was suffering, mired in despair and begging his God to help him to comprehend it, to endure it. In the silence of the cell, this word echoed around us, and I thought that even had Herr S been entirely lucid when he arrived in this place then merely a day of this would have delivered him into another state of being. When I looked again, he was staring into space, having assumed once more an expression of dull defeat.

'You were interested in the General Hospital. Why is that, I wonder?' I said.

'I am not sure. The thought of it frightens me. I see it as a place of suffering and death.'

'It is common to feel like this about hospitals.'

'Perhaps I was there once. Perhaps I was ill.'

'Herr S, you are an educated man. Earlier you discussed internal bleeding with confidence. Perhaps you have worked at the hospital?'

'I am not sure.' Now he began rubbing his forehead again. I could not tell what the man might have looked like in a happier era. Perhaps in his youth he was stout and fair, though he would even then, I imagine, have been balding and with a tendency to corpulence. I could see he might once have responded passionately to elements around him – his work, or a beloved girl, or his friends. His moods shift-ed constantly, and this might in youth have made him rest-less, precocious perhaps. I was uncertain how old he might be now. He was bent and wrinkled, and his remaining hair was white. But his voice was firm; his movements unencumbered by decrepitude. I suspected he was a prematurely grizzled man of fifty or so; that he had perhaps suffered from a traumatic experience which had etched lines upon his face.

'I think perhaps I have been ill for some time,' he was saying, as he rubbed his forehead in his desperate way. 'I am not sure. I have such scenes in my brain . . . I cannot . . .'

'What sort of scenes?'

'It is as if everything happened a very long time ago. Something dreadful occurred. I have a sense of a terrible crime. I think I committed it, but there were many accomplices. I wonder if I have committed it and hidden the evidence, and this is why I am here. They will interrogate me, will they not? They seek to unearth my secret, I trust?'

At that, his dull eyes turned towards me.

'You are in an asylum,' I said, again. 'There are many inmates here who do not deserve the epithet "mad". Indeed perhaps all of you. Yet your keepers are woefully uninterested in your inner thoughts. They seek merely to suppress you.'

'You are not being honest,' he said. 'I know I am to be tortured, and you are lying to me.' He was preparing to rage but then I said very quietly and calmly, 'I assure you, I will not lie to you. Essentially I do not know anything about you. I am merely telling you what I think is the case. If you disagree with me that is perfectly understandable, but I am not lying. Because I am not an insider, they will not tell me anything about you. Herr Meyer is a corrupt man, but he does not like me. So he has not told me your name, and he will not inform me of any of the particulars of your case.'

At this, he stopped rubbing his forehead and placed his

hands on his lap. Then he looked down at his hands.

'All you are saying in your . . . pretty words . . . is that you have no power and they will torture me anyway.'

'With respect, I am not saying that at all. I am saying that I should like to talk to you, that I seek to understand you, if you will permit me to stay here a little while.'

'You will understand me!' he said, scornfully. 'I do not think you would like that very much. There is something within me – I have a dim recollection of it, and it makes me shudder with fear . . . I am not sure I want to remember the rest . . . I long to sleep, but it is so uncomfortable. I long to sleep and be oblivious . . . But it seems I am always awake, and always there is this sense . . . of something . . .'

'Do you think you have fallen into your present condition as a response to a particular event, to something dreadful that has occurred?'

That seemed to irritate him once more. He snapped back at me, 'I do not know, how should I know? I am in darkness, and you ask me what I think?'

'I am sorry if my questions seem inappropriate to you. I do not want to upset you.'

'You have no power to upset me at all. Your voice is very faint, very distant. There is a roaring in my head, I can barely hear you beneath the roaring. I am adrift on a . . . poisonous . . . boiling ocean. I cannot see the shore. I have been cast off, sent to drift until I drown . . .'

Professor Wilson, do you not think this conversation was relatively cogent, if you will permit a qualified use of the word? I have had many a discussion with the inmates of asylums, and it is rare that they speak in this manner. By this I mean that they are usually far less self-aware, far

more deeply ensconced in the private or other world to
which they have gained access. They have nearly forgotten
the language of their former lives, the cadences of conventional speech. But Herr S was still quite fluent in such
everyday modes. He was aware of his condition, to a notable
degree. Naturally, he railed and lapsed into symbolical
utterance at times, when the moon was working its mischief
within him; he was moving constantly between worlds, the
lunar and the solar: he was neither of one nor the other. I
wrote down some notes, trying to express some of this and
also to record my immediate impressions of the man, and
all the while Herr S was sitting thoughtfully in his chains.
The only consistent sign of distress was the repetitive
movement he made with his hands. This was a horrible
motion, as if all his suppressed energies were finding an
outlet through his hands. Yet in many ways he was surpris-
ingly measured. When I asked him a question, he often
thought about his answer before he spoke. He was struggling to use his addled brain, though it was clear that organ
had indeed suffered a form of injury – whether before or
after his arrival in the asylum I could not ascertain – that it
was not functioning correctly. I suspect that he knew his so-
called reason had deserted him, or been terribly compro-
mised. Most inmates of these institutions have no more
notion of reason, and what it is to be in a 'reasonable' state,
than you or I have of what it means to have fallen into
unreason. If one accepts that it is in dreams that we
encounter our inner madness, these ordinarily fettered
forces of misrule, then the inmates I meet are living in the
world of dreams, and cannot return to the daytime realm.
Nonetheless Herr S was in a lucid dream, aware that he
was dreaming, and sometimes, briefly, he woke altogether.

He woke and stared around, recognised familiar objects, then he slipped into his dream state again. This must have been most distressing for him, and I think this was the cause of his sudden rages. Yet I am not sure.

I said, 'Why do you believe that you have done something awful, in the past? On what do you base this assertion?'

'I dream of blood,' he said. 'I dream of torrents of blood. A sea of blood. I am swimming in a sea of blood. I am wholly encased in blood. Yet I am not drowning. I can breathe in the blood. Blood is my natural métier, in my dream. I imbibe the blood and am nourished by blood. I am very peaceful and happy. Perhaps I am smiling as I drink down blood. When I wake from these dreams I am sweating and crying. I wake in my cell to the sounds of others screaming and though I try to summon the memory of this blood – to understand its import and also because something deep within me craves it – I cannot.'

'You say that you are glad of the blood. What do you think this means?'

'I am not sure.'

'What other dreams do you have? Are there any others of significance?'

'There is one, in which I am searching for something in the blood. In this dream I am not in the blood, I am outside it. But I am reaching my hands into it. When I take out my hands they are coated in blood. There is something in the blood that I must find. I feel it is very important that I find this thing quickly. If I do not, I feel something terrible will occur. It is of the utmost importance that I find this thing.'

'Do you ever find it?'

'No,' he said. 'Sometimes I think I am about to, that soon

it will become clear what it is and yet . . . I cannot see it. It is lost in the blood. I fear I have lost it myself, that I am responsible for the loss of this thing. In my dream I feel a dreadful sense of grief and as if I must die of guilt.' Then he fell silent. He was still wringing his hands, and with each of these movements his chains rattled. The rattling was persistent and annoying, but I could not ask him to desist. He seemed to find the hand-wringing somehow comforting; certainly I rarely saw him stop it. As I made my notes, I wondered if it was not the case that these dreams of blood suggested a fear of life, of the conditions of living. I was thinking of the classical notion of the contamination of the soul by birth: the suggestion of Origen, for example, that everyone who enters the world is afflicted with a kind of contamination – because they reside in their mother's womb, and because the source from which they take their body is the father's seed, and thereby they are contaminated in respect of the father and the mother. I thought perhaps Herr S perceived life as a form of contamination, that this dream represented the striving of his confused soul for something higher than the life around him, and that this striving had severed him from ordinary human congress.

I have seen such self-loathing before; indeed such sentiments are often regarded as perfectly necessary and even devout by many of those who follow our major creeds. I have seen these beliefs become rigid in the asylums, drawing many into terrible visions of damnation. It begins with mere conventional piety, and descends into individual mayhem. Thereby believers come to despise the blood which flows through their bodies, and which sustains them. They come to despise it and to hope for a time when it will cease to move in their veins and they will be purged and resurrected clean. For does it not say in the teachings of Ben Sira, 'Of the woman came the beginning of sin, and through her we all die' – through birth we all die into life, torn from the side of our father God? The mother betrays us, drags us away from our spiritual parent, the invisible Father. So millions of humans have been persuaded that the questing soul must deny the mother and the earth; that the divine is not present among us but lies far beyond us. I wondered if Herr S had simply allowed his heart to be commanded by such teachings; and thus he feared this blood he imagined, believed his yearning for it was treacherous and must condemn him.

My good Professor Wilson, these are rather vague musings, and I hope you will forgive me. I have often been criticised for the diffusion and inconsequentiality of my thought, and I am quite aware that my opinions are not widely held. And indeed even to those who may agree, such proposals might well seem superfluous to the sad case of Herr S. I am only recording them, indeed, that you may perceive how I have tried to understand him, how many theories I have fashioned. This was how my thoughts ran at this time, and I allowed myself a few moments to note them down.

When I lifted my head, and stopped my pen, Herr S had fallen once more into silence. Hoping to rouse him again, I said, 'Do you have other recurring thoughts?'

'Oh yes,' he said. 'Many thoughts.'

Then he shuddered, horribly, so violently that I thought he must be falling into a fit. He rattled the chains and his whole body convulsed, and he said, 'Oh I cannot speak about them, they are too . . . They are . . .'

'Can you disclose any of them at all?'

'There is a name. A name which hammers in my thoughts. It is the name of a woman – I dread to tell it.'

'If you can, then perhaps we can shed some more light on your condition.'

'My "condition"? That is a fine word for it!'

'Why are you afraid of telling me the name of this woman?'

'She is a woman with bright blue eyes. Flaxen hair, I think. She is very angry with me. I fear I shall anger her further. She is furious and I believe she is tormenting me. I am being punished for the death of this woman.'

'You know she is dead?'

'I know it because I killed her.'

'Why do you believe this to be the case?'

'She appears to me – she was here just the other day, and she accused me with her eyes. They were piercing my flesh. My body burned when she looked upon me. And there was a pain at my core – here' – and he pounded on his chest – 'as her eyes burned into me.'

'You think you knew this woman?'

'I did not know her. I met her somewhere, I cannot remember where. I met her and then shortly afterwards – a few days perhaps – she was dead.'

'Herr S, I would be most interested to know what you call this woman.'

'I cannot tell you,' he said. He was shuddering; the man was shaking in the depths of his dread.

So I said, 'Are there any other names you remember?'

'Not names but faces and they are all screwed up in agony and there are red marks on them, around the hollows of the eyes and on the gaunt cheeks. They are women's faces and they are stricken with pain. They appear to me on the wall. I wake and I see them arrayed on the wall before me. Thousands and thousands, perhaps, I am not sure, and I think they are all this woman . . .'

'All of them are the same woman?'

'No they do not look the same. They are not physically the same. But somehow they are all her, I believe them to be her. When these women appear before me they are not like her though they are somehow her but these women have their eyes screwed up in agony and I am fearful, so very fearful, lest they open their eyes. I am writhing in torment, waiting for them to open their eyes and burn me. If they all open their eyes, I am quite sure I must die. So I watch them, and always so far their eyes have been closed. But soon, soon they must open. Then I will burn. Do you understand me?'

'I am not sure that I do. But I am determined to help you, if I can.'

'You?' he said, staring at me suddenly. 'Why?'

As I began to speak he remembered once more, and said, 'Yes, yes, of course. It is this cloud. The cloud disperses my recollections. So then I must speak to you alone?'

'You are under no obligation to talk to me.'

'You are preparing a document against me?'

'No, I am not.'

'My words have always been twisted and used to testify against me. I have a sense that it is very dangerous to speak, to explain, because my words will be misconstrued.'

'You feel you have been traduced?'

'I feel I am guilty indeed, mired in blood. But somehow I have been unfairly judged nonetheless.'

'Do you want to become well again?' I said.

'But what is well?'

'That is a very pertinent question, Herr S. You are right to query my idle expression. I mean do you want to leave this place?'

'How will I leave? They have confined me here. To be rid of me. I am quite sure they want to be rid of me.'

'Who are they, to your mind?'

'I do not know. I know they have acted decisively. I am aware I am ill, and I think I have done many dreadful things. Aside from the crimes of which I am rightly accused – oh somewhere I am accused, I know – I have done dreadful things to other people, and – oh my wife!' And now his features were mangled by longing and grief, and he twisted in his chair.

'You remember your wife?'

'I am not sure. I think I . . . I think perhaps I dealt foully with my wife. I have – I think I was, oh I remember another woman, someone I fled to. But I was not fleeing from my wife, I was trying to hide myself.'

'But it is not your wife you see in these dreams?'

'No no, it is not her face.'

'Perhaps it is an aspect of your wife you see. Or an aspect of this other woman you speak of.'

'No! No, that is quite wrong.' And now he was terse, as if I was being obtuse and must be castigated. 'This woman who visits me here has nothing to do with my wife! And why do you presume to mention her?'

'You were telling me just now about her. That you see her frequently, and that you could not tell me her name.'

He paused for a moment, and passed a hand across his eyes, as if trying to clear his vision. I said, 'Do you remember if you have a family?'

'Children?'

'Yes, do you think you have children?'

'I think I have many beautiful children but I am not sure.'

'When did you last see your family?'

'I do not know. I cannot remember.'

'Do you have any idea where they might be?'

'No, I do not. And must I die without seeing them again?'

And now the man suffered a substantial collapse, and for a while he sobbed wildly, and I said nothing. I sat in his gloomy vicious cell, the darkness seeping from the corners, and waited. When his sobs appeared to be diminishing, I said quietly, 'Herr S, you are not dying.' I said this, though I knew nothing of his condition. My intention by such a remark was simply to calm him, so I might continue to speak with him. But I am afraid my words gave him hope, and he lifted his ravaged face and said, 'You are sure?'

'I am not sure, but I do not think you are dying,' I said. 'But please do not take me as any sort of an authority. I am not, as I said before, a medical man.'

'No, I think you are not, after all,' he said, looking at me carefully, as if he was seeing me clearly for the first time. I submitted myself to his gaze – I was there, assessing and observing him; it seemed only fair to permit him to do the same in return. He stared at me in silence for a time, and then he said, slowly, still in a contemplative mood, 'It is as if I have lost a portion of my brain. My thoughts run into holes. Do you understand?'

'I do understand.'

'They are very far away, I know that. My wife is a good and virtuous woman.'

'Do you think she knows you are here?'

'I hope she does not.'

There was a pause, and then he said, still quite calmly, as if he were expounding a scientific theory, 'When I dream of blood I think because I crave blood and love blood in the dream then I must have in the past been a bloodthirsty man. In the dream I am drinking blood. So I must have thirsted after blood and this is why – or one of the reasons – I think I committed a crime. I think I have spent years in a deep reverie, a criminal reverie and in this deranged state I have committed acts of violence and now I have fallen out of that reverie and yet I cannot remember my former actions. As if I have experienced two lives in one body.'

'But you say that you are also looking for something in the blood?'

'I am delving into the blood,' he said, and he briefly stopped wringing his hands and instead made a horrible grasping gesture, as if he were probing deep within something, his hands opening and shutting and finding only empty air. 'I must find it . . . I must . . . I must drag it out . . .'

Now he stopped this delving and fell silent again. His hands for one brief unnerving moment were entirely still, and the clanking of the chains stopped, and the dank cell was silent. Then he began to wring his hands again, and the jangling resumed.

'You remember elements of your past but it seems there are

significant gaps in your recall,' I said. 'The one place you remembered was the General Hospital. Perhaps they will know you there. I would be glad to make enquiries, if you did not mind me doing so.'

'I am not sure that is a good idea. If they do know me then you too would be their enemy.'

'I do not think I would. Besides, it does not matter.'

'You do not know how powerful they are, how they will unite to destroy you.'

We had reached something of an impasse. He was deep in the domain of the symbolic, and though I was content to observe him in this domain – it is always a privilege and a matter for awe to witness the human mind unmasked, dis-gorging mysteries – I also felt a great sense of curiosity about his true identity. I wondered what he had done, and if there had truly been a campaign of any sort to dismantle his reputation. I wondered about the real or symbolic nature of his Great Reversal, the moment when all he had worked to achieve was undone. I wondered if he must have experienced a particular shock, the final catalyst, which had thrust him from the lucid realm into twilight and dream. I did not know. I was torn, indeed, between a suspicion that it might be most comfortable for him to remain in this twi-light state, in the 'wolf-light' as Homer so beautifully describes it, and my own urge to draw him into the daylight. I was not sure if he wanted to return to the harsh glare of day. It had made him dreadfully unhappy to stand there, I imag-ined. Illuminated by the glances of other men, until they had turned away from him. I must confess that I did not know what to do, and was deep in thought when he turned to me and said, 'What did they tell you my name was?'

'Herr S, that is all Herr Meyer would say to me.'

'Do not speak of that man,' he entreated, with all the trembling desperation of before. In the wolf-light, Herr Meyer loomed large, like a monster conjured from the darkest reaches of the human soul, and I apologised for my thoughtlessness. I had no desire to torment this poor man. Yet he had quickly recovered, and was saying, in a neutral tone, 'My surname then begins with S, perhaps. I wonder what it could be?'

'You really do not remember?'

'I am afraid I do not.'

He had lost himself. The man had lost his very name, and a man without a name – well, he is indeed in limbo. The nameless man has symbolically reverted to the time before we are named, when we are residing in the womb or perhaps drifting in the spirit world, waiting to be summoned to earth. You are a scientific man, Professor Wilson, and will think all this nonsense, I suspect. It is just my way of alluding to mysteries which might otherwise be inexpressible. Herr S had his own theory, and he was saying, 'I have no name because I am a malefactor. I should have a number, not a name. Because of the crimes I have committed. We should all be stripped of our names.'

I was preparing another question, when he suddenly said, 'Klein.'

Thinking he was merely using the adjective, I said, 'What do you mean by this word?'

'I mean it is a name,' he said. And he had begun rubbing his forehead, his motions once more frenzied. 'It is not mine. It is the name of a man. An enemy. I cannot remember my own name, but I remember his. Johann, that is it. Johann Klein.'

'You believe he is your enemy?'

'I believe he is my darkest foe. And I believe he visited me last night, and gloated over my ruin.'

'I do not think he visited you in body, but perhaps you dreamed of him,' I said.

'He has been here. He spoke of the quality of the air, and how that had caused it all, and how unfortunate it was that I had not accepted his theory, and then he left.'

'And you remember nothing more of him?'

'I do not. It is only because he was here yesterday that I remember him at all.'

While speaking of this man, Herr S's appearance changed altogether. Before, he had been slumped in his chair, wringing his hands in his habitual way and staring at the floor. Now he straightened his back and looked directly at me. His face darkened. For a moment I thought he would try to rise, and certainly he writhed in his chair. Yet he did not rise, though as he spoke it became clear he was furious; he spat out his words.

'It makes me very – that man – you must tell me who he is.'

'I am afraid I do not know. I can make enquiries, however.'

'I am sure – it is he who has killed them all.'

We stared at each other for a moment. Something was beginning to clear. Herr S was still rattling his chains and grimacing towards me but now it seemed as if there was content to his rage, a tangible argument we might draw out. Before I had been merely trying to understand the particulars of his state and I had considered it largely a matter of the intimate and mysterious workings of the mind, but now

I had a further sense there might be facts involved and, perhaps, even individuals. I said, 'You are accusing this man Klein of murder?'

'Yes. I believe he is among the worst of them.'

'The worst of whom?'

'Of the murderers. He presided over the greatest massacre of all. It is – in my deadened brain, something is sparking – if I can only – if you will help me. You must tell me something else about this man – anything, his appearance, the details of his dress, how he spoke, any detail which may . . . help my memory . . .'

'I am afraid I do not know anything about him.'

'Ah, I could gouge a hole in my skull, if it would release the truth . . .' And he was tearing at the skin on his forehead, so frantically that he scratched himself and released a thin trickle of blood. I said, 'Herr S, you must calm yourself. I am trying to help you but . . .'

'I cannot be calm. There has been a massacre, you must understand. And every day it continues . . .'

I was about to explain to him that this massacre he perceived might well be suggestive of something else, that the question might not be whether to 'prove' it but rather to understand the significance this concept held for him, but I must confess that I was now uncertain of my own theory, and I feared suddenly that Herr S might hold the key to a genuine crime, a real series of murders. Before I could speak again he slammed his fists together, and he struggled to break out of his chains. He hammered on the chair, screaming, 'You must help me you must help me to stop it.' And then he seemed to entertain a vision, an awful, dark vision, because he began wailing in terror, and he stretched out an arm and said, 'But you must forgive me, you must! I beg forgiveness.'

He whispered something which sounded like 'Mea culpa', and then slumped down in exhaustion.

To my consternation, the sound of raging had caused Herr Meyer to return, and once he arrived Herr S retreated into his earlier catatonic state and would not look at me, and certainly not at Herr Meyer, though the vile man addressed him in his sneering way, demanding to know what he had 'been doing' and whether he had been 'behaving himself'. As if Herr S was a wicked child, to be punished with the rod! And poor Herr S was hunched over, surrendered to his impotence, occasionally muttering or wringing his hands. Sometimes he pressed his hands to his head, as if to protect himself from blows. It was sad indeed to see him there, cowering like a dog, and I turned in my anger to Herr Meyer and said, 'Herr S is – to my mind – poised between the worlds of reason and lunacy. It is imperative that you are gentle with him. His condition is most precarious. If he degenerates further, you will be responsible.'

Naturally, Herr Meyer did not like that at all, and glared at me in his vicious way, as if he was sizing me up for a strait-jacket, and then he said, 'I do not require your opinions on how to treat my patients.'

'You do not, if you perceive them as such. However I fear they are prisoners to your mind, malefactors, not patients at all.'

And Herr Meyer snorted and turned away from me.

It was futile to continue the interview, that much was plain, and so I informed Herr Meyer that I would return in the afternoon. I wondered if I should endeavour before my

return to find out more about the man Klein, simply
because his name had caused Herr S such agitation, and
had indeed precipitated his decline. I was curious, naturally, though I was not sure if I should indulge my curiosity,
because Herr S seemed so fearful of being returned to the
world of names, of categories and limitations. Yet how was
he to be released, how could he escape this horrible prison,
if he lacked any recollection of the real nature of his circumstances? Grappling with these notions – Herr S's fear
of knowing himself, my sense that it was wrong for him to
remain in this squalid cell, my loathing of the viciousness
of the asylum and my conviction that no man could live
long in such a place and not degenerate entirely – I
returned to my house. I was pensive throughout luncheon.
I had various pieces of work to finish, and though I sat at
my desk with my papers in front of me, I found I could not
consider them. My thoughts turned constantly to that man
trapped in his cell, his hands chained, and I wondered just
what treatment Herr Meyer was administering to him now.
I was thinking of Herr S's patchy recall, his oscillations
between ordinary lucidity and something more revelatory
and perilous, something which might bring forth everything or nothing at all, and I recalled again the devastating
effect upon him of the name 'Klein'. My moral sense was
confused. If the man genuinely wanted to remain undis-
turbed, then perhaps his wishes should be respected. If the
man were a murderer, as he claimed, then he should be
brought to trial. If his thoughts of blood and murder were
– as I strongly suspected – symbolical, then it would surely
assist his recovery to supply him with the means to dismiss
these darker elements of his being. Besides, at one point,
before he was afflicted by his terrors, he had clearly asked

me to find out who Johann Klein was.

I folded up my papers and placed them in a pile on my desk. It was early afternoon when I left my house again and walked through the crowded streets towards the hospital. I did not know precisely what I was doing. I merely remembered that Herr S had been agitated by the thought of the hospital, and that, along with the name Johann Klein, it was the only tangible clue I had unearthed from our conversation. I know of a man there – you know him too, perhaps – called Professor Zurbruck, and I wondered if he might be able to help me to ascertain the real identity of Herr S. It was a random hope, and I imagined it would prove fruitless. Yet I had no real idea of how else I might proceed, and so I went to the registrar's office on the first floor, and asked if he had seen Professor Zurbruck that day.

Vienna General Hospital is a vast edifice, the sort of place you might vanish into and never emerge from; a labyrinth, and I trod carefully, clutching my tenuous thread. The hospital was founded as a benevolent enterprise and I am sure a great deal of good work is performed within its confines. Yet there is something about it that nonetheless disturbs me, and, because of this, I have never spent much time there, except when there has been an interesting case on one of the wards, and I have sought an interview. I have a few acquaintances among the doctors there, but my connections are not strong. Professor Zurbruck I know simply because his brother was a friend of my brother when they studied at the university here in Vienna. We have met a few times, at gatherings and suppers, though I had never previously sought him out at the hospital. A young doctor directed me towards Professor Zurbruck's quarters, and I walked swiftly along the corridors, thinking that this really was the sort of place in which one might need a ball of twine yet all the while trying to keep my thoughts firmly on the matter in hand.

At Professor Zurbruck's door, I knocked and waited for a response, but my knock sounded hollow and as if I summoned no one, and I perceived that I must wait. Indeed I was obliged to pace the corridors, avoiding the milling hordes of students, for a good hour before Professor Zurbruck returned. I had almost given up hope, when he emerged abruptly around a corner. Even then he was hurried and rather gruesome – he is like his brother a man of great height and unusual thinness, and yet while his brother is rather jovial and thereby reassuring, Professor Zurbruck lacks his sibling's warmth. He extended a fleshless hand to me and suggested I explain my cause as succinctly as I could. He was polite but he emphasised – in his slow monotone – that he could only offer me a few minutes of his time, as he had an appointment very shortly.

In his room, as he busied himself finding materials for his next lecture, I laid out what I knew of the case of Herr S. I explained that he had been disturbed and transfixed by the notion of the General Hospital, and that he had also produced a single name, Johann Klein. I explained myself as precisely as I could yet it seemed to me that Professor Zurbruck was scarcely attending to my words. He was about to stand up, indeed, and announce that he must depart, when I mentioned that Herr S had accused himself and others of murder and had claimed there was a conspiracy to silence him.

'Ah,' said Professor Zurbruck, with a slow nod of his head, as if something had just fallen into place.

'You recognise something in this case?'

'I may do. He talks of a massacre?'

'Yes, oceans of blood, he says. The massacre of women.'

'He accuses specific professionals of murder?'

'Yes,' I said.

His manner was curious, as if he knew the answers to his questions already, and was rather contemplating how much to reveal to me than seeking enlightenment. I began to grow most eager, and I said, 'My dear professor, if there is anything you know of this case, I entreat you to inform me. Herr S is in a very grave position, and if you were to see how dreadful are the conditions of his confinement, you would pity him.'

'I have no doubt I would pity him. I am simply wondering if he might be – there is a chance he might be Professor Semmelweis. You might ask him if he is. Perhaps this would prompt his memory.'

'Who is Professor Semmelweis?'

'I must emphasise that I do not want to slander a former colleague, by suggesting he must be this poor lunatic you describe. Yet it is possible. Certainly Professor Semmelweis had become eccentric in recent years, and there were fears for his health.'

'On what were these fears based?'

'He had written a very rambling book, justifying himself, explaining to everyone that he had been right when they had all been contemptible fools, essentially. Or so I heard, I never read it. It is not my area of expertise. And when that was not received with the acclaim he thought it deserved, he took to haranguing his colleagues through personal letters, strewn with vicious accusations.'

'What sort of accusations?'

'This is why your remarks conjured the name Semmelweis. Because Professor Semmelweis has acquired a reputation for accusing his colleagues of murder, individually, in these letters, and in general in his book and other published works. And he claims, I believe, that there has been a massacre.'

'Why does he claim this?'

'He takes upon himself – and expects others to do the same – the burden of guilt for those women who die each year in our hospitals of childbed fever, or puerperal sepsis as it is known within the medical profession.'

'He thinks he has killed them?'

'Yes, I believe he claims that their deaths were caused by his actions, and by the actions of his colleagues. He calls childbed fever a global epidemic, spread by doctors. He suggests doctors are unclean, and the bearers of contagion, and this assertion has irritated many of his colleagues. Also, I believe he is not rigorous and therefore his theories have been queried. He does not enter into reasoned argument, he does not prove his case by amassing evidence through experimentation. He merely insults his opponents and slanders their reputations. In this way, he has lost his few supporters.'

'What were they supporting?'

'His theory about how puerperal sepsis is spread by the hands of doctors. It has been generally refuted, and anyway, it does not much concern me, as I am a surgeon.

41

Professor Semmelweis's focus is the woman in labour and after labour.'

'What is his theory?'

'A colleague once suggested it is rather like the example of Columbus's egg. It is not a work of grave complexity. Perhaps he might have persuaded his colleagues to adopt it, purely as a cautionary measure, had he not been so bombastic. Yet his manner angered Johann Klein, Professor Johann Klein, who was the head of the lying-in department of the hospital. Yes, the theory, you are anxiously waiting, and I really must attend to my business, concerns the washing of hands in chlorinated lime solution. Professor Semmelweis talks of, now what was the expression – ah yes, "cadaverous particles" – festering particles derived from the bodies of those who have recently died of puerperal sepsis. Infection, he claimed, could be carried from a dead body to a living body through these particles. You know it is still quite usual for students and doctors to perform autopsies of women who have died in childbirth shortly before they go to examine the lying-in patients in the First Division. And Professor Semmelweis proposed that these doctors and students must wash their hands in chlorinated lime solution after they had dealt with corpses and before they conducted an internal examination of a living woman. He claimed this would prevent puerperal sepsis.'

'And did it?'

'The theory has never been proven by experiment or systematic investigation. Professor Semmelweis however is adamant that it is the solution. He is adamant that those who refuse to adopt his preventative measures are wilfully slaying their patients.'

'So this is why he was cast out?'

Professor Zurbruck was pacing the room, in a long-limbed, leisurely manner, and now he came to rest – staring at me with his sunken eyes, and placing a long hand upon his desk. 'He was not cast out, my good fellow. He has behaved very strangely. He fled from Vienna many years ago. It was something about debts, I think; I cannot remember the details. I think he went back to his native Budapest. That is perhaps right. You must remember I have never known the man well. Yes, I heard he reigned supreme over a lying-in ward somewhere in the Hungarian Lands, though his techniques infuriated many of his colleagues. He is a hectoring angry man, you may have noticed.'

'He is much reduced.'

'I am sorry to hear that.'

'So his wife and children are in Budapest now?'

'I do not know where they are, I am afraid. This is all I know of the man. Now I really must go. Perhaps it would be useful for your further enquiries if I refer you to my colleague – Professor Hebra. I think he knew Professor Semmelweis well. Professor Hebra can be found at this address . . .'

He wrote it down for me on a piece of paper. I thanked him, and he nodded and waved me away. When I hurried to make enquiries of Professor Hebra, I was disappointed to discover that he had gone to Paris for a conference, and would be absent for a week. The lying-in ward, which I went to immediately I had failed to locate Professor Hebra, was equally unhelpful. I pushed open the heavy doors. It was an unusually hot day, and there were hardly any medical students in the wards. There were rows of women lying in beds – the blankets moulded around the swollen forms of those who had not yet delivered, and their faces taut with pain. Row upon row of them, about to cross the threshold, not knowing if they would survive. In suspense they lay there, and they had looked up fearfully when I opened the door. I had little time to gaze upon them before a midwife hurried up to inform me I could not stay there. She held up her hands, as if to shield the modesty of these women. So I bowed and turned away. I was pursued along the corridor by a strange volley of sounds, some like war cries, and some like the lowing of cattle. Then I found some terse doctors, who told me they knew nothing of any Semmelweis and hadn't time to consider the nature of his accusations. When I asked them about chlorinated lime solution, and cadaverous particles, one of them – a stern man of forty or so, who had just come, he said, from delivering a healthy boy, and who had to hurry to advise a midwife on a troublesome birth – said he had heard mention of something of that nature, but it was blatantly apparent – as Professor Klein had always argued – that puerperal sepsis was spread by a foul atmosphere, and all that was required was an extensive ventilation system, such as Professor Klein had installed. 'Chlorinated lime is simply superfluous, though any man should feel entitled to use it if he wishes,' he added, and then hurried away to his duties.

Feeling hot and rather tired, I went to take a glass of lemonade in a café nearby. As I reviewed my recent enquiries, I wondered if the best course of action would be to inform Herr S of what I had found and thus – perhaps – prompt him to further recollections. I suspected I held the key to his human identity, his social existence and the nature of his profession. I was confident further details of his life could be gathered: I had only spoken to one man, and he was no expert on childbirth, and he had already told me a great deal about Professor Semmelweis. Once Professor Hebra returned, he would clarify matters further. Had I the time, I thought, I could make a decent study of this man Semmelweis, and discover something of the controversy over his assertions, the battles he had fought, those colleagues who had supported and later deserted him, and no doubt, in the end, precisely who had committed him to the asylum. I was quite convinced I could hunt much of this information out, if I devoted some time to the case.

Yet I am not a detective, naturally given to harvesting facts, craving resolution simply for the neatness and purity it affords. I was mindful, furthermore, of Herr S's own reluctance to regain himself, his fear of the harshness of the solar realm. While some might say this was a symptom of his distress, I do maintain that, for some unfortunate individuals, the 'lunatic' condition is a respite from reality, and it is plain cruelty to force them to return to the world of absolutes. There had been some moral imperative upon me to ascertain that Herr S was not a murderer – in a sense which would interest the law. This achieved, there was no clear justification for further enquiries, unless they were to the benefit of Herr S himself. More practically, I perceived that for the sake of his reputation, and his family, I must not wander around Vienna proclaiming that he had been placed in an asylum. While I perceive no shame in this epithet 'mad', I am aware that for most it carries a terrible stigma, and if

Herr S's family subscribed to this opinion, I did not want to distress them. Professor Zurbruck I knew to be a man of discretion, for all his ghoulishness, but others might not be so careful.

After much thought, I decided I should refer the dilemma to the man himself, Herr S or Professor Semmelweis. I would inform him of his name and lay the case before him – that I had garnered some other details about him, or rather about his non-lunar existence, and that they could be revealed to him as he chose. I would be directed by his desires, unreasoning though they might be. I hastened back to the asylum, weighted down by the many implications of what I had discovered, uncertain as to the effect my words might have on this desperate man.

I am cursing as I write this last sentence, as there is someone below who I simply must see. I will continue with this letter as soon as possible . . .

The Empress

15 August 2009 and London was clad in heat and dust. The day hung still and close; there was no breeze. The tarmac was burning to the touch; everything was harsh and over-lit. People were moving, but listlessly; the heat had gradually sapped them. They were walking with their hands at their eyes, trying to block out the sun. From time to time it rained, in violent bursts which made everyone run for cover, though the dampness was a relief all the same. After the rainstorms the city gleamed, as if someone had polished the buildings.

It was barely mid-morning and Brigid Hayes felt already as if she had been awake for a dozen hours. She was smiling at her son, trying to please him, struggling against a latent sense of failure. She was not certain, but she feared this was failure, that she was failing her son. There was a gulf between them: on one side his dynamism, brightness, his vivid urges to do, to consume, to understand; on the other her basic attempts to subsist, to endure the day. He was ambitious, incessantly curious; she was faded, fading before his eyes, though still she was smiling and holding out her hands to him. She had left childbearing late, and so at thirty-nine she set about it zealously, but fearing the worst. Twenty months later, she had Calumn. Seventeen months after his birth, she was expecting another baby, as yet unnamed. As yet invisible, trapped within her though due any day. This child would be the last, she was sure of that. She had hardly expected to have one child, when she began 'trying' three years ago. Two was more than enough. Two was extraordinary, if she took the time to think about it. But she rarely took the time. When she wasn't dealing with her son and the physical demands of pregnancy she was working, dull copy-editing work but she did it because they needed the money. She had given up her teaching job but now she pored over manuscripts and wrote symbols in the margins. She was precise and disciplined in her work, chaotic and self-critical with her child. It didn't make any sense.

She was tired and not quite well. At night she could not sleep; she would lie for hours in the dark, waiting for exhaustion to drag her under. She could scarcely breathe or find a comfortable way to lie. So she listened to the nocturnal whispers of the radio, watched the sky change; often it was dawn before she slept. That had ruined her well enough, and then during the days Patrick went out to work and she stumbled around the house. He was worried about her, she knew; he told her she must stay inside, rest whenever she could. Still, the other day she had aimed at defiance, she had grown so bored at home. She had forced Calumn into his pushchair and walked to the local park. After that, she coughed her throat raw; she had scarcely slept at all.

Worst of all, Patrick kept praising her; he said he didn't know how she managed it all. He was trying to encourage her, though it made her feel alone, too, that her experience was untranslatable, obscure to him. He did not perceive that she was half-mad with fatigue, and yet she rose each day and knew she must play her part, she must be a mother to her son, she must be measured with him, never raise her voice to him, even when her blood was curdling with frustration. Yet often she felt so happy, so over-whelmed with love – everything was incoherent and ragged and she could not explain it to Patrick; she mostly blamed him when things were hard. She wanted him to experience it too – the relentlessness, how it did not end, and you could never rest, how it was beautiful and it smashed you to pieces at the same time – but he usually came home after Calumn was in bed, found her collapsed and monosyllabic on the sofa. She told herself each day, she must remember, he was a wonderful father, a wonder-ful husband, this would soon be over – then everything got clouded, this chemical exhaustion took hold of her, and she slipped again.

She felt a low pain in her belly, the sort of grinding cramps she had been experiencing for a day or so. In her com-plaining body, she was desperate for her pregnancy to end, so she hesitated to question this augury, fearful of mis-diagnosing it as labour. She didn't want to attract any attention from vengeful gods or in any way leave herself open to charges of hubris. She rubbed her belly, felt the baby kick, a palpable swelling which was a foot, a tiny vengeful foot, she thought, because the kick was so hard and probing. A reproach, perhaps. Impatience or appre-hension, if a foetus could feel either. The pain was surging within her, and she tried to remember how it had been last time, how it had felt. Then, she had been optimistic; in the final weeks of her pregnancy she had phoned the hospital at the first sign of a contraction. They had rushed off, she and Patrick, like eager neophytes. They arrived and were sent away again. Braxton Hicks, the midwives told them patiently. The body practising for real labour. Nothing to worry about. Do call if you're concerned about anything. Three times they tried to scale the ramparts and found the hospital fortified against them. The entrance was barred; she was not ready. When she finally gained access to her sterilised room, things moved efficiently, to a timetable. A nice quick birth, the doctor said.

Another pain, and Brigid breathed more deeply, her instincts beginning to help her. She was planetary in her girth, an ancient breeding cow. She was whole with child, swollen beyond any size that seemed proportionate or reasonable. She was entirely child, she felt; her body had been colonised. It was not herself, as she had been, she had become someone else; it made her uncertain if she really had a self at all. She was surely half-mad, her brain stewed in hormones, yet now she took Calumn in her arms, tickling him under the chin. He turned to her, smiled toothily, said 'Mamma,' and she said, 'Hello baby. Hello, hello lovely baby baby,' and he said, 'Ahdoorschnefatibumaha,' some proto-talk she couldn't interpret. She kissed his warm soft skin, breathed in the wafting beautiful smell of him, baby shampoo and milk. She kissed him and held him to her, whispering in his ear, telling him how precious he was and how much she loved him. Though she felt spiky and savage within, she never doubted that she loved her son. Her love was infinite; she sensed there was a deep infinite core of love, and then a lesser love, her surface emotion, where everything got sullied by quotidian demands, and mingled with guilt.

'... *The Moon*, a novel by Michael Stone ... its central subject the ... epidemic of childbed fever ...,' she heard the radio say, and that made her shake her head. If Patrick had been here, he would have acted swiftly, banished the voice. Instead the phone was ringing, so she said to Calumn, 'Come on sweetie, let's go and see who this is.' He beamed up at her, made a sound like a siren, his current favourite noise. 'Nee-nar nee-nar nee-nar,' said Calumn, as Brigid led him slowly along the corridor, knowing she had twelve rings to get the phone. She caught it on the final ring, heard her mother saying, 'Hello Brigid,' as she lifted the handset. Calumn dropped to the floor and began picking at a piece of fluff. Brigid smiled at him. 'Hi Mum, yes, fluff, Calumn,' she said. 'It's called fluff.'

'Feeff,' he said, glancing up at her, seeking her approval.

'That's exactly right. How are you, Mum?'

'Fwuff,' said Calumn, taking the phone book from a shelf and opening it, glancing down the pages as if in search of something.

'How are you feeling dear? Any signs?' her mother was saying. Yes, there was a star above the house last night, Brigid wanted to say, and an old crone shook her stick at me this morning. But she said, 'No, no signs. I feel as usual.'

'Oh, it must be awful to be so overdue,' her mother said. 'So terribly boring.'

'It's not that overdue,' said Brigid. She had been saying this to everyone for two weeks, ever since her baby had been diagnosed as late. As if there was a deadline, as if they were falling behind. Below her, Calumn was meditatively tearing at the pages of the phone book, while Brigid watched and couldn't face bending down to salvage it.

'You can't have heard about Dorothy, about poor Dorothy's baby,' said her mother.

'Yes, I did hear. I must send her a card.'

'You know, she thought like you. And she was much younger. At your age Brigid, you have to take care. You sound terribly tired.'

'I'm not too bad. I could last another week or two, if necessary.' She didn't believe that at all. She had plainly established that it was bad, that she could barely suffer another hour of it. Yet there was something within her, some instinct she couldn't entirely command, which made her disagree nonetheless. She said, 'I'll write Dorothy a card today . . .'

'You do understand that it's another person's life, don't you? I always think there are points to make and points to waive, Brigid. Battles to fight and battles to cede.'

'How are you, Mum?'

'I'm not the subject under debate, Brigid.'

'Nee. Nar,' said Calumn. 'Aidahadabok.'

'Look, it's all fine. I'm fine. That's right, sweetie, it's a book,' said Brigid. Now Calumn dropped the phone book, having torn it to his satisfaction, found a ten-pence piece on the floor and stuffed it into his mouth. There began a mighty struggle between mother and baby for possession of the coin, mother with her fingers in the baby's mouth, baby throwing back his head, trying to clamp his lips shut. Prising open his mouth she seized the object. He began a screaming protest so she gave him a pen to chew. He sat on the floor, instantly mollified, busy with the wonder and strangeness of a pen.

'There's absolutely no need to play the martyr. At your age they would induce you like a shot. Nobody in their right mind would deny you an induction.'

Calumn had dropped the pen and was trying to drag the phone away from her, accompanying his endeavours with insistent little yelps and squeals.

'What on earth is up with Calumn this morning? Is he ill?'

'No, no, he's all right,' Brigid said, trying to smile at Calumn. 'He just needs his morning snack. And a friend is coming soon. I'd better go.'

'Oh, OK. Well, I was phoning to say I'm just at the hair-dresser's. So I can drop round after I finish here.'

'Really Mum, there's no need to put yourself out.'

'Oh no, I'll just drop round with a couple of things.'

It was improbable; her mother was coming to assess her. Now she took the phone back from Calumn again, tried him with the pen but he shook his head, knocked it out of her hand.

'What about later, later today? It's just, I have a friend coming this morning,' said Brigid, as Calumn's wails rose in pitch, and he lunged for the phone again.

'Oh, I won't stay long,' said her mother.

Defeated, Brigid put the phone down and turned to her son. She smiled down at him, though he twisted in her arms, kicked against her. 'Come on sweetie, come on,' she said. She took his hand and danced him along, 'Bouncy bouncy bouncy. Bouncy bouncy bouncy boy, look how we're bouncing along.' He began to chuckle. He lifted his head and looked delighted again. His energy amazed her, especially now she had slumped so consummately. It made her glad, that he was so enchanted by everything, so eager to know it, feel it, eat it – his appetites were robust and she admired that. She watched him, from far away – as if he was a beacon on a hill, and she was in the shadows, far below. He was radiant; he really burned with life – and she wondered if this unborn child – kicking now within her, pushing against the prison walls – would be as radiant as her son.

'Shall we go and have some grub grub?' she said to Calumn, kissing his ear, and he recognised the words and smiled back. 'Dah,' he said, nodding.

'Let's bounce into the kitchen,' she said. Bouncy, bouncy, gub gub, they said – Calumn with his awkward little stomping movements, pausing from time to time to examine some fleck of dust. Gub gub, they said as they passed into the kitchen. The baby world of Calumn required her to communicate in monosyllables, to submit herself to these simplified versions of her own language. 'Bek bek,' she said to Calumn though her mother always told her – and would tell her again, no doubt, when she arrived later – that this would stunt his development. 'I never baby-talked to you,' her mother would say. 'That must be why I was such a prodigy,' Brigid would reply, laughing. Her whole being was tempered for Calumn, maintained at a level he could understand – though sometimes she felt he understood far more than she thought, was even in touch with something primal and significant. She didn't really know why she thought that but sometimes when he became pensive or when he looked at her as if he could see her more clearly than anyone else, she wondered just what he knew, what he saw.

In the kitchen she grabbed the protesting form of her son, bundled him quickly into his high chair and when he began to kick and flail his arms around she said, 'Bek bek, gub gub,' in a loud jovial voice, kissing him. When she gave him a book he flicked through the pages, smashed it on the table then dropped it on the floor. 'Bek bek, gub gub,' she and Calumn said to each other, as she put some fruit on a plate and directed it towards his scrabbling hands, and he began to paw at it and drop it and sometimes eat it. Now she had a few minutes, perhaps even ten minutes, while he sat there, playing with his food, so she put water in the kettle, found some chocolate in the fridge and ate it quickly, as her son chewed on a piece of apple. She made some tea, and now she heard the radio again. Brigid listened but only in a distracted way, making encouraging faces at her son and handing him chunks of apple. Occasionally she said, 'Yum yum,' pointing at her food, at his food, exaggerating the movements of her mouth so he would think it was fun to eat. And on the radio she heard people talking and didn't entirely understand them, or she absorbed a few sentences then lost the thread while she said, 'Yummy scrummy yum,' to Calumn.

'. . . debut novel by Michael Stone . . .' one of the radio voices was saying.

'A sort of historical novel . . .'

'Very loosely defined . . .'

Brigid put bread in the toaster, drank more tea, said, 'Yes, sweetie, that's right, that's absolutely right. Would you like a piece of toast? Toast and honey, yes? You like a nice piece of toast and honey don't you?' she said, as she waited for

the toast to pop up and on the radio another voice said, '...
yes, a doctor ...'

'This man ... Semmelweis ...'

' ... rise of modern obstetrics ...'

'Nee-nar gub gub,' said Calumn.

'Yum, yum, delicious. Mummy has some. Mmmm, delicious. Calumn has some ... Mmmm delicious ...'

'Dah,' said Calumn. 'Dah.'

'The imposition of technology on ancient process ...'

'Hardly fair . . . hospitals founded with benevolent intentions ... Often the women were birthing illegitimate children ... nowhere else to go ...'

' ... but the midwives fared better ...'

'Well, they weren't doing the autopsies ...'

Brigid shook her head, spread honey on the toast, presented it to her son. His face was smeared with food and his hands were sticky, but he was babbling happily, enjoying the small rituals of the morning. She thought it was poignant, how much he enjoyed simply being with her, having her to himself. So she felt one more stab of guilt, even though she was having this child partly for Calumn, to give him a sibling, a life companion. She had a sentimental idea that one day he would thank her. But now, he didn't understand and simply wanted her. He smiled at her, waving his fingers towards her, trying to grab her as she leaned over him. She kissed his hot face, smoothed his hair. 'Lovely little boy. So beautiful.' Then she sat down beside him at the table, holding her tea. She thought of Patrick in his office, typing emails, fielding calls from strangers. Leaning over his desk, a photograph of Calumn among the books and clutter. Living through time, elsewhere, apart from her. Perhaps he would be looking at the photograph of Calumn, in an idle moment he would glance towards it . . . and then the phone would ring.

'. . . Budapest. Moved to Vienna as a young doctor. Failed in every other department, so had to go into obstetrics . . .'

'Facts have been changed . . .'

'Became obsessed with saving the lives of mothers . . .'

'. . . like a plague . . .'

'Ahhh ahhh ahhh . . .' said Calumn, banging his spoon on the table.

'Ssh, sweetie,' said Brigid. She wondered if this was a message, if the radio was telling her something – if she must beware. She was superstitious and not reasonable at all. When the voices said, 'A massacre of mothers . . .' she trembled and didn't want to listen any more. She was scaring herself, trying to hold back her fears, and sometimes saying 'sweetie' and sometimes 'bek bek bek'. Still she couldn't flick the switch, in case it was important, in case there was something she should understand. Then she wanted Patrick to be with her. She remembered now that he had an important lunch today. It was dreadful timing, he had said this morning, but they wouldn't move it. This morning he had rushed out of the house, in his smartest suit, bearing a folder thick with papers. He carried this off towards the Tube, looking determined and as if his preoccupations mattered to the world, while she stood in the doorway, heavy and becalmed. Now Calumn put a finger to his lips, tried to 'shush' her back. She smiled back at him, even as she heard the warning from the radio –

'. . . swathes of orphans . . .'

'. . . called the hospital a charnel house . . .'

Calumn dropped his cup on the floor. That stopped him
from eating, while he peered into the depths beneath him,
searching for the cup. Instead of leaning down to pick it
up, Brigid went to the cupboard and took out another,
filled it with water. Swathes of orphans, she thought, and
shook her head again. Then she missed what they were
saying, as she splashed water at the dishes, stacked them
on the draining board. It was clear that her brain had been
rearranged by months of baby care and then the fatigue of
pregnancy. Two rounds of pregnancy and all the sleepless
nights with Calumn had made her kinder, more altruistic
perhaps, and yet more easily unnerved. Often she took
refuge on the surface: she considered the business of baby
mush, she considered that carefully many times a day, and
she pondered the complex question of whether her son
needed more protein, or whether protein pained his stomach, and sometimes she thought, 'Hey diddle diddle the
cat and the fiddle the cow jumped over the moon . . .'
Despite all that, she sensed something else, she had not
been aware of it before, some ancient force that kindled
life within her. All her enterprises, her tangled hopes, were
nothing, against this force. It made everything so very
strange, and these phrases on the radio – these sanguine,
clever voices – seemed to come from a world she had once
inhabited, spoken in a language she had once mistaken for
her own.

'Here you are, sweetie,' she said, placing the cup in
Calumn's urgent outstretched hands. 'More water.'
    'Wahatar.'

'Yes, very good. Water.'

'. . . ever more distant from original events . . .' said the radio, but Brigid had lost track of the debate. She breathed out slowly. Briefly she had been absurd, she had been frightened, and now she had returned to the morning, her son, the water she was pouring into his cup. It was just this fatigue; it made her nearly hysterical. She was forty-two and there wasn't much to be done if you were tired at forty-two and about to birth another child. How much more exhausted would she become? She couldn't quite imagine it, the period after the birth. There would be the baby, a tiny thing, with its simple needs – milk, love, a warm place to sleep. After a few months she would no longer be able to imagine that she had grown the child within her; it would seem so vital and present, as if it had always been in the world. When she thought like that, she thrilled to a sense of anticipation. She was simply glad, at those moments, but that was before her thoughts strayed into plain logistics: how would she carry her babies, feed them, clothe them, wash them? How would she tend to their basic needs, when she found the needs of one so entirely engrossing? She could fill a day with Calumn's needs; where would she fit those of another child? She could oscillate from apprehension to excitement in a minute. Now, she was thinking, she would manage. There was no alternative, and besides there were people who managed with four children, five children. They didn't die of exhaustion. No one ever died of sleepless nights. They might lose themselves for a time, enter a shadow world of bewilderment, but they didn't die. So with a bright smile she said to Calumn, 'Are we finished? Have we finished second brek? All done with your second brek? Good good. Can I take your bowl and spoon away?'

'Dah.'

'That's right, sweetie. I'm taking your bowl and spoon. And now I'm putting them in the sink. There's the sink, that's right' – as Calumn pointed at the sink.

She cleared up some of the mess though not much of it, just enough to keep things reasonable and not entirely sordid, and then she wiped Calumn's mouth, though he bucked against her.

'There we are,' she said, stroking his hair. 'All clean. Good boy.'

And Calumn turned to her and with his arms outstretched, kissed her wetly on the chin.

'Thank you, sweetie,' she said, kissing him back. 'How lovely, a kiss for Mummy.'

'. . . let's turn to the next . . .' said the radio, and then Brigid felt a deep pain within her, harsh now, quite searching, asking her if she was ready to go through the whole thing again. The pain stabbed at her, severely and in this questioning way, and then it receded. A contraction, if ever I felt one, thought Brigid, but still she was superstitious and tried to dismiss the thought. But it must be. She was contemplating the real possibility that this was labour when she heard the doorbell. She said to Calumn, 'Come on sweetie, let's go and see who's at the door.' She wondered if it was Stephanie, arriving early; Stephanie who had gone through five years of IVF before she conceived. A walking miracle, she called herself. More likely, it was her mother already. Hastening to her, with something to say. So Brigid lifted her son down from his chair and set him on the floor. He grabbed at her trousers, wanting to come up again, but she kissed him and tousled his hair. 'Come on sweetie, have to hurry. It's the doorbell.' He raised a hand and put it into hers.

Brigid opened the door and greeted her mother, who was looking particularly small and determined, her hair newly dyed, her skin creamed with some expensive unguent, her jewellery sparkling and everything about her expressing a firm resolve that try as the universe might to upset her she would prevail. She was carrying a lot of plates and bowls, in plastic bags, each of them neatly capped with a piece of tinfoil. These she thrust into Brigid's hands.

'Several meals,' she said. 'I thought you would need them.'

'Thanks Mum, that's really amazingly brilliant of you,' said Brigid, brightly, taking care to smile. She took them into the kitchen and stacked everything carefully in the fridge. A procession followed along, her mother and her son. 'Hello darling,' her mother was saying to Calumn, kissing him and rubbing his fat hands. 'Darling boy, aren't you looking nice in your red trousers. What lovely red trousers! Come and kiss your old grandma . . .' Calumn burbled back, flung his arms around her neck. No idea at all, thought Brigid. He has no idea at all. Assumes adults are consistent, uniformly kind. One day he would realise – or would he? – that there were certain ambiguities, that his grandmother was a complicated woman, giving with one hand, taking with the other, that his mother was herself a wary daughter, and that Calumn was a battleground. Across the battleground of this small boy they mounted their respective campaigns, attacked and retreated, or suffered an uneasy truce. Calumn never noticed. He only saw a smiling woman who plainly loved him. It was his simplicity perhaps, it helped others to become simple too.

'I made you and your mummy lunch, yes I did . . . I made you and your mummy a lovely yummy lunch,' her mother was saying to Calumn. 'A delicious lunch, oh we'll have a lovely lunch.'

Brigid made more tea, while her mother settled herself into a chair and said, 'Oh, what a funny little boy you are!' and Calumn clapped his hands and said, 'Gan gang gan gan.'

'Gran, gran,' said Brigid's mother. 'That's what I am yes! I'm your gran, yes I am.'

'Hilabsnroortshammablapa,' said Calumn, turning circles.

'What's all that? What on earth is all that?' laughed Brigid's mother. 'Good Lord. What an amazing word, not a pause for breath at all.'

'Mewirddeeteo.'

'Absolutely, dear little boy. Absolutely, I agree entirely. Thank you dear,' said Brigid's mother, as Brigid put the tea on the table. 'Dreadful weather isn't it, all this rain? They say it's global warming on the news. Hotter and wetter summers. It's like a rainy season, really. I find it so sad. So sad that poor Calumn will be growing up with these horrible wet summers. Poor little boy. When I was a child the summers were so beautiful and ceaselessly hot. Bright blue skies, little wisps of cloud. It was the same for you too. I remember spending every day with you in the garden, John too after he was born. Endless blue days.

And the evenings were balmy and long. Then you had a proper cold autumn. Even in October you were cold, and you knew that winter was really on its way. But it was a proper year with seasons. I like seasons. Don't we like seasons, Calumn? We like a nice hot summer, don't we? Yes we do!'

'Dah,' said Calumn, smiling. Then he grabbed a saucepan – left on the floor for his entertainment – and smashed it on the tiles.

'Oh, that's a bit loud,' said Brigid's mother. 'Really too loud, Calumn.'

'Rowd rowd,' said Calumn, and then he wailed when the pan was taken away from him. 'Have some more apple,' said Brigid, trying to bribe him. 'Yummy apple, would you like some, sweetie?'

'Nnnnnear,' said Calumn, with his eyes shut.

'OK, sweetie, don't have any apple. But let's be a bit quieter. Hush hush, a bit quieter, please.'

'AHHHHGANNNGANNNNNGANNN,' said Calumn, in his loudest voice.

'It is bad,' said Brigid, trying to speak over him, while her mother smiled as if to say that she understood, that it was impossible to be a perfect parent, she understood that Brigid was doomed to fail. 'It is bad about global warming. Calumn, do you want a banana instead?'

'Neeeearrr.'

'I don't think he wants it, Brigid. Now, have you been speaking to your midwife? What's her name?'

'Jenny.'

'Yes, her.'

'I have regular appointments with her, yes.'

'Why don't you call her up today? See if she can't

speed things up for you?'

'Thanks Mum, but really Tuesday's not so long away,' Brigid said loudly, confidently, even though she didn't believe it. Just then the pain surged within her and she gritted her teeth. She turned away and fumbled in a cupboard. Breathe, she thought. Remember to breathe. Oblivious anyway her mother was continuing, determined to convince her.

'I think you've been very heroic and so on, yes Mummy has been a heroine hasn't she Calumn, but I think we should let her have her new baby now, shouldn't we? So we can all meet it, so Calumn you can see your new friend, yes you can . . . Mummy hasn't wanted to let the baby out yet because she likes having it in there so much. But perhaps now she might let it out. Perhaps she'll let the doctors help her soon. Won't that be exciting?'

'Shall I pour you some tea, Mum?' said Brigid.

'Oh let me do it, dear. Really, you should go and lie down. Come on Calumn, you and I will pour Mummy a cup of tea, yes? Shall we? And would Mummy like some pineapple with it? Is Mummy having her pineapple?'

'Mummy has eaten quite enough pineapple, thank you,' said Brigid. 'Not that it helps.' Her mother was busy with the teapot, smiling periodically at Calumn, who was holding onto her trouser legs.

'It's true, isn't it Calumn, that pineapple seems not to have helped your mummy. So now she needs the nice doctors, that's what Grandma thinks. That's what Grandma thinks, though Mummy doesn't believe Grandma. Poor Grandma!'

So Brigid bridled, even in her weakened state. Even as

another pain threatened to evolve, she bridled. She was exhausted and irritable; certainly she felt she could neither surrender fully to her mother nor could she stand firm against her. Anyway her mother had innumerable strategies and was clearly in a better state to marshal her victories. She was staring blankly at her mother, thinking about what she would say, how she would neutralise the latest line of enquiry, she was phrasing something when she felt the pain again, deep, rising to a peak and then breaking and receding. She remembered this, this rhythm of pain; she had once lived a day to this rhythmic rise and fall.

'More juice?' her mother was saying to Calumn, holding up his cup while he shook his head. And Brigid was trying to grasp the pain she had felt, hold it close. She longed for pain, more pain, a still more direct and inescapable pain. That was just one of the small perversities of her state. And now her mother was talking about the floor in her kitchen, how she needed it re-tiled, how the tiles she wanted were so expensive, while Brigid thought about how she craved pain, a pain which would drag this pregnancy to an end. This was how you became glad about labour. It was the only possible release from this discomfort, this enslavement to the overgrown body. You longed so urgently for release that you accepted agony, welcomed physical distress. She smiled, as she thought how absurd it was, that she was nursing this pain to herself, feeling friendly towards it.

'I have various things I should do, sorting out the house and making sure I've sent away all my copy-editing,' she said. 'And a friend of mine is coming round for coffee quite soon. But of course you're very welcome to stay. You might like to play with Calumn.'

'Who's your friend?'

'Stephanie.'

'Stephanie?' said her mother, imperiously. A stranger! And she the gatekeeper, the guardian of the front door! It was that sort of expression, thought Brigid.

'Yes, a former colleague, from school.'

Her mother was peering into the fridge, rustling through the bags of mouldy vegetables. 'Your fridge is rather empty,' she said. Calumn was behind her saying, 'Rid-rid-ridd-rid.'

'Well, I haven't been to the shops for a while. Calumn, come over here, sweetie, let's have some milk. A cup of milk?' He put out a hand, took the milk.

'I remember when I was pregnant with you, I was so busy in the final days,' said her mother. 'I made two months' worth of meals and put them all in the freezer. Labelled them all. Lasagne. Shepherd's Pie. Fish Pie. Rhubarb Crumble. All in labelled containers. I was determined not to be caught short after the birth. I cooked for days and days, hour upon hour. I wasn't quite as big as you, but still, it was a major undertaking. I dragged myself around our kitchen, without all these labour-saving devices everyone relies on these days, and morning to dusk I cooked. And when I'd put the last container in the freezer, I felt the beginnings of labour.'

'Very precise timing,' said Brigid, though she had heard the story before.

'So precise. My body knew it could let itself go. I had finished the cooking. And we ate so well after the birth.

Not too well, naturally, because I wanted to lose my baby weight as soon as possible. But your father, God rest his soul, ate well. And I had enough. I always think when I look at photos from that time, how slim I was, even just after the birth,' said her mother, who was far from fat now but had perhaps sagged a little in recent years. Age had dragged her skin down, though there wasn't much flesh on her bones. She was a handsome elderly woman, Brigid supposed. Carefully set hair, dyed a blonder shade of white. High cheekbones, tastefully applied make-up. She wore pastel shades which suited her well enough. Well-cut trousers, low shoes. She was small but she held herself well. She had shrunk in recent years, but she wasn't bent-backed. She was cleaning the surfaces with a regal air, as if she rarely had to stoop to such work but was doing it for her daughter.

'Don't do that, Melissa will clean tomorrow,' said Brigid.

'Nee-nar nee-nar,' said Calumn, racing out of the room, and Brigid's mother went to fetch him. There was a cry as he was retrieved and the kitchen door was shut behind him.

'Thanks Mum,' said Brigid.

'You shouldn't be carrying him around in your state. Not a big boy like you, Calumn. Such a big strong boy! Can't Patrick take some time off work?'

'It's very busy at the moment. Besides, he's saving it up for when the baby's born. He'll only get a couple of weeks.'

'What does he do all day in that office anyway?' said her mother.

'Well, somehow he passes the time,' said Brigid. 'The hours pass and then he comes home again.'

The doorbell rang again, and Brigid waddled off to answer it. Stephanie was on the doorstep, with a baby in a pram, a tiny grub-like creature, its eyes shut, occasionally making little grumbling noises and sucking its fingers. The grub was called Aurora, but really it was a pre-human, with its furry body, its asymmetrical skull. It was still foetal, with its jerky little movements, its utter dependence on the mother, everything involuntary, unmeditated. It hardly needed a name, it was still so clearly an extension of its mother.

'Oh, how beautiful she is,' said Brigid, kissing Stephanie, adoring the baby for the requisite amount of time, picking up a little finger and holding it, careful not to wake her.

Calumn was trying to peer into the pram.

'Gently, gently, Calumn,' Brigid said. 'Don't wake the baby.'

'Bah bah bah,' said Calumn, loudly. The baby stirred but didn't wake.

'Ssssh, Calumn, very gently. Speak quietly, ssshhh,' said Brigid.

'Don't worry,' said Stephanie. 'But can we bring the pram into the kitchen? Just so I can push it backwards and forwards, make sure she stays asleep as long as possible?'

'Of course,' said Brigid. 'Just wheel it along.'

'Aren't the wheels wet?' said Brigid's mother. 'Shouldn't you dry the wheels?'

'Don't worry about the wheels,' said Brigid, before Stephanie could bend down. 'Don't worry at all. I don't care about them.' And she started pulling the pram through the door, while Calumn bounced along beside it, saying, 'Bah bah,' and making the baby twitch and stir.

Stephanie sat down in the kitchen, the pram beside her, moving it backwards and forwards, the wet wheels making a swooshing sound on the kitchen floor. 'Is she sleeping well?' said Brigid's mother. 'Calumn, darling, don't grab the side of the pram.'

'No, not really,' said Stephanie. 'Up every two hours to feed, then feeds for an hour, that sort of thing. But I hear that's pretty usual.'

'Oh yes, absolutely normal,' said Brigid's mother.

'Breastfeeding is a nightmare of course,' said Stephanie. 'I hadn't realised what a complete nightmare it was. Brigid you were so good, you never told me how ghastly it is, how painful, how desperately you think, "God, why not just give the poor little brute a bottle," but then the health visitors treat you as if you are Satan for even suggesting it, and so for some reason you carry on.' She laughed, vividly, showing her teeth.

'I'm sure I told you many times how tough it was. I must have, I moaned bitterly to Patrick,' said Brigid.

'How long do I have to do it to earn my little gold badge, "Good Mummy"? How long, please tell?' said Stephanie. She was looking pretty good, thought Brigid. Flushed cheeks, from pushing the pram along, and her hair was still glossy and thick from pregnancy. Auburn, streaked with grey, curling over her shoulders. She was striking certainly. At school she had a reputation for saying outrageous things. She sometimes swore in front of the pupils. Teaching *Romeo and Juliet*, she said things like, 'Romeo and Juliet simply fancy the bloody pants off each other,' while her pubescent class tittered and blushed.

'I breastfed both my children for a year,' said Brigid's mother. 'Twelve months each. Then I stopped. I was happy to stop when I did. I felt I'd done the best I could for them.'

'A year, Mrs Morgan. That's amazing,' said Stephanie. 'That's so amazing. God, I'll think I deserve a bloody medal if I get to three months. I told Jack that the World Health Organization recommends three months. He never reads anything so he doesn't know any better. Also men never discuss these things with their friends, do they? They don't sit around having earnest conversations about whether breast is best, or do they?'

'I don't think Patrick does,' said Brigid. 'But he definitely thought breastfeeding was important.'

'Oh yes, Jack says that. But where has he got that from? I just don't understand,' said Stephanie, kicking off her heels, causing Calumn to wander over to look at her feet. But he was shy and wouldn't touch them. And they were strange, thought Brigid, trying to imagine – as she often did – what Calumn saw, how things appeared to him. Gnarled bent toes with glistening nails at the end. Soft skin and hard nail. He stood over them, pointing at the shining nail polish.

'Yes, my toes,' said Stephanie. 'Where are your toes, Calumn?'

Calumn looked up at Stephanie's face, smiling coyly, then gazed down at her feet again.

'How are you feeling in yourself?' said Brigid to Stephanie.

'Oh, pretty trashed. Big weeping Caesarean scar, that sort of loveliness. Can't imagine I'll ever get back to normal. I'm just trying not to think about it.' Stephanie was wearing a loose orange dress, still in her maternity clothes, so you couldn't really see what she looked like. Underneath, Brigid imagined she was bloated, still carrying piles of weight.

That was how she had been. And her face had been so full and fat, like a girl's. It made her look improbably well on all the post-birth photographs. She was wallowing in agonised surprise but she looked like her teenage self, puppy fat on her cheeks. Stephanie took a sip of tea. 'Anyway Brigid you're looking great. How are you feeling?'

'Fine,' said Brigid. 'A bit bored. A bit impatient, but then apprehensive at the same time. You know, you'll remember it so well.' And in pain she thought, trying to shrug off a rising surge, moving so she was facing away from them, crossing to the sink and running the tap. As the water ran she breathed. The pain rose. It was nothing, she knew. This pain was nothing compared with the pain to come. Later she wouldn't be standing around thinking about the varieties of pain. She would have her head down like a dying animal, simply trying to endure. But now, she stood by the sink, pretending to wash her hands, wondering how long it was lasting and whether she should start to time the contractions.

Breathe and breathe, and now the pain peaked and began to ebb away.

'No, my brain has already been wiped. I've forgotten pregnancy already,' Stephanie was saying.

'It's nerve-racking for Brigid, because she's so overdue,' said Brigid's mother.

'Not nerve-racking because of that,' said Brigid, grimly. 'Anyway, I'm not necessarily overdue.'

'You can always get the little swine induced anyway,' said Stephanie in her matter-of-fact way. 'I went for an induction. But then I had my gross Caesarean, so don't do anything I did.'

'A friend of mine's daughter had a very successful induction the other week,' said Brigid's mother, looking irritated. 'It was over in a few hours, and she hardly needed any pain relief.'

'Lucky her,' said Stephanie, wrinkling her nose. 'There's always one, isn't there?'

'More than one,' said Brigid's mother.

'How's Jack adapting to fatherhood?' said Brigid, with Calumn tugging at her trousers. 'Hello sweetie,' she added. 'How are you? How are you sweetie? Do you want a drink?'

'Neaaarrr,' said Calumn. He was restless and she knew he really wanted to go outside. But she stroked his hair, tried to calm him.

'He's very proud. Keeps emailing photographs of Aurora to everyone. Very doting. Not so keen on the sleepless nights of course – who is? But you know, he's pretty smitten. Rocks her to sleep, puts her in the bath; the man even sings to her. And he rushes home from work and cooks dinner – can you believe it, he actually cooks dinner every night?'

'Well that's very nice of him,' said Brigid's mother. 'Lots of men wouldn't do that.'

'I think he was so amazed by labour. He tried to get down and dirty, help me to push, that sort of stuff. But often he stood there watching, as if he just couldn't believe what he was seeing. Not wanting to stress you out, Brigid,' said Stephanie, flexing her toes and laughing. The baby stirred again, briefly opened its eyes, then settled back to sleep.

'Mum, do you want to take Calumn for a walk?' Brigid said, thinking how much she wanted to talk to Stephanie on her own. 'You could take an umbrella? Or maybe he'd like to hear a story?' She wanted to confide in her friend, tell her how weary she was feeling, how she thought she was in labour, how there was a weight upon her, crushing her so she could hardly breathe and then she felt as if her mother had come to observe her, to spectate at her annihilation, she wanted to say all these things and listen to Stephanie laughing them off. 'Can't be that bad! Just let her make Calumn's lunch and ignore her!' She wanted Stephanie to be outrageous, 'Oh mothers, I never see my mother. Callous witch that I am!' She wished she could just ask her mother to leave them for a while. Come back in an hour, she wanted to say. Or in a day. Come back later, much later.

'Oh no,' said her mother. 'I think he's fine here, with his mummy. Aren't you, Calumn?' Calumn nodded back, and so Brigid's mother settled in, watching Brigid and Stephanie as if they were enacting a bad play, which she had bought her ticket for and might as well see to the end. And Brigid was too polite and didn't insist. Useless, she thought to herself. You are useless.

'How's Patrick?' asked Stephanie.

'Oh, fine. Busy at work. Wants to change his job.'

'It's a good job, he's very lucky,' said her mother.

'Of course, Mum,' said Brigid. 'We're all very lucky. But he still feels like a change.'

'I always thought Patrick's life was rather glamorous,' said her mother. 'Always forging contacts, making deals or whatever it is he does.'

'I think that's fine for a few years, and then it palls a bit,' said Brigid.

'It's a perfectly good job,' said her mother.

Now Brigid looked down and saw that Calumn was curled at her feet, playing half-heartedly with a stuffed toy. He looked listless and she felt a surge of love and pity for him. Poor Calumn, conjured into existence only to be ignored, that was how she felt when she saw him at her feet, uncertain and somehow sad. 'Calumn, sweetie, how are you?' she said. 'Do you want to play a game?' It was still raining outside, or she would have suggested they all went into the garden. 'Do you want to play with tins?' He lifted his head and smiled at her a little. Always he forgave her. He smiled and stood up, bashed her knee in an affectionate way. 'Let me,' said her mother, and took some tins from the cupboard. Now, at least, she went to work immediately. A pile of tins appeared on the floor. Calumn sat down by it. Even though he had done this a thousand times, perhaps even more, he applied himself to the business of knocking down and reassembling the tins.

'Good boy,' said Brigid, kissing him on the top of his head. 'What a very good little boy you are.' She imagined him feeling ambivalence, but she was sure no such emotion had ever troubled her as a child. She had felt joy then sadness, bold and certain states, fleeting in their effects. She didn't feel diffident, or troubled by something she couldn't quite express, or any of these confusing relative states of the adult brain. In childhood she regarded her mother with awe and dependent love, with desperate need. 'You were always crying for me, all day, all night,' her mother later told her. 'You were such a furious little baby, always fuming about something or other.' Brigid had accepted this for years, had told her friends what a difficult baby she was, how her mother had perhaps never entirely forgiven her. She joked about it, though she felt it, too, as a rebuke, something she could never atone for. Having a child had made her reassess the story, or aspects of it now resonated differently. After a few months, she began to think that babies raged not because they were inherently furious, or inherently anything at all; they cried because they wanted to tell you something, and when you didn't hear them, didn't respond or comprehend, they simply cried more loudly. She wondered if her mother really meant something else, if really she was saying that she had been overwhelmed. That she had felt her baby was displeased with her, because she was so uncertain of herself. 'In the end I gave up,' her mother said. 'I couldn't stop your shrieking, so at night I put you in a cot at the end of a corridor, and shut the door. At least then I could sleep.' This had once shocked Brigid, but now she thought there might be something else her mother wanted to tell her – something about losing your grip on things, becoming detached from events you could no longer control. Calumn had never slept through a night, and this had made her more tired than she had ever been before. Yet she understood that his needs were simple; he only wanted her, or Patrick. He was lonely in the darkness. She had always loathed sleeping alone, and if Patrick went away she found it hard to sleep. So how could she blame her son for being lonely at night? For the first year, he slept in a cot by the side of the bed. If he cried she simply lifted him out and took him into bed with her. She stroked his hair and kissed his soft face. Even when she could barely open her eyes, when she moved as if drugged, she felt compelled to kiss him, to hold him as he fell asleep again. She wasn't sure she could have done things differently, and anyway it was too late. Now she had become so huge, they had moved him into his own room. He still cried in the night, but now it was Patrick who consoled him. If it had still been her – if, like her mother, she had never asked her husband to help, or he had never offered – what would she have done?

Whatever she thought, however her thoughts swirled and would not settle, her mother was here. She was here and she was trying to help. This was worth noting, thought Brigid. Perhaps she had always worried that her mother didn't love her much. She had certainly been an unpredictable woman. But now, here was the evidence. She loved Brigid and she loved her grandson, Calumn. She was brimming over with love, some of it revealed clumsily, in these forays and in her determination to advise her daughter, but it was love all the same . . . Now Calumn was grumbling, so she handed him a carrot, said, 'Would you like this, Calumn?'

'Gub,' he said, as he took it.

'A carrot! How lovely,' said her mother. 'A delicious carrot!'

'Awott,' said Calumn.

'Very good,' said Brigid and her mother, together.

'I suppose I'd better go in a minute,' Stephanie was saying, though she had only just arrived. 'I suppose I'd better go before Aurora wakes and we have to embark on the terrible business of breastfeeding once more. You don't want to witness it, I'm afraid. At the moment I have about forty-five minutes from one breastfeed to another. Blissful breast-free minutes, and then it's back to work again. Basically I might as well just put her on my breast and lie in bed all day. It would probably be less hassle.'

'It'll get better,' said Brigid. 'It'll get much much easier.'

Stephanie smiled as if she didn't believe her. 'That's what they say. They say that about everything, really, don't they? The first six weeks are hell, they say. Well, that's certainly true. The breastfeeding is hell at first but it gets better. The first five years are hell but they get better. The whole thing is hell but it gets better. Well, I sure hope it does.' She laughed again, her big round laugh, though it sounded hollow this time.

'Are you enjoying it a bit?' said Brigid. She looked at her more carefully. Stephanie seemed so indestructible, you assumed she would always be OK. But looking more closely, well perhaps after all she looked chastened, as if she hadn't been prepared for this. It was hard to be certain. Her eyes were puffy, but that was just fatigue. She was holding herself carefully, as if she was very delicate, but that was the Caesarean and all her post-natal pain. Then she was bleeding, of course, and she had her heavy breasts, and her nipples all cracked and sore and she was only slowly understanding what had happened to her. The body understood but somehow the brain took a while to catch up.

'I love her very much,' said Stephanie, looking down at her baby, smiling at the sleeping little form. 'I do love her. I just wish these weeks would rush on by. They seem to go so slowly. I wish we could all wake up in a few months' time, with everything established and running more smoothly.'

· 'The ironic thing is, later you'll feel really nostalgic about these early days, when she was so small and completely dependent on you, and all she wanted was to be with you,' said Brigid. 'You really will feel nostalgic when she gets more and more autonomous.'

'I find that hard to believe,' said Stephanie. 'I don't want her to depend on me for everything. I'd quite like her to depend on someone else.' Now she was smiling but Brigid knew she was completely serious. She had been serious throughout, but she had been dressing it up, pretending it was all a joke. 'I just wonder when things get sane again. But perhaps they never do get back to sanity.'

'No, they don't,' said Brigid's mother, firmly, from the floor, where she was showing Calumn how to balance a colander on top of a pile of tins. 'They never do.'

'Oh, that's not true,' said Brigid. 'They get back to a different form of sanity. In some ways it's a richer sort of sanity. I'm not saying it's simple. It's not at all. But the beginning is by far the hardest part. Aside from the bodily stuff, you're struggling to process what has happened to you. You're in a sort of existential crisis, as well as the rest. But it gets better and better, until you decide things are clearly running along too smoothly and you had better cast everything into chaos again by having another one . . .'

'Brigid has had a wonderfully easy baby,' said her mother to Stephanie.

'I don't know if I have or not,' said Brigid. 'I've always thought that people must enjoy it in the end, mustn't they? On balance they must think it's all worth it? Or people wouldn't have more kids, two, three, four kids? They wouldn't keep producing children, if there wasn't something about it they enjoyed.'

'Perhaps it's just that they lose any sense that they once did other things,' said Stephanie. She looked uncertainly at her baby, still sleeping, eyes tightly shut, pink mouth open.

The baby looked serene, even confident, and yet Stephanie looked uncertain nonetheless, as if the sight even of its serenity was troubling to her.

'I just worried all the time,' said Brigid's mother. 'All the hours of the day I was worrying.'

'Well, you didn't need to,' said Brigid.

'Perhaps I did. Perhaps if I hadn't worried then you wouldn't be here now,' said her mother, defiantly. 'Colander, Calumn, it's a colander. We put salads in it and pasta. To dry them off. CO-LAN-DER.'

'Oblambar,' said Calumn.

'Very good darling,' said Brigid.

'I don't worry about Aurora,' said Stephanie. 'I feel somehow she'll be OK.'

'Oblambar coblandar oblandar.'

'Well of course she will be,' said Brigid's mother. 'She's a sweet little thing.'

'She's gorgeous,' said Brigid, quickly, because her mother sounded so tepid.

Always she was trying to force her mother back, or counteract her perceived effects. And Brigid thought how much she wanted to love her mother simply and virtuously, because she was afraid otherwise her children would grow up feeling varieties of ambivalence towards her. They would learn from her poor example, experience the same confusion of emotions as she did. And perhaps this was her mother's fear too, that despite all her work she had only received this imperfect love from her daughter. Perhaps this was why she came round and couldn't quite leave, couldn't stop coming round and staying too long, because she was still trying to earn something better.

'Would you like another cup of tea?' she said to Stephanie.

'Oh no, I really have to go. I really do have to feed Aurora. Thanks anyway,' said Stephanie, struggling to get up. Calumn turned and watched her, a tin in his hand. Then he stood on tiptoe to look at the baby again, still sleeping in the pram.

'Well, thanks for dropping by,' said Brigid.

'Nice to see you, Mrs Morgan.'

'You too dear,' said her mother.

'Bye bye Calumn boy,' said Stephanie, bending towards him, ruffling his hair. Calumn looked up, didn't smile, and then went back to his tins. Under-stimulated, thought Brigid, and Stephanie thought how little she understood babies, how she couldn't understand her own and certainly not Brigid's. For a moment Stephanie felt appalled and longed to beg for help, but then she was kissing Brigid, saying, 'Best of luck darling,' and pushing the pram back along the hall.

'Send greetings to Patrick,' Stephanie said, as she waved goodbye on the step.

Brigid turned back towards the kitchen and now she felt the pain so harshly that she almost cried out. Involuntarily, she stiffened. Her mother was doing something in the kitchen and couldn't see her. Calumn was there, picking through the vegetables. Lacking any sense of what was to come, or perhaps he was somehow attuned to her, sensitive to her shifting moods. She wasn't sure. At that moment the only thing she could be certain about was this pain. A very rising pain, shrill at its heights, really making her nerves scream and then just when she thought the note would go on forever, this jangling shrillness, it began to diminish, slowly it faded, and then there was silence.

In the silence of the hall Brigid knew – there was no longer any doubt – that she was in labour. The battle had begun and now her body would rip itself in two.

She heard the radio in the background; her mother must have switched it on again. The pips of the hour. It was one o'clock. Through London, ordinary people were eating lunch, oblivious to the trials that awaited her. Then there were women, countless women she didn't know, experiencing something similar, the earliest beginnings or the climactic agony or the final relief. Throughout London, and that consoled her a little even as she dreaded the hours to come. Her body was trying to douse her fear, dilute it with consoling hormones. Yet she felt it all the same. And she heard the newsreader saying, 'And today' – today the prime minister travels to Washington. Some sportsmen have won glory on the pitch. Some wars are raging and an earthquake has taken thousands of lives. In his office, Patrick Hayes checks his watch, and now he is taking his jacket and setting off for his important lunch – and now she heard her mother calling, 'Brigid darling, do let me make us both another cup of tea.'

The Hermit

For years he had failed and failed again; he had been disappointed a hundred times and then he had the book in
his hand. They told him this was the one; Sally told him.
So Michael Stone put on an unfamiliar suit, and in the
sweating interior of his small flat his hands trembled as he
pulled a tie around his neck. He was nervous and his sense
of vindication – even triumph! – had ebbed away. His
nerves were bad and threatened to spoil it all, but he drew
his tie into a knot, tried to smooth his lapels. He took his
hat and settled it upon his head. The night before, he had
sewn up a tear in his shirt. He had even clipped his beard.
Yet when he glanced in the mirror he saw a grey-faced
unkempt man, ravaged by anxiety and something else he
couldn't quite understand. An incongruous pink tie slung
around his neck. He saw it all, in the glass before him, then
he wiped his hands on his trousers, and turned away.

He had been waiting a long time – it was terrible to contemplate – but really he had been waiting all his life for
this day.

In the upper dining room of an expensive London club, a
gathering of literary men and women. Four of them, and
Sally. They pulled out a chair for him. 'How nice to meet
you,' they said, their hands outstretched. Sally said their

names and he nodded. Yet his nerves made everything twist and shift around him. It was as if a chasm had opened up; he was stranded on the edge, and before him was deep empty space. They were on the other side, far beyond him. They sent words across, they smiled towards him. 'How nice to meet you, come and join us! You only have to jump!' He was stranded on the other side, though he had longed for years to be rescued. He had written his books; again and again he hoped that one of them would find an audience. It was a ritual he performed, a devout observance. He finished something, something of which he was proud, then laboured in the photocopying shop, bound it all proudly, addressed envelopes and waited. Urgently, later in despair. He lifted his head, they shot him into his hole again. It had been like that for years. His universe was predictable, the rules seemed firm and fast – he tried, then he failed. Again he lifted his head – but this time they had seized him; Sally had drawn him upwards, into the light. And he should have been glad, but everything had moved so quickly, his consoling realities had been shattered, and this chasm had opened up before him.

'Some wine, sir?' said the waiter.

'Thank you,' said Michael Stone, and watched as wine was poured into his glass. Then the waiter twisted the bottle, and moved away.

'Michael,' Sally was saying. 'This is Roger Annais, who was speaking about your book this morning on Radio 4. Roger, I haven't yet been able to hear the programme but I've been told you were excellent.'

'Well, I don't know about that,' said Roger Annais, a man with black hair, a sunken face, as if his features had been carved from wax, and were melting slowly. 'I was just trying to voice my genuine admiration. It's often easier to demolish something than praise it, I find. One can at least be wry when something is bad. Admiration can start to sound a little . . . dull . . .'

'Thank you for doing that,' said Michael Stone, in his very soft, dry voice, which, though he cleared his throat, would not resonate, sounded merely like dead leaves crackling. 'I really am . . . most grateful.'

'No need for gratitude. You wrote it, it's my job to comment on it,' said Roger, firmly. He took a sip of wine. Michael noticed his veins bulged on his arms, as if he was malnourished. But he was more likely a driven, energetic man. He imagined him, rushing from the studio to his office, his day portioned into meaningful segments. Always he must have an eye on the clock; he must move swiftly, purposefully; a radio interview and then a lunch, and then – Michael wondered what this man would do later. But he was looking back at Michael as he put down his glass, so Michael said, 'I have been . . . in recent days I have been a little nervous. I keep wondering if . . . perhaps . . . I should not have published this book at all . . .' as Sally shook her head.

'Ah, the misgivings. The opening-night jitters,' said a man Sally had introduced as 'Arthur Grey, reviewer and friend . . .' And Arthur Grey continued – resting his stocky arms on the table and speaking slowly, careful in his phrasing, as if he was dictating a letter – 'With my first published book, a novel, I woke at dawn on the morning the first reviews were due. I pulled on my clothes, dashed out, bought all the papers. Dashed back, heart pounding, ha ha! Read through them, couldn't find a word about it, finally found the briefest imaginable review in *The Times*.

"Not so much a promising beginning as a horrible threat that further carnage may be yet to come . . ." Ha, ha . . . !'

And the table laughed. Michael joined in, a false laugh because the story only made him more afraid. If that could happen to Arthur Grey, if this compelling man could be so emphatically dismissed, then what did he think he was doing? But they were lifting up their throats and laughing together, and he didn't want to show them how he had lost his nerve. So he laughed and tried to swallow some wine.

'The best review I ever wrote, the most honest, began: "By Mary and the blessed saints, this is a dreadful book", said Roger Annais, and they laughed again.

On his right-hand side was Sally Blanchefleur, his agent, co-director of Blanchefleur and Scott, wearing a deep-green dress, gaunt and beautiful, striking at fifty or so, more striking than anyone else in the room. She drew attention away from Michael, with her beauty and her deep-green dress. Just some of the glare, directed towards her elegance; that was a relief. On his left, his editor Peter Kennedy, who had taken up his book, rescued it – he was meant to call him his saviour, he knew. And then an order of the just around him, like a secret society. In recent days he had been ushered around, people gripping his arm, directing him. Shielding him from something – he was not sure what it could be. One moment he felt revived, better than he had in years, and then he simply wanted to run. He didn't want to be at the centre of anything, felt it might even have been a bad idea, to write books, only tenable when your works were never read. If they printed them up, distributed your efforts – that was a different matter altogether. And then he wondered what it had been for, all those years of suspense and futile endeavour, and being knocked back a hundred times; he wondered why he had bothered with it all. Why had he persisted, and raged against his detractors? He had been so urgent and angry about it all. For years he could hardly read a book, because he was not published. He could not really take pleasure in anything, and then he had grown so angry with his family – really his mother – because she was so foul about it all, told him he was wasting his time, that he would never achieve anything worth the years he had taken over it all. And his father and the callow rest of them backed her up, stood firm against him, as if he was an enemy they must vanquish. A few years ago he wrote a novel in the depths of his rage, hurled everything he could at their piety and hypocrisy, and – even though that novel sank without a trace, like all the others – they never spoke to him again.

He had almost stopped thinking about his mother, until that phone call from James. That had been unexpected, a little disturbing, because James had sounded upset, and he was usually so quiet and cold. He had talked about dementia, how their mother had been diagnosed with it, 'a bad case of it,' James added, as if there might be another, better sort of dementia. 'I'm sorry to hear that,' Michael had said. But he was surprised to discover he felt nothing at all. It was as if they were discussing a distant relative. A month later, James had called again, saying that it would be 'nice' if Michael went to see her. 'She won't be at home much longer. She has a nurse but soon she'll have to go into a home.'

'She'll hate that,' Michael had said.

'She barely knows where she is. She may not notice.'

He thought it was odd, that his mother was finally passive, an invalid, to be shunted from one place to another, on the advice of doctors. It was hard to imagine. The only time he felt truly sad about it all was when he received the first copies of his book. Beautiful in their dust jackets, his name on each spine in bold letters. It was an extraordinary moment, and there was no one apart from him who cared. So he sent a copy to his mother, one to his brother. He bound them up, spent a long time writing his mother a little note. Then he took the note out. He put a press release in with each copy, so they might think a functionary had sent them, some hard-working publicity person, not him at all. He hesitated in the post office, then he handed the parcels over.

He had received no response.

Yet this morning he was rushing to the door when the phone rang. He grabbed it, thinking it might be Sally, but then he heard James saying, 'Ah Michael, I thought you might not be at home.'

'I'm just about to leave . . .'

'I was just sent a copy of your book,' said James. 'For which, my thanks. I see that today is the date of its official publication. You must be busy . . .'

'Yes,' said Michael, wondering why his brother was always so formal, but then he supposed he was too. 'How is our mother?'

'She is being moved into a home in a few weeks' time. I'll send you the details of her address when she has settled in.'

'All right.'

'Then if you want to visit . . .'

'I don't think she would . . .'

'She's very different now. You'd see if you came.'

The call made him late, so then he had been forced to hurry to the Underground, sweating and certain he would offend them all, but everyone was late, apologising to each other, and it hadn't mattered. They had drawn him into a private room in an expensive restaurant, where there was a waiter at his elbow, asking would he like the fish or the lamb.

Lamb, he said.

For the question must be answered.

Sally was saying something to him, and he turned to listen. 'The first reviews,' she said. 'I have them in my bag. I must warn you . . .' and she leaned closer to him, dropped her voice to a whisper. 'They are not marvellous. Not quite what we hoped for. But there are many more yet to come.'

'What did they say?'

She shook her head at him. 'I'll show them to you later. Dismiss them from your mind. Now, Michael . . .'

'Yes?'

'Drink up. We've a long day ahead.' And she clinked her glass on his.

Briefly he panicked, felt his heart fluttering in his breast, thought how difficult it was even to breathe, to lift the chest, fill the lungs and empty them again – he sat there, looking at his hands, paying careful attention to the rising and falling of his chest, and after a few minutes he was able to lift his head. Someone was speaking, but not to him. 'I liked your programme about George Lamott,' a woman was saying. Alice Mortimer, he remembered now, a woman with auburn hair, tiny arms wrapped in silver. She was speaking to Roger Annais, who was nodding back at her as she said, 'One element which has become apparent during this episode is that we are losing any sense of values worth fighting for. Because we have no sense of these values, we are constantly buffeted by the values of others, or by our perceptions of these values. We are over-conciliatory, imagining these values to be more and more absolute the more confused we become.'

'I agree,' said Roger Annais, nodding still. 'When the religious tell us that their "beliefs" must be respected, we acquiesce carefully. We don't dare to ask "Why?"'

'The funny thing is, that even on your programme, Roger, they were so reluctant really to discuss the heart of the matter. I was amused to see how nervous they were, how they censored themselves even as they debated the issue of self-censorship,' said Alice Mortimer.

'George Lamott's point is very simple, as I understand it,' said Arthur Grey. 'He argues that it has become usual to fudge the whole thing. Instead of being prepared to say, "No, this is wrong, it is simply wrong-headed to find any of this offensive," we say, "Well, there may be those who misinterpret these words, and thereby, we cannot proceed."'

'It's not entirely their fault,' said Roger Annais. 'Things sometimes do get blown out of proportion. Suddenly, the thing becomes a cause célèbre. Perhaps someone says something misguided in an interview, irritates someone or a group of people.'

'Nonetheless we are losing our grip,' said Alice Mortimer, with a wave of her arm, so her bracelets chimed and sparkled. 'So many ideas are mediated for people. So you can have a small enclave – a highly intelligent enclave – deliberately misrepresenting something, in order to get people fired up. They know that these people won't ever read the original. They will just respond to the call to anger, in essence.'

'It's the way of elites everywhere. The ordinary people never know what's really going on,' said Arthur Grey.

Michael listened, though he wasn't sure what they meant. He had a sense of drama, something they all regarded as significant. They leaned towards each other; they had forgotten him. It was right, too, that he should be so easily forgotten. He had sequestered himself for too many years, he had never heard of George Lamott. They had opened the door to him – just a crack – he had squeezed himself through. He had crawled into this elegant lunch, because the door was slightly open, and he had been hammering on it for years.

'It will be interesting to see whether this type of affair becomes quite common, whether publishers will continue in this vein,' Arthur Grey said.

'And then you will have authors censoring themselves before anyone else does,' said Roger Annais. 'Perhaps this is already happening.'

'All you need is fear. You don't even need legislation. You just need everyone a bit worried, glancing over his or her shoulder. It's a marvellous way to change a society, without having to go through the boring process of campaigning for legislative change,' said Alice Mortimer.

'It will be interesting to see what the response of the

reading public is. Whether they buy this book, simply to see what the problem was.'

'I hope they do,' said Alice Mortimer. 'That would annoy a few people.'

'I don't think it's fair to blame the religious in this. Not one of them has voiced any objections to Lamott's book. This is not a question of religious extremists versus liberal democracy,' said Sally.

'... It is the suicide of liberal democracy. It's self-annihilation by degrees ...'

'Like lemmings, we jump,' said Arthur Grey. 'We jump before we are pushed. There is no one around, even, but just in case someone appears, someone who might – or might not – push us – we jump.'

'They are not liberal, in the true sense,' said Alice Mortimer. 'They are double agents, working to smash the edifice from within.'

'Well, you don't hear swathes of the religious denouncing the whole thing.'

'That's not true, some of them have.'

'Not enough of them,' said Roger Annais.

Their voices merged, as Michael sweated and twisted his fork in his hand. They said, 'Naturally ... One need hardly say ... Of course ...' All that he did not understand was clear to them. They nodded at each other, ate with gusto, splashed wine into their glasses. They clashed vividly, or concurred suddenly – everything was emphatic, determined. Then it was as if they suddenly remembered they must include him, and so they issued a general murmur, '... but however ... Let us not ... We oughtn't ...' Alice Mortimer nodded her auburn curls towards him. '... Now,

The Moon . . .' she began to say.

And he nodded back at her.

'Yes, I wanted to ask you about your title,' she said, with a wave of her silver arms. 'Odd title, I thought, considering the subject of your story. And then I wondered, is it *la lune ne garde aucune rancune*, the all-forgiving moon? Or Diana and the hunt? What did you mean by it, if you don't mind my asking?'

'I don't mind at all,' said Michael. In the silence that settled around him, he fumbled with his words. 'I meant . . . well, something about madness of course, and then . . . something about . . . unknown mystery, something which is intuited but not . . . precisely . . . something which can't show itself . . .'

'Who intuits it?' said Roger Annais.

'I hoped that might remain . . . a little ambiguous . . .' said Michael. They paused and nodded, as if to encourage him. Then Arthur Grey was saying, 'I thought it was a most interesting book, but there was something I wanted to ask you about. This poor man Semmelweis – who I confess I had never heard of before – is opposed to one sort of dogmatism – the adamant beliefs of the doctors around him, their particular theories about childbed fever. This dogmatism is ruinous, we are made to see. But then he develops his own opinions, and though they are right, it turns out later, he is relentless in his arguments, dogmatic himself, one might say. He insults his opponents, bombards them with invective, and won't submit to the rules of scientific experiment. Essentially he is as dogmatic as his foes, is he not?'

Michael lifted his head. They were waiting, expecting him to answer. Yes, he wanted to say. It is not coherent.

Naturally when I began, I hoped my book would be lucid and true, and yet as I wrote it – even as I wrote it – I sensed it was spiralling out of my control. And then I thought perhaps it did not matter, that – like everything else I wrote – it would not be read, nothing would come of it. He wanted to say this; he wondered briefly about saying it, but then he wasn't sure how it would sound to them, so he wiped his hands and said, 'It is true that Semmelweis is very angry . . . Perhaps this anger loses him the argument . . . But somehow, to me, I think . . . Well, I think there is – surely there must be – a difference between the lone figure . . . and the many. The one and the confident many. Perhaps the many are so confident – dogmatic – only because they are among the many. Not because they have thought really – truly thought – about what they say. The solitary man must either say nothing . . . or shout to be heard . . .'

Michael took a gulp of wine, pushed his greying hair from his temple. There was a lingering pause, while they hesitated, not wanting to curtail him. And he tried to fill it, but something – his shyness, native anxiety, or Sally would have told him it was stress – he didn't know what it was, but something mangled his words. They waited, while he said, 'Really . . . that was . . . I think that was what I meant . . .,' and then they resumed.

'I felt Semmelweis was an anti-hero,' said Alice Mortimer, briskly, as if trying to show him how easy it was, just to talk, to speak and be understood. 'There is a distance between us and him. I felt he was essentially unknowable, as a man.' That set Michael trembling again, because he thought they might want him to answer, and he wiped his palms together, but Roger Annais was saying something about a fatal flaw. '. . . Something quite classical about his downfall. Perhaps that's what you mean, Alice; he isn't a modern character, as we now understand characterisation. He's too archetypal. But, I should really let Michael reply . . .'

He was sweating though the room was cool, full of manufactured cold air. Like the other men, he had taken off his jacket, and undone his tie. As if they were saying, now we are among friends, that was what he thought it meant, all their loosened collars, their jackets slung over the backs of their chairs. With the trousers of his suit wrinkled, a smart suit he had been forced to borrow, never having had much need for one before, Michael saw their faces blurring and re-forming, and he tried to say, 'I rather enjoy . . . hearing all of your opinions . . . For a long time I lacked readers . . .' He wiped his temple again, and because he was floundering, Sally stepped in.

'Michael is very tired. He has been working on this book for many years. He is a little overwhelmed, I believe.'

They nodded and murmured back at her. And Michael breathed more easily, because Sally had granted him a respite. So he slouched a little in his seat, and took another slug of wine.

He only had tenuous impressions, warped by his nerves. Peter Kennedy, head of Giraffe Books, the imprint which had finally published him, was leaning towards him – they were all leaning towards him. He was embarrassed to dis-

95

cover that they were trying to encourage him. So he leaned forward politely because Peter Kennedy was saying, 'I'd like to propose a toast anyway. To *The Moon*.'

Michael tried to smile, and while Peter added a few more words of praise he pushed his grey hair back, and fiddled with his cuffs, and there was a general murmur as they all lifted their glasses. And Sally said, 'I am just so glad you decided to publish it, Peter.'

Under the table, Michael wiped his palms together. The talk continued; he was glad when the debate surged around him. And while they talked, he saw the room was filled with soft afternoon light; furtively he watched Roger Annais marking his words with a beat beat of his hands and Arthur Grey nodding twice in return, and there was someone else saying, 'I'm writing to *The Times* about Lamott today; anyone want to sign it?'

Yes, they said. 'Email me the letter when you've drafted it,' said one, and another said, 'Don't you want to wait, to see if there is any more fuss?'

'No, I think I'd like to speak now. I know my opinion already.'

'One can only hope it will strike a general chord.'

Roger Annais marked his words with a beat beat of his hands and Michael caught Arthur Grey staring towards him – their eyes met, and Arthur Grey half-smiled, half-nodded, then looked away.

One can only hope, thought Michael. For them, there was an intellectual point to be made, a debate for the letters pages. Beyond him, a controversy raged, something he did not understand. More important than his book, something which reverberated widely. For him, there was the business of the reviews - this sense of judgement, of a public reckoning – perhaps this was why his hand kept trembling when he lifted his glass, why he was drinking such a steady stream of wine. And Sally was pressing his arm, to let him know she was there. 'It's hard, the first book,' he had heard her saying earlier, to a friend of hers. Into her mobile, she had said, 'Especially at his age.'

There were reasons why you became a writer. Diffidence, a fear of social events. An affinity for solitude. Perhaps even misanthropy. You had to like sitting alone in a room. You had to be able to conjure your best thoughts and phrases alone. It seemed to Michael that some people were writers because they wrote better than they talked. He talked very badly, and had never – until now – been asked about his books. He had hardly been called upon to justify or explain them. He had not minded this much; he thought such explanations would be redundant anyway. How could you express something more plainly in a hasty phrase than in a meticulously worked sentence? Surely you were more likely to traduce yourself, to expose all the inner contradictions of your crafted prose? Yet recently they had been asking him to parse his phrases. They had been saying, 'When you wrote . . . what did you mean?' 'When you said this . . . what did this mean?' Sometimes he tried to explain that it was not him, it was a narrator. 'But you wrote the narrator,' they said, which was true enough. 'But I am not the narrator.' 'But what did you mean when you made him say . . .?' 'Can you be more plain?' they asked, but he wasn't sure he could.

He had become a writer so he could avoid his kind, so he could evade the false intimacy of the office and days spent in the company of others. He had been a solitary child; his own mother had told him so. 'People need you more than you need them,' she once said. In youth he suffered through a few office jobs; he shuffled papers and was ignored by his colleagues – he had been too quiet to interest them, so they left him alone. He dragged himself through these jobs and then he spent years as a language teacher. I am, you are, he is. We are, they are. John likes to go to the cinema. Do you like to go to the cinema? Then he got a job teaching creative writing at Hendon College of Further Education, when he simply wanted to be alone with the thoughts in his head. He wanted to live within these thoughts; they were compelling enough to him. If he could have made a living from writing, he would perhaps have never left his room. He might have been a true recluse, his desk turned away from the window, oblivious to everything except the page. His pen moving through space. The hours moving onwards.

'Sally tells me you have spent years writing?' Arthur Grey was asking, as if he had read Michael's mind. It was a benevolent enquiry, he heard the kindness in the man's voice, and so he said, 'Yes, most of my life . . .'

'You were struggling? I mean . . . to earn money?'

'I did odd jobs . . . But it was not . . . very elegant . . .'

'Michael has been rather ill,' said Sally, protectively. 'He wore himself down writing and – now – worrying.'

'It is the uncertainty,' said Michael. 'The sense that one's words . . . are not one's own; that they might mean in ways one . . . didn't expect . . . It was not my intention . . . all of this . . .'

'Of course it wasn't. Art was your intention,' said Arthur Grey. 'But I interrupted you, you were saying . . .'

'I was trying to write about conviction . . .' – and the table nodded – '. . . about those who propose something that is not generally thought, and how they are dealt with. About those who are convinced of what they say, to the point that they continue to speak, even when everyone has turned away. And I felt that . . . all things being unknowable, all real things, all real mysteries, then . . . well, who can stand, really, and say, "I know; I understand"? I wanted to write . . . something about this . . . impulse . . . to tell others what is true . . .'

Their polite silence made things worse, kept surging into the cracks in his sentences.

'I wanted to ask why some people are raised . . . aloft, and others cast down . . . into darkness,' he said.

They nodded back at him.

He wanted to tell them that he couldn't remember precisely what he had been thinking of at the time. That it was a long time ago, a few years, that he started thinking about this book. He could not quite remember what it was, the original spark, the kernel he had begun with. He had been interested, for a long time before he even began his book, in the history of medicine, and then he read about Ignaz Semmelweis, this man who had driven himself mad. He was gripped by the story of Semmelweis, that was sure enough. So he started writing about Semmelweis, perhaps he intended to write only about him, but then other strands emerged. The whole thing took months, then years. His narrator rattled on – he supposed it was himself, some aspect of himself – so he set this man rattling on, and the whole story became – or to him it seemed this way – a metaphor, for any system of belief. It might be Christianity or it might be evolution, or the idea that humours governed the body. While he was writing, it occurred to him that there had been a time when medicine was founded on entirely different principles, then accepted as persuasive – the beneficial properties of leeches, or the uses of phrenology. And people had been convinced of these ideas. And there had been a time when mainstream science assumed that continental drift was impossible, and Wegener was branded eccentric. History was littered with such characters, proposing theories that offended the norms of their profession, finding themselves ostracised. And he thought the same was true of religions, in the end, that each new religion set itself up against others that had gone before, that the history of mankind was littered with discarded gods and goddesses. Something about Semmelweis's frantic talk of mothers, his obsessive devotions, made him think of all the crones and goddesses who had been worshipped for thousands of years and then shoved aside. Artemis, Isis, Ishtar, Ashtoreth, Brigid, Cybele: their temples burned, left in ruins, their powers spent. And there was something else he didn't even manage to formulate entirely, something which lurked beneath, but he wrote because it was a habit and he couldn't stop himself, and he wanted to be published because he was vain – perhaps that was it, he simply wanted to be able to look at his published books, feel the glossy covers.

He wanted to tell them all – Arthur Grey and Alice Mortimer and Roger Annais – that he only meant – his narrator only meant – that much had been forgotten, much remained obscure and perhaps unknowable. That it was madness to presume to know. Even to speak – to write – was perhaps madness, and he hardly expected anyone to agree with anything he wrote. Even as he drove words onto the page, he assumed his opinions were his own small maniacal perceptions, and he didn't think they would necessarily chime with anyone else's. Because of this, he felt quite alone.

He wrote his novel, and sent it to his agent, Sally Blanchefleur, who was impatient with him at the time and thought he would never do well. She had been his agent for years and it was clear her patience was wearing thin. The previous novel he sent her, she had not liked at all. She had taken months to respond, and finally she wrote, 'Michael, I am sorry, but frankly I am not convinced.' Nothing more than that, a terse note, after all his years of writing and the months she had taken to reply. He wanted never to speak to her again, after that, but she was the only agent who had ever replied to him, and he knew no others. So instead he badgered her on the phone, begged her for answers. 'You are an intelligent man but you have to decide what you want,' she told him, a trace of boredom in her voice. 'Either accept your circumstances, or try to write something more . . . palatable to the general reader.'

Palatable, he had thought, sitting in his little room, in his flat in South London. To become palatable. That was the challenge she had set him. At fifty-five, to live in a small flat in South London pursuing unwanted projects; it was foolish to resist. But he found he was intractable, he couldn't do it. He didn't want to masquerade as someone else, and anyway he lacked the necessary daring. He simply couldn't do it. 'It wouldn't hurt if you became a little more digestible' – that was another phrase Sally used. The public appetite, the general palate, had no taste for him. Sally had been loyal, but now her loyalty was laced with fatigue and perhaps an element of pity. Poor old Michael Stone, better ring him. 'Never mind, sometimes you can create your own audience,' she would say. 'Perhaps you'll be the exception.' But he felt she didn't really believe it.

He had been writing for himself, that was the thing. He had been alone in a silent room and he had forgotten there was any chance of being overheard. Like being schizophrenic. You spoke to yourself and then you answered. You did not need to clarify your words; you were content with suggestions, half-fashioned thoughts. And then someone else invaded your cosy talk, this conversation you were having with yourself. Someone eavesdropped, heard half of what you were saying, or even less perhaps, and then they began to talk over you. They said, 'So this is what you mean.' Not even 'what I think you mean'. Simply 'this is'. First one, then a group of them, saying loudly and firmly, 'This is the meaning of your rambling indecisive prose. We will explain.' They got more loquacious. They talked and then they condemned you.

With *The Moon* everything had been different. 'Well, Michael,' Sally said. 'Perhaps we might finally find you a publisher.' He wanted to sob with relief. 'There are many problems,' she added. He listened, gripping the phone. 'Men are unlikely to read a book about childbirth. It's unfortunate, but there's not much to be done. Women might just, but they'll get put off by your obscure doctor. And the title too – the title is rather awkward.' But he didn't want to change the title. 'It sounds like a dreary symbolist novel,' said Sally. 'And this rambling narrator, who seems mad himself. It's as if you want to talk about everything, in one book. You can't talk about everything in one book. It's boring and it bores the reader.'

But he did want to talk about everything, the universe as he found it, not that he was much of an interpreter. He wanted to cry out how beautiful he found it, but how he was mired in darkness and knew nothing at all. Perhaps he wanted to find a way to express his ignorance. Sally explained to him – rather sternly – that he should take her advice, she was trying her best – she had been ringing around everyone she could think of, and finally – she could hardly believe it herself – she had found him a publisher. That sent him into nervous joy for a few days, and then they backed out. The editor was sorry. 'Terribly sorry. Not my decision,' he wrote. On second thoughts, they had decided it was not right for their list. They had thought carefully – 'agonised long and hard', wrote the editor – and they simply didn't want the book. 'They don't think it's worth it,' said Sally, and now she lined up beside him. She phoned him regularly to give him progress reports. Finally she found Peter Kennedy who told him he loved the book and paid him almost nothing, but no one else would consider it at all, and so - Sally explained - he really had no choice.

Sally was brisk and unsentimental. 'It's a good novel, I'm not saying it isn't a good novel, but it will be tough to find it a large readership,' she said to him on the phone. 'I've been talking to Peter, we were discussing the vogue for historical dramas, perhaps there's something in that – but still, there's only so far they can go.' Michael tried to explain – once again he tried, though of course he was never persuasive – that wasn't the point, but she was already talking over him. 'Look, you have to relax a bit,' she said. 'I'll get some friends to throw a launch party for you. And we'll have a nice lunch on the day. Then you just have to hope the reviews are kind.' And now she had them, hidden in her bag. She would not show them to him, she did not want to spoil their nice lunch.

'Would you like some more wine, sir?' the waiter was saying in his ear. He nodded and held out his glass.

'How is the lamb?' said Sally.

'Very good,' he said.

They were speaking quietly, and the talk continued around them. She put her hand on his arm again. 'You do look pale, Michael. Is there anything else you would like?'

'I wish I had done everything much better,' he said. 'I wish I had . . .'

'It's important to sustain a sense of humour about all of this,' said Sally. 'It's a sort of game. Not the work, the work is very important. But the launch, this, the business surrounding you. That's a sort of game. It can be fun, even.'

'Yes.'

'If you are too worried about what people think of your work, you will only be disappointed,' she said.

'I am not disappointed,' he said. 'I am . . .'

She waited politely, with her fork raised.

' . . . in shock,' he said.

Then the waiters came and began to clear the plates away.

'Michael, what will you do after this?' said Alice Mortimer.

'Perhaps . . . I would like to go on holiday,' said Michael.

They smiled at him, laughed a little.

'Are you working on another book?' said Roger Annais.

'I don't have any ideas at present. I have been . . . well, it has been hard to focus on my work . . .'

'Of course it has,' said Alice Mortimer. 'I remember that, you feel you have to test the water, before you start again.'

'We need more wine,' said Sally, holding up her hand. 'We really should have another drink.'

Michael looked down. They had taken his plate away. He had hardly touched the food, he had merely drunk the wine. So now his head was thick with wine and if anyone wanted to speak to him this afternoon, he would be drunk.

He would pass the rest of the day stewed in wine, and tomorrow – perhaps tomorrow – things would be different. It was an irony that after all these years of hoping for an audience, of imagining that was what he needed, he found these people so bemusing. He longed for the privacy of his room, where he sat for years without anyone noticing. Unsullied, immaculate in his obscurity and failure. The river coursed along beneath him, dragging everyone else along. He saw them dragged along each morning, surging towards the Underground, and he thought of them being poured into London, into their offices. And then they flooded home at five and six and seven o'clock, short and fat and tall and broad, conveyed by the current, subject to its force. He surveyed everything from his tower and thought he had escaped it. He surveyed them from the safety of the shore. He had been voluntarily beached for years. And now, somehow, he had been dragged in. Here they all were, these people who swam with the current and he was there too, but they were swimming along, buoyant and accustomed to their state, and he was drowning even as they spoke to him.

The waiter was putting something down in front of him. A crème brûlée, perfectly glazed on top.

'How delicious,' said Sally. 'Dessert wine, anyone?'
    'Down the hatch,' said Peter Kennedy.
    So Michael Stone lifted his glass and received another splash of wine.

Everything had been soured by that phone call. It was the peculiar tone in his brother's voice, something almost police, when for years James had treated him as if he was pathetic, unspeakable. Polite and yet cold all the same, as if hostilities were off for the time being, while their mother declined, out of some sort of warped notion of decorum – yet he did not want to have to think about James, or his mother. They always made him feel anxious about things he had previously enjoyed. Even his childhood had been nervous, because of his mother's godliness and determination, because she always had so much to say about even the smallest things. She ordered the world so convincingly, classified everything as either 'good' or 'bad'. He couldn't believe she had really changed. Things were better when he ignored them, but then the chilly voice of his brother had intruded, making him uneasy again. It made him think of an ancient patriarch, some ogre of his childhood, standing in judgement, far above him. He saw himself clambering towards this venerable prophet – perhaps he was on a mountain, by a stone temple. Michael saw himself struggling up to the peak, approaching with his head bowed, and there was the old sage, swinging his hoary locks towards him, saying, 'You have done wrong. You have done everything wrong and for this wrong you must be punished.'

As he had always done, in childhood and even in adult life, Michael felt uncertain, guilty even, found himself saying, 'But what is it? Just what is it I have done?'

The Tower

Transcripts of interviews with members of the anti-species conspiracy of Lofoten 4a, Arctic Circle sector 111424

Part 1, 10.00–11.55 a.m. 15 August 2153
Interview with Prisoner 730004

At time of commencement the prisoner will not disclose her real name.

I do not understand. Just what is it I have done?

Prisoner 730004 you are aware that your crimes against the species are very grave and you stand under a charge of conspiring against the Genetix and thereby against the survival of humanity?

I am aware of the charges but I do not understand what I have done to merit them.

The Protectors are very disappointed with you. They perceive that you have behaved in a reckless manner, dangerous to all. What do you say to this?

I am sorry the Protectors are disappointed. Yet I remain confused about the nature of my offence.

They regret to inform you that while they seek to assess all matters reasonably and dispassionately, your case and that of your co-conspirators must be considered a crime. We are appointed to discuss with you the precise nature of this crime and to relay information to the Protectors on your behalf. Do you understand?

I do not really understand, no.

Could you firstly explain how you came to be living in Lofoten 4a, Arctic Circle sector 111424, in the Restricted Area?

You mean on the island?

Lofoten 4a, Arctic Circle sector 111424, yes. Can you explain how you came to be living there?

We were living in the land of our mothers and fathers . . .

Correction, for 'mothers and fathers' the record will read egg and sperm donors.

. . . Generations were born and lived their lives there. We merely wanted to be at home.

You were not happy with your accommodation in Darwin C?

Naturally I should have felt fortunate. In our perilous times, Darwin C supplied me with everything I should need. I had my allocated role in the struggle for the survival of the species. I had my own small room which is called a space. A regulated lamp which functioned from nightfall for a regulation hour, during which time I could arrange my clothes for the following day, pull my bed down from the wall. I had a thin window with a view of all the other towers. I took my meals in the collective dining centre, like everyone else. I washed in the collective hygiene centre, and I received my daily allocation of drinking water. On Sunday mornings, I was granted three hours of relaxation time. I liked to read in the collective data hall. Despite all this, I became aware that Darwin C was not my home.

But you had lived there all your life, is that correct?

Yes, my parents were taken there before I was born. They were removed forcibly from their home and taken to a space on the twenty-eighth floor, sector 1125, Darwin C. My mother was harvested and then sterilised and I was the product of her Genetix treatment. As you know in those days it was the custom for Genetix children to live with their parents.

Correction, for 'mother' the record will read egg donor. And for 'children' the record will read progeny of the species. And for 'parents' the record will read sperm and egg donors.

Now of course this is no longer the case.

How did it come to pass that you left Darwin C, Prisoner 730004?

I had a dream. I dreamed of torrents of blood. I was swimming in a sea of blood. In my dream I was encased in blood. Yet I was not drowning. It was astonishing but I could breathe in the blood. I was drinking the blood and I liked the taste of it. In my dream I understood that the blood held all the nourishment I needed. I felt very peaceful and happy. Perhaps I was even smiling as I drank down blood. When I woke from this dream I was sweating and crying. I woke in my space in sector 1125 Darwin C and I thought of all the millions of souls waking in their small spaces too and I cried out in anguish for something I had never known.

And you attached significance to this random twitching of neurons?

I was profoundly affected by it. My life changed utterly. I could no longer perform my job – my allocated role, I mean.

Please explain what your allocated role was.

I worked at the nurture grounds, in sector 1126.

Your area of specialisation?

I cared for babies of six months to a year. I loved what I did though I felt deeply sad that I could not have a child myself.

Correction, for 'child' and 'babies' record progeny of the species. Your eggs were classified as deficient, Prisoner 730004?

No, I believe they passed the test.

So they have generated many progeny of the species.

I do not mean children that I will never meet and who were generated in a laboratory using sperm from men I will never know. I mean children of my own womb, grown and nurtured by my own body.

On behalf of the Protectors we are obliged to advise you that the expression of such statements will not help your case at all, as they constitute a grave threat to the survival of the species and cannot, for the common good, despite the generosity and forbearance of the Protectors, be sanctioned.

I am sorry. I was trying to answer your question.

These dangerous anti-species opinions were shared by all of your group?

It was not something we spoke about. It is a private matter, the yearning of the sterilised body to procreate . . . I do not know how other women endure it.

We assume that other egg donors understand that it is necessary for the survival of the species that we regulate procreation. That we select from a crop of harvested eggs and only place the most superior in the Genetix, fertilised only by the most superior sperm. That we filter out genetic deficiencies. Such deficiencies and your egomaniacal fixations are luxuries the species can no longer allow itself, if it is to survive.

I am aware of the arguments for the Genetix. I am merely explaining my own emotions.

I am afraid this is where you and your group have been in error. You have glutted yourselves on emotions, without a single thought for the Collective. Did you consider what would happen if everyone behaved as you have?

I am afraid we did not. We were compelled . . . I was compelled, I cannot speak for the others, by an overwhelming desire to leave Darwin C.

And if everyone left the Protection Zone and set up farms in the Restricted Area what would happen?

I do not know. I am no prophet.

You don't need to be a prophet to understand the basic laws of supply and demand. I assume you attended Species Survival Courses A, B and C?

Yes, I did. They were compulsory.

And you were taught there that given current climatic instability and the grave perils of overpopulation and shortage of

113

resources, we must make various personal sacrifices for the species to survive the current crisis?

Yes, I was taught this.

Were the arguments persuasive?

I lacked the knowledge to disagree with them. I have no idea what is really happening to the planet, even now.

But you acknowledge that the climate has changed violently.

Yes, I think it has since I was young. But I do not know what this means.

What it means, Prisoner 730004, is that the Collective and the Protectorate and the proposals established for species protection must prevail. It means that to defy these proposals is to aim at the annihilation of the species. Under Proposal 113 of the Darwinian Protectorate auto-genocide is forbidden, you realise?

Yes, I have been told this.

You were taught it in Species Survival B part 7, were you not?

I can't remember exactly when it was that I was taught it but yes I know I have been told it.

And do you understand that the reason we are all accommodated in cities such as Darwin C is to conserve as much land as possible for mass-scale farming to support our species?

I have no real knowledge of anything but yes this is something I have heard.

You were taught it in Species Survival B part 2, were you not?

I can't remember the details. I was a poor scholar. But I have a recollection that something like this was explained to me, yes.

So, when you left the city to set up your own farm you knew you and your group were disobeying the most serious proposals of our Collective? Proposals which have been established to protect the species as a whole?

As I said, we knew that it was not what we had been told to do, or rather I knew, I cannot speak for the others, but such was our – my – craving . . . I was guided by desire, by my yearning for the island . . .

Correction, Lofoten 4a, Arctic Circle sector 111424.

. . . and for the countryside and besides it was becoming too great a torment to work at the nurture grounds any more.

Because of your egomaniacal fixations?

Because of my sense of profound grief that I would never birth my own baby . . .

Correction, progeny of the species. Had you been taking the advised doses of hormone readjustment, Prisoner 730004?

I had.

So you are arguing that you felt this craving despite taking the advised daily dose?

Yes, my yearning transcended these suppressants. My yearning burst out and made me wretched.

115

So this was when your group was formed?

I had remained in contact with friends from my homeland.

From Lofoten 4a, Arctic Circle sector 111424. And who was it that devised the plan to abandon your posts and desert to the Restricted Area?

I don't think there was a single person. I think gradually we came to understand each other. We had so many ancient ties in common. Our understanding was very profound. I am not sure we ever really spoke about our deepest yearnings, to depart. But we understood each other anyway.

You are proposing that you never planned to leave? That it just happened spontaneously?

It was not spontaneous. It happened slowly. But yes, it happened amongst us, without anyone really saying anything. For a long time no one dared to speak. But then there came a time when everything was clear to us, when we knew – we knew everything about each other, without having spoken much at all.

Prisoner 730004, you are making no sense. Why don't you tell us – in plain speak – who the woman known as Birgitta is?

I am not sure I can.

The Protectors value truth and it pains them to hear lies. Please do not insult them by lying in this way. Your lies are wasted anyway as we are searching for this woman known as Birgitta throughout sector 111243. So we ask you to explain exactly who she is, before we take her and ask her ourselves.

She is many things.

Such as?

Well, she is entwined with many forces. There is an old idea we found out . . . someone knew of this phrase – the Magna Mater. Somehow Birgitta is entwined with this phrase.

You will explain yourself in plain speak, Prisoner 730004.

She is an ordinary woman, a terrified girl. But there is something else about her. I am not sure what it is. We have been deprived of tradition and ritual and therefore we are not entirely sure who Birgitta is, and what she might mean.

Once more we must ask you to explain yourself in plain speak, Prisoner 730004. And turn your face towards the screen.

When I was working at the nurture grounds, each day I would hold these beautiful little babies – 'progeny' you would say – in my arms and feel how monstrous it was that my living body had been rendered barren, that the eggs had been ripped out of my womb when I was merely eighteen and taken to a laboratory somewhere, where I didn't even know, and fertilised without love or passion. And if not fertilised then thrown away, discarded. When I thought about this I felt a terrible ache, the mourning of my body, and I always consoled myself – or tried to – with the thought that something might go wrong. The Genetix might fail. Society might collapse. And afterwards, from the ruins, women might regain our former power, to create life within our bodies.

You actively wished for the ruination of our civilisation?

I thought it might be the only way to escape from this . . . this . . . I do not know what it is . . .

It has been clearly explained to you. In Species Survival C. That this is the only option for the species. That all available land must be converted to intensive farming. That city population density must be 13,500 persons per square kilometre. That for farming requirements and also for the most efficient implementation of the Procreation Regulation Programme individuals must live in their allocated accommodation in the cities. Prisoner 730004, you were aware of all these proposals, were you not?

Yes, in truth I was. But somehow I couldn't accept that this is the only option left to humanity.

So you admit that you have desired the ruination of the species and that you have favourably contemplated societal collapse?

Only because I could see no other way that humanity might return to a more natural way of . . . being. Only because I had come to feel that if this denial of nature was required for species survival then perhaps . . . I am speaking only for myself . . . but perhaps it wasn't worth it.

Worth what?

Worth surviving. But I don't know, naturally.

Prisoner 730004, we must warn you that such statements constitute a grave threat to the survival of the species and will only harm your case further. Let us return to the question of Birgitta. Explain what you mean by your talk about her.

I mean that a girl who originally also came from my island . . .

Lofoten 4a, Arctic Circle sector 111424.

. . . became pregnant.

Be very careful what you say, Prisoner 730004. We have already warned you about the harm you are doing to your case.

It is the plain truth. She was harvested at eighteen and had her womb 'closed up' in the so-called ordinary way, and yet twenty years later she had become pregnant.

Who is Birgitta?

She worked in the Sexual Release Centre. Once upon a time she might have been called a whore.

There are no such people in Darwin C.

No, by the terms of the day she was not a 'whore' it is true, she was an 'expert in the administration of sexual release' – and she specialised in the loveless sex that is now encouraged. Not merely encouraged, that is not what I mean. I mean that lifelong coupling is now frowned upon as . . . you would say it is one of those egomaniacal fixations we can no longer afford. Also children are no longer raised at home but in the nurture grounds by strangers . . .

You are digressing and your words are meaningless. Who is Birgitta?

She had been supplying 'sexual release' for many years, and then she became pregnant. At first she had no idea what was happening. No woman of my generation has ever become pregnant. We are of course the first complete generation of 'egg donors' – with us the process has been completely successful, you would say.

We would. You have not yet told us who Birgitta is.

She wasn't sure what was happening to her body. She was experiencing awful nausea, nausea so she could barely function as a supplier of sexual release, and her belly appeared to be bloated which some of those she sexually released found unsightly anyway. She thought she must have a problem with her digestive organs, and she took various remedies and hoped that would cure it. She didn't want to lose her position at the Sexual Release Centre; after all she had never worked anywhere else and didn't know quite how else she would be able to serve the Collective and the Protectorate. She was even afraid she might be regarded as extraneous and sent to the mass-scale farms and no one ever comes back from there.

They do not return because they are happy there.

They do not return because they are worked to death, that's what I have heard.

You heard a myth, an irrational fable told by simple people. Please do not digress.

Birgitta grew still more nauseous and still more bloated. No one she knew had ever experienced these symptoms and she was too afraid to go to a Corporeal Scientist. She was mystified and feared she was dying, until she went to her mother.

Correction, egg donor.

Well, actually Birgitta was conceived just before her mother was taken for harvesting and sterilisation. Things were a little more lenient in those days and so the pregnancy was permitted to continue. For many years Birgitta felt that it would have been better had she never been born. Because of her beauty, her long limbs and her flowing blonde curls, she was taken from her family at the age of eighteen and consigned to a life of whoredom.

She was allocated her role in the struggle for the survival of the species. Though the Protectors wish in their virtue to give you a reasoned hearing, we cannot permit these rambling digressions. Correct for the record instances of 'children' and 'mothers' in the appropriate way. Prisoner 730004, you were telling us of a supplier of sexual release, Birgitta, who believed she was pregnant.

At the time she did not believe it. She was very frightened and didn't know what was wrong. Then she went to her mother and she lifted Birgitta's top garment and saw the swollen belly, and she said, 'My daughter, this is no disease, no sickness of the body, you are pregnant.'

Correct for the record 'mother' and 'daughter' as before. How very unfortunate that this poor woman should be so deluded.

That is what everyone said. When Birgitta finally – reluctantly and in great fear – went to the Corporeal Scientists they said she was having a phantom pregnancy, that she was sick in her mind, that she must cure her mind and the body would follow, because as the Protectors tell us the body is mere matter, to be controlled by the faculty of reason, with a little help from our technologies . . .

You are digressing again. Please explain clearly what happened to this woman Birgitta and why her delusions are linked to the selfish anti-species activities of your group.

Even when she could feel the movements within her, the little flutters and tentative kicks which were once called quickening, even when it was clear that there was something alive, they told Birgitta it was just her imagination, that her mind was – they told her – confused by the unbridled urges of her body. Not a single Corporeal Scientist thought it was even worth scanning her: they knew from her records that she had been harvested and purged and closed and so they were entirely convinced that it was a mental deficiency, taking over the body. Indeed they explained to her that for her own good – for her protection – she must be committed to an Institution for the Improvement of the Reason. Which in the old days we would have called a lunatic asylum.

Prisoner 730004, you are once more mistaken in your reasoning. You must not simplify everything and draw it into your mythical and non-scientific worldview. The Institutions for the Improvement of the Reason are a necessary element in the protection of the species. The Protectors are wise and just. Now continue with your account.

It was then that we acted.

At this point you were already in a state of delusion about the nature of Birgitta's illness?

I already knew that she was pregnant, yes.

So how did you 'act'?

A group of us decided to leave Darwin C and take Birgitta with us. At the time she had not realised her power. She was just a very distressed person. She was still in a state – induced by her upbringing – of self-fear. She feared the bulging of her body. She feared being cast out from the con-

122

fines of the Collective, from the world she had known all her life. She felt freakish and wanted to hide or to be cured. Indeed she basically accepted that she should go to an Institution for the Improvement of the Reason and it was only because of us that she did not. It is in a sense fortunate that none of the Corporeal Scientists would believe that she was really pregnant, otherwise she would – I think – have been easily convinced to have a termination. If you have been constantly told that something is true, that a particular reality is true, if you have grown up in a society which has disposed of the natural function of the female body, then it is quite understandable that you would regard pregnancy as a sickness. And Birgitta also felt that whether her illness was a sickness of the mind as the Corporeal Scientists told her or the ordinary symptoms of pregnancy, she was alone. Either she was mad or she was the only pregnant woman in Darwin C. And Birgitta was in such a state of self-fear that she thought either state was undesirable and terrifying.

You are digressing again, Prisoner 730004. Please explain precisely what happened. Though the Protectors seek to understand you, they are in truth less concerned with your vague musings about reality as you see it than they are with the plain facts of the case.

I am sorry. Lacking the analytical brilliance of the Protectors I find it hard to disentangle actions and thoughts.

We are talking of the circumstances of your departure from Darwin C.

Yes I understand, though in my weakness I can only perceive the circumstances of my departure as bound up with my gradual disaffection with the mores of our civilisation and

123

my mounting sense of unease at the prospect of further years spent in the nurture grounds of Darwin C. In a sense I could not have physically departed from Darwin C had I not already become detached in my mind from the place. I came to realise that I could no longer accept my allotted role in the so-called war against nature and I therefore had to desert.

You accept then that your actions constitute a dereliction of your duties?

By the terms of our civilisation, as you call it, by the standards of the life in Darwin C, by the standards of the Protectors, then yes, I see I shall be punished.

You will be allocated a new role in the struggle for the survival of the species. Now Prisoner 730004, please return to the circumstances of your desertion of Darwin C.

It was very sudden. We never planned it, we just realised we had to leave.

Can you clarify at this point who 'we' is?

No, I'm afraid I can't.

Why not?

Because I made a promise not to reveal the identities of my friends.

Prisoner, the Protectors, through us, assure you that it is categorically in your interest to co-operate fully with this process. Indeed a failure to do so will make things even more difficult for you and your co-conspirators.

I am grateful to the Protectors for their kind reminder. However, we swore an oath of secrecy and allegiance and I am afraid I cannot break it. In case some of my friends are still out there.

Out in the Restricted Area?

Yes.

You do not know where they are?

I have had no contact with anyone since the army came to our village.

Correction, Protection Agents. So you made no arrangements for reconvening if your camp was dispersed?

No such arrangements at all. Things weren't like that. We felt free. We were among mountains and the sea. Infinite rocks and water. We felt as if our lives were peaceful and blessed. We certainly never imagined our village would be set upon and destroyed, that our huts would be burned, that they would beat and coerce us and that I would be sitting here in prison, being interrogated.

You are not being interrogated. The Protectors merely seek to understand your actions so they can better protect our Collective. The actions of the Protection Agents are always proportionate to the magnitude of the threat represented by the activities against which they are deployed. We cannot afford to be sentimental in our dealings with exceptional cases such as yours, lest we imperil the majority. This is a question of billions of lives.

I understand that humanity has destroyed the planet.

Nature has declared war on humanity and we must evolve and use all the technology at our disposal, or be vanquished.

You are more knowledgeable than I am.

Prisoner 730004, you are claiming that you have no idea of the whereabouts of your co-conspirators?

I do not know where my friends have gone, those that are still living.

You are aware, Prisoner 730004, that while the Protectors seek to understand you, the better to protect the Collective, they also insist on honesty as a central value of our civilisation. They cannot protect us unless we confide in them. So why will you not tell us, and thereby the Protectors, precisely who else was living in the Restricted Area?

I would like to be as honest as possible, and have no desire to hide our activities where my explanations can harm no one. Yet in this instance I have made a promise. You can torture me or threaten me with the mass-scale farms but I will not break it.

Prisoner 730004, your remarks have been noted. They will sadden the Protectors. Can we now return to the precise nature of your departure from Darwin C?

It was very exciting. I had never gone beyond the two sectors – the one in which I lived and the one in which I worked. In Darwin C I had the view from my space and that was as I said nothing but towers and by night there were red lights flashing from the tops of the highest towers. As far as I could see, there were towers. And the small figures passing beneath, all in their little dark smocks. And always the whirr of the air processing, I had never been anywhere without this constant whirr. I went from this constant mechanised whirr to the sound of waves. The cries of birds. The wind in the trees.

Can you tell us the precise chronology of your departure?

We met at the base of a tower. We had discovered there were supply trains running to and from the Arctic. Birgitta's brother . . .

Correction, DNA relative . . .

. . . worked on one of them. He is gone now, as is Birgitta's mother, so I can tell you that they helped us. Birgitta's mother came with us, though she perished later. But the joy she felt at returning was so immense, so wonderful to behold, so I think it was a good thing she came, even though it killed her. I am certain it hastened her death. Conditions at first were very hard.

Correct 'mother' for the record as before. Prisoner 730004, we ask you to apply yourself only to the question of how you departed from Darwin C.

Yes, of course. Birgitta's brother told us we must be at the loading bay at 3 a.m. He said he would load us into his section of the train. He was the porter for that section and so he could put us in a crate and say the crate contained special equipment going up to the mass-scale farms. He told us the passengers on that train were a desperate horde: those judged mentally unwell, former workers in the Centres for Sexual Release who were too old to attract people any more, or others who had exceeded their usefulness and could no longer be housed in Darwin C. They were all going to the mass-scale farms of course. We couldn't see them but the worst thing was that we couldn't hear them either. They were silent and I thought of them the whole journey, lined up in rows and knowing where they were going and that they would die there. They had been discarded. They were the discarded rubbish of our so-called civilisation. Stripped of any sense of individuality, or worth. They were merely being thrown away.

Such remarks cannot be permitted, constituting as they do a grave threat to our species. Correct 'brother' for the record as before. Please continue with the basic facts of your story, Prisoner 730004.

Then there were the so-called Protection Agents and we were very frightened of them. Every time their footsteps thumped towards our crate we expected to be discovered. We were in there for three days. We had some water and a little food and we couldn't sleep at all. Birgitta was halfway through her pregnancy then, and the claustrophobia and the stale air made her sick. It was a terrible journey. In some ways I can't remember much of it, because I was so stricken by fear and horror. For myself and Birgitta but also for all those doomed souls beyond our crate.

Prisoner 730004, must we remind you again?

I am sorry, I keep forgetting about the restrictions upon me.

They are for your protection and for the protection of the species. What happened when you arrived at your destination?

By the time we arrived our limbs were locked, our bones aching. The crate stank of vomit and urine. It was a descent into the body, being stewed in fluids for two days like that. The Protectors would doubtless have judged us mad or in need of mental readjustment.

The Protectors do not judge, they only protect.

Yet there was something cathartic about the process. We who had been bred in sterilised sparkling machines, in the pristine technocratic sanctuary of the Genetix, we who had lived our days in perfect towers coated in shining solar shields, so everything was always glittering in the dangerous sunshine, suddenly we were dirtied, reborn into viscera and filth.

Once more on behalf of the Protectors we must emphasise that such digressions are not relevant to your case or suitable in your circumstances.

I am sorry.

Please continue with your account, taking care to adhere to the facts.

I will try. Let me think. The facts of our arrival. I am not sure. I think that we were all afraid. And uncertain. Perhaps this is not a fact. We were unsure about what we had done. Birgitta's brother dragged us out. I think he was also afraid. Again I am not entirely sure of this. I was disoriented by fatigue and nerves. I do not remember who was there, beyond the members of our group and Birgitta's brother. Others were there, though: I felt hands on my shoulder, on my arm, guiding me along what I think was a dark passageway but could equally have been a tunnel. Perhaps someone wept. Perhaps we all did. But this is not a fact, or not one I believe would be useful. Birgitta's brother disappeared before we could thank him – I never saw him again and now I strongly believe he is dead. Though I do not know this for a fact I am almost certain it is the case.

Correct all instances of 'brother' for the record. Prisoner 730004, why do you believe that Birgitta's DNA relative is dead?

We were told later that they discovered our urine and vomit in the crate. Only traces but it was enough to condemn him. I believe, though I am not sure, that it is considered a grave threat to the species to assist fugitives, so he was sent to the mass-scale farms. There the average survival span is six months, I have heard, though I am aware this would not qualify as a fact.

It is a myth, a foolish unscientific myth.

Of course. I am sorry. I have no clear understanding of our world. Just impressions, emotions. I believe, intuitively, that he is dead. And if not dead, then his condition cannot be worsened and I imagine death might even be a blessing to him. I have heard – again you will not regard this as a fact – that life on the mass-scale farms is so dreadful that some there stop eating even their scanty portions of food, to die more swiftly.

This is another irrelevant digression and a blatant untruth.

Of course, I understand.

Please continue with your account, Prisoner 730004.

We went along the tunnel which may not have been a tunnel for what seemed like hours. I had no clear notion of time as it was dark and I was also unsure if we were outside or inside. There was a heated wind gusting at my body. My arms and back were doused in sweat. I think I felt very hopeless then, as if I had made a mistake. We didn't speak, I am sure of that. Our unknown guides led us at a relentless pace, and we needed all our energy to control our stiffened limbs. Birgitta was very hungry, though we had given her most of our food. In thrall as we are to the demands of the body, it is a fact that we were ravenously hungry. We walked and walked and I thought I was too weak and weary to continue, but always the guides encouraged us along, and finally when my mood had sunk close to despair, we came to a boat. To the water. The sea. I had never seen the sea before and it was such a beautiful sight, such a vision of infinite vastness and natural power – though I knew the waters were polluted beyond redemption – that for a moment I was mesmerised and forgot everything else. It was dawn. The sea reflected the orange morning sun. The waves surged and rose, became full and white at their crests, foamed brilliantly and then crashed against the rocks. The water bubbled and churned. There was a deep roar, a sound I never thought I would hear on this planet. The air was full of the smell of salt and the wind made me breathless, as if my lungs could not hold much of this unprocessed air. And under the sound of the waves I could hear Birgitta's mother weeping. Our guides were moving quickly, leading us onto a boat which rocked on the swell. I had naturally never been in a boat before and I remember feeling an acute sense – as we moved away from the shore – of the fragility of our vessel and the relentless force of the waves surging around us. The boat was just a small wooden fishing boat and one of our guides told us the summer was stormy and the seas unpredictable. 'Ill-tempered,' he called the ocean, I remember. Birgitta was very sick. A few of us were also leaning over the side to spill bile into the water. I do not know how long the journey took. I remember Birgitta's mother holding her daughter, cradling Birgitta's head and saying, 'Peace my beautiful girl, peace my love,' and I felt a great tearing pain and grief for the parents I had lost and the child I would never comfort in this way and I felt . . .

Prisoner 730004 on behalf of the Protectors I must remind you that such remarks are not required and you must confine your account to the basic details. Correct 'parents', 'mother', 'daughter' and 'child' as usual for the record. Continue, Prisoner 730004.

After a stormy crossing we arrived. The boat was dragged onto a sandy stony beach with mountains rising all above. There was grass on the lower slopes, and trees. Then the upper slopes were purplish, ancient rock, like something I had seen only in dreams. Our guides turned back as soon as they had unloaded our supplies. We had some basic food resources and some guns and ammunition. We had some fishing rods and some seed. It looked to me as if we would die quite quickly. I had no sense of how we could possibly survive.

How long ago was it that you came to this place?

I think it was some years ago. I measure it only by the passing of the seasons. And as you know the seasons are less clear now than in former days.

Prisoner 730004, the Protectors are curious about how precisely you built your community?

Through grave hardship and loss. The island was much changed. We had hoped we might live by fishing as our predecessors had done but the few fish remaining in the sea were gravely polluted and made us ill. Birgitta we thought must not eat them.

The myth of her pregnancy had continued among you?

Birgitta was burgeoning by the day. Her belly was an object

of wonder for us, even devotion. She was always tired, because there was so little food at first. We were about to starve when we learned how to take eggs from nests. That was a great advance. At least then Birgitta could get nourishment. That was how we thought during the summer. We thought if Birgitta and a couple of others survived then that would be an achievement. We ate the poisoned fish simply to quell hunger pains, but then we were sick – it was like fighting an addiction, ignoring the desperate promptings of our stomachs. We found abandoned houses and tried to repair them. We were fortunate in that respect – the houses had been fashioned to withstand the old Arctic winters, and though these severe temperatures have become a thing of the past, perhaps never to return, the houses were sturdy and we were comfortable in them. It was just the food. We were not short of water – the summers had become very warm and wet and we gathered rainwater and drank our fill. We were not thirsty. But hunger sapped our strength and nearly broke our morale. It ate our flesh until we were gaunt and ill. A diet of eggs and grasses, poisoned fish and rainwater is not enough to sustain the body. Gradually we learned to shoot and then sometimes we killed birds. On a few glorious occasions we shot a fox or two. But our fortunes only really changed once we had developed our farm.

And how did this happen?

As I mentioned before, our guides had left us with some sacks of seeds. At first we did not understand. Then we realised what we must do. The process was arduous and full of errors. A storm washed half our crops away. The birds took some of our seed. But gradually our vegetables grew.

133

That was a wonderful thing, to see how the earth could grow food. How it nourished us in the end, once we understood its workings a little better. In the season before the army came . . .

Correction, Protection Agents.

. . . we had grown enough food to be comfortable. We knew then that we would be able to stay there for the natural course of our lives. We knew these lives would be shorter than the span we might have expected in Darwin C. We would have no cell therapy, no gene readjustment. Our bodies would age naturally and sicken and die. But we were content with this. If I die tomorrow, then I am content. I would trade decades of life in Darwin C for a year of this life among the rocks. I think, though I cannot speak with any certainty, that the others would have agreed. Before Birgitta's mother died she said as much.

Correct 'mother' for the record. How did this egg donor die?

She had been ill in Darwin C. She had been on cell therapy and so in deciding to go with Birgitta she had effectively sacrificed her life. We did not know this until the last days of her life. Finally she told us, and she said that she was so glad she had come. She wept, with Birgitta holding her and kissing her and crying onto her face. She died slowly and in pain. In Darwin C she would of course have had every medicine available and the Corporeal Scientists would have judiciously shortened her life at the point at which they deemed her no longer functional or worthy of resource use. We were more profligate and we fed her to the last and kept a fire burning in her house. By then it was winter and though the climate shift meant that this winter was not cold at all,

Birgitta's poor dying mother . . .

Correction, egg donor.

. . . was convinced that she had returned to the winter fastness of her childhood and kept saying, 'Keep the fires burning, don't let the fires go out.' Everyone who sat with her sweated and grew parched, but she believed the snows were driving against the windows, that the sea was frozen solid and that the roof was being rattled by icy blasts. She told us stories of trolls and berserks, the old mythical characters of her . . .

Prisoner 730004, do not insult the Protectors with these nonsensical digressions.

I am sorry. There is so much I remember. I remember Birgitta's mother saying goodbye to her daughter, knowing that they would never meet again, and I felt such a sense of the depths of love passing between them and the beauty and sadness of this bond between parent and child, and how we have betrayed ourselves.

It is tedious to have to remind you again, on behalf of the Protectors, that such digressions are inappropriate. Correct 'mother', 'daughter', 'parent' and 'child' as usual for the record. How many of you deserted Darwin C?

I am afraid I cannot tell you.

You cannot or you will not?

I cannot because of the promise I made.

We are obliged to remind you for your own protection how very important it is that you co-operate with us.

135

I understand. But I am afraid I cannot tell you.

We hope you will see reason before it is too late. When did Birgitta's egg donor die?

She died in the winter after we arrived. She never saw the birth of her grandchild.

Correction, progeny of the species. And, Prisoner, do not digress into these absurd fantasies.

I am sorry but I do not regard them as . . .

How many of your camp died?

Several in the early months. From starvation. We all denied ourselves food in order to feed Birgitta. We all went without. So some of us could not survive. The sacrifice was necessary.

Please do not call your species-threatening actions a sacrifice. That is a very grave offence and trivialises the efforts of all those working for species survival. Will you explain who the guides were?

I am afraid I do not know.

How can you not know?

We never knew their identities. We never saw their faces. I do not know where they came from and where they have gone.

Yet they supplied you with seed and guns?

Yes, they did.

How did they procure these things?

I do not know.

You did not ask?

No, I did not.

But did you not think it strange, that in a civilisation in which access to all resources is necessarily restricted, for the protection of the species, these guides of yours had acquired guns? And bullets? And seeds?

Everything was strange. It all seemed like a dream. The crate, sweaty and vile. The passageway or tunnel and my confusion about whether it was day or night. The incessant beating of the waves and the vision of a landscape I had never seen before but somehow recognised, and all the suspense of our crossing and the shock of our arrival. And so when our guides, who we knew only as our guides, unloaded the boxes I barely noticed what they contained and definitely didn't consider the meaning of the objects. I was transfixed by the mountains and the vastness of the sky. I didn't ask any questions.

Did anyone in your camp know anything about the guides?

I don't think so.

But someone made contact with them?

Yes, perhaps someone did.

Is there anything else you can share with the Protectors about the identity of these guides?

I am afraid not. I know nothing else about them.

What did you do in this camp?

After the initial months when we were merely trying to survive, we settled into a rhythm, a very ancient rhythm I believe, of rising with the sun and going to sleep with the dusk, of passing the days collecting food and tending our crops and the evenings singing songs and telling stories. And in general we were preparing for the birth.

How were you preparing for this imaginary event?

We were trying to make Birgitta as strong as we could, so her body would withstand the trials of childbirth. Only one among us knew the true nature of these trials – Birgitta's mother.

Correction, egg donor.

But she told us the body was grievously tested and Birgitta must be as strong and nourished as possible. So in the evenings we brought Birgitta presents – things we had found or made for her, extra foodstuffs, treats, and in turn she would show us the great roundness of her belly, the skin taut across the mound, the navel stretched and almost inverted, and we would take it in turns to place our hands upon it, and to feel the movements within. The sudden thrust of a foot. The probing exploration of a hand. Sometimes, a great ripple of the flesh as the miraculous cargo turned. Of course once these things had been commonplace but now they were to us a matter for great awe.

And you thought she was the 'Magna Mater', as you called it?

No, we didn't think Birgitta was the Magna Mater. We were not sure of anything. But we observed something – some creative power – within her. And this force, or presence, whatever it was – made Birgitta stronger and more serene by the day. She was no longer cowardly and reluctant. She no longer found her body revolting. In Darwin C she had only wanted to rid herself of the signs of her improbable state, but on the island, among rocks and trees and water, she somehow understood the force that was within her. Among these natural forms, in the natural flow of life, perhaps she came to accept what was happening to her. It was something like that. Birgitta is not the Magna Mater. The Magna Mater – or whatever life force is suggested by this term – is something that I believe exists within her and within all humans. But it is just a phrase somebody heard, or remembered. Its deeper meaning is lost to us at this time. We have our instincts but we have been encouraged to suppress them and it is hard for us to name such ancient forces.

You believe this Birgitta is alive?

Yes I think so. I do not know however. Her existence is not to me a fact, or not something you would perceive to be a fact. But I have a sense she is still in the world. And so is her son.

What do you mean?

The son she bore. The son she held up to the winter light and wept to see. The son who screamed and whose newborn cries were so piercing and wonderful. The son who was a tiny packed mass of life and energy, reddish purple and covered in gore, but the most beautiful thing I have ever seen. The son she fed with her own body.

For 'son', in all instances, record progeny of the species. You are mentally ill, Prisoner. There is no progeny in this instance. This woman's so-called pregnancy was nothing but a collective delusion. Your group should all have been in an Institution for the Improvement of the Reason.

I am sure without the evidence of the son this is a perfectly rational argument. But I have seen the son.

Correct 'son' as before. It is impossible for a woman whose womb has been harvested and closed to bear a progeny of the species. It simply cannot happen.

And yet it did.

You are gravely insulting the Protectors with these lies.

I am sorry you feel like that.

You must concede instantly that there was no progeny.

I am afraid I cannot. I held him in my own arms. I wiped gore from his eyes and mouth and I kissed him. I saw him. I wept to see him. His hair was richly perfumed with uterine blood. He was beautiful.

You are lying.

I am not. He was the most extraordinary thing I had ever seen. I long to hold him.

Prisoner 730004 will be taken back to her Protection Cell. There is no point continuing at this time. She needs the attention of a Corporeal Scientist.

I don't want their drugs.

It is for your own protection, Prisoner 730004.

. . . Over the Earth and the Loud-
echoing Salt Sea

The Moon

Professor Wilson, I have now returned to my desk, and can resume my account. The heat here is fetid, and works against the concentration. But naturally one can write a letter, even under such conditions. I believe I had described to you how I decided to return to the asylum, to seek further conversation with Professor Semmelweis. It was late afternoon by the time I arrived back at that foul place, and I rang the bell for some time without gaining a response. Finally when the door opened it was clear that my return displeased Herr Meyer. He met me in the anteroom, and there was none of his false friendliness. Rather he was intractable and surly, and claimed at first that Herr S could not see me.

'It is simply not possible,' he said, shaking his head. 'He has suffered an unfortunate relapse.'

'I would like to see him anyway, if you would be so kind,' I said, briskly.

'You do not understand. He is in no fit state to receive visitors. Your visit this morning induced his collapse.' As if otherwise poor Professor Semmelweis was kept in pristine conditions, in sublime equanimity, and it was only my visit which might be blamed for any diminution in his general health . . .

'Then I should like to try to help him, to revive his spirits a little.'

'I do not think that is a good idea,' said Herr Meyer.

'I assure you, I have information about his state that must be conveyed to him, if you have any compassion.'

'The man is not to be informed of anything. The man is to be restrained from harming himself and others, and to be treated as I see fit,' said Herr Meyer. He was becoming quite agitated himself, his face glowing with something I feared was combative glee, for men such as Meyer are oppressed by various forces themselves, and if they have the opportunity they enjoy a chance to assert themselves.

'The man is called Professor Semmelweis, by the way,' I said. 'He is an esteemed doctor and I suggest you show him more respect.'

'I shall receive no instruction on how to conduct myself in my asylum.'

'You should need none, had you any moral sense to guide you.'

Had one of my friends not been a benefactor of this ruinous place – a matter which has been the cause of many disagreements between us, on the occasions when I have mentioned the maltreatment which is quite ordinary in this asylum – I do believe this vicious man Meyer would have thrown me out. As it was, he really had little choice, and so, clicking his tongue in fury, and refusing to speak further to me, he conducted me along the corridor. This time, Professor Semmelweis was slumped in his chair, his chin against his chest. He was still in chains. He was wringing his hands as he had done earlier, and I now realised this must represent washing, and must refer to his former researches and to his yearning for a cleanliness which his vile sur-roundings denied him.

'Herr Meyer, would you be so good as to provide this man with some hot water, and soap, and a towel,' I said. Herr Meyer looked at me in disgust, as if no inmate of his could have any cause for such things, but I repeated my request in a sharper tone, and he retreated with a bad grace.

I stood there, still uncertain about how to proceed, as the poor man wrung his hands and gazed into space. Or perhaps he was fixed on a vision I could not apprehend, but he looked inert and unstimulated, and for a while I felt quite overwhelmed by his state and the hopelessness of his situation.

Then I said, 'Herr S, I visited you this morning. I do not know if you remember me.'

There was no response, and so I stood there silently once more, watching him for a time. He seemed quite unaware of my presence. I wondered indeed if he had suffered the final Great Reversal, and would never return from his wolf-light existence again. I thought it might be the case, that he had passed to the other realm, and could hardly comprehend me at all, just as his motives and beliefs were now obscure to me. And indeed I was not sure if this was so dreadful a fate for a man as troubled as Professor Semmelweis, to lapse entirely from the world that perplexed him, though I pitied his wife and children who longed, no doubt, to see him cured.

I was thinking perhaps I should leave the man to his demolition of the self, and hope that he found some consolation along the journey, but then something interesting occurred. Herr Meyer returned with a bowl of water, and a piece of grimy soap and a towel that was almost too disgusting to handle, yet I was obliged to accept them, having nothing else to assist my cause. Expecting little from the gesture, yet moved to try nonetheless, I turned to Professor Semmelweis and said, 'Sir, I thought perhaps you might like to wash your hands?'

At that, he looked up and regarded me with vague interest. The blankness, the emptiness of his expression, was replaced with something like recognition. He looked at the water, and then he took the soap. For a moment he paused. Then he placed his hands in the water. He shivered with relief. The effect upon him of the water was very palpable. He rubbed his hands vigorously with the soap and dipped them many times in the water.

'You can leave us now,' I said to Herr Meyer, and he departed with an angry scowl.

'Sir, I think I understand your dreams of blood,' I said.

'I am afraid I do not know who you are,' he said. He was still dipping his hands in the water, removing them to rub more soap upon them, dipping them again.

'I came to visit you this morning. We discussed your dreams of blood and also your fears that you had committed a crime. Also you mentioned a woman with blue eyes whom you feared. Do you remember any of this?'

'You came to visit?'

'Yes.' And I told him – once again – my name and the nature of my studies.

There was a splash as his hands entered the water again. He looked down at his fingers, moved them in the water, applied soap carefully to each finger. I pressed on, while he was relatively attentive.

146

'You spoke of a man who had disturbed you greatly. Indeed the mere mention of his name caused you to fall into a sort of fit. So I shall not say it again. However, because of this name I believe I know who you are. I could tell you your name and your former profession, if you would like to know.'

I thought this would cause him to descend again, but he remained calm. He was splashing his fingers in the water, almost like a child, watching the ripples and bubbles he caused. Then he turned to me and said, 'I believe I have already regained those details.'

'You do?'

'Yes, I have been thinking more clearly. I came round, as if from a long sleep. I do not know when I woke, but I was not alone. That man' – he nodded his head towards the corridor – 'was with me. I said nothing to him, yet I knew that something had changed. I had a kernel, just a kernel. It was as if someone had cried out to me, and they had spoken my name.'

'Who are you, will you tell me?'

'Of course, I have no regard for my reputation any more. It is simply not important. I believe my name is Semmelweis and I was once a doctor. I was a doctor but then I was quite rightly and justly deprived of my profession. It is right that I should be incarcerated, quite right, and better for everyone.'

This was a transformation I had not anticipated. Indeed I was unsure what to say for a moment, not wanting to disturb his new state. He was now almost measured; certainly there was something pensive, contemplative about him. He was splashing his hands, but there was nothing frenzied about the gestures now; he was moving his fingers quite gently in the water.

'I have been thinking about Aristotle's concept of the soul,' he was saying. 'That its residence is in the heart, yet it is also the form of the body. It permeates the entire body, though emanating from a single point. And somehow I remembered the beat of a heart, heard through the skin. Two hearts, I recalled, the mother's and the galloping pace of her unborn child's. I remembered the beat of these two points, two souls, contained within a single body. I was thinking how curious it is, that a philosopher such as Aristotle had failed to consider what it is to be a pregnant woman, who contains another life point, another point emanating life to a body, within herself. Surely this must change our notion of the human form? Surely this must change our sense of bodily autonomy, when many a woman spends decades with another self – various other selves – contained within her, as she moves successively from one pregnancy to another? And I began to remember. Myself, I remembered myself, leaning over a woman who was rounded and immense with child. At first I thought it was my wife. I thought I must be remembering the birth of one of our children, yet then I saw a number of these women, and I saw myself again, passing from one to the other.'

'What do you think this meant?' I said.

'I realised I had been a doctor. That was the first small revelation I was permitted. That I had been a doctor and that I tended to women in childbirth. Then suddenly I knew my name. I heard the women saying it to me, their voices full of fear and hope. At first I could not hear them clearly, but then their words – the single word – became clear to me. They said it in tones of relief, that I had come – these women trusted that I could assist them, perhaps even save them. And all the while another voice was saying to me, "Do not approach them, do not, in your arrogance, approach them!"

'In my vision I ignored this voice entirely, I continued to move from one to another, and gradually as I pressed my ear against the rounded mass of their bodies, I heard the hearts stop. The tiny galloping baby hearts stopped, and then the women threw up their hands and died.'

'This is a dreadful vision,' I said.

'I think I have done something very grave, which is that I – in my small person – have somehow changed the course of many women's lives, and of the lives of their children. And it is wrong for a single human to have wielded such power. Thereby I have insulted God, the ledger is marked, and I must suffer.'

'You have done a great deal of good, I suspect.' I said. 'I can tell you, Professor Semmelweis, that you developed a theory about the way in which puerperal sepsis is spread. You argued that it was spread by the hands of doctors. That doctors infected women with this disease during internal examinations.'

'Puerperal sepsis?'

I thought for a moment he would not be able to recall his medical expertise, and indeed for some time he stared at his hands, as he splashed them in and out of the water.

Then he shook himself, or shook involuntarily, and turned to me. His aspect was more animated now, and he said, 'I forget your name.'

'Robert von Lucius.'

'Herr von Lucius, I must thank you. I confess I have

wandered greatly in my thoughts but now everything is clearer. You have supplied the crucial element I lacked.'

'I am sorry but I do not understand.'

'I am Professor Ignaz Semmelweis and my field was obstetrics. You are quite correct.'

'And you worked . . .'

'I worked in the First Division of the Vienna General Hospital. For several years. I am not sure when it was. I do not know the year at present.'

'The year is now 1865.'

'Then it was some time ago that I arrived at this hospital. Perhaps twenty years ago. I was young and I was a student doctor. I had not chosen obstetrics as my first profession. I would have preferred to study something else, but I think my family was not a wealthy one, and I had to accept whatever position I could obtain. I was an assistant to . . .' Herr Semmelweis was now rubbing his forehead avidly, spreading dirty water across his face. And I hesitated, for I suspected this must be Johann Klein, and I did not want to lose him to another fit.

'To the head of the lying-in ward,' I said, hurriedly.

'That is correct. His name will come to me. It is not important at the moment.'

'But you worked as this man's assistant during the 1840s?'

'I believe at the time there was a terrible epidemic – when I arrived there was an epidemic. In the First Division it raged, this epidemic of puerperal sepsis. Childbed fever, that is what the midwives called it. Naturally we thought our definition more precise, yet the women died all the same, however we defined the disease. And it was clear that they died in greater numbers in the First Division, where the teaching hospital was. The doctors worked there and their students. In the Second Division, which was staffed by midwives, and only rarely by doctors, childbed fever did not kill so many women. It was a mystery which tormented us all. The women would weep when they were told they must come to the First Division. I remember that. They knew they were being sent somewhere dangerous. They begged for their lives. The allocation was random – it depended on the day you arrived. They tried to wait, I remember. Some women would try to wait until the Second Division day before they came into hospital. Often they were too late and they birthed their babies on the streets. They brought them into the world while squatting in the gutters, but even this was less likely to cause them to die than coming to the First Division.'

'This cannot have been the case.'

'During times of epidemic, yes. The First Division was a charnel house. It was a breeding ground for death. It was horrible to see it. And yet now I forget the word they gave it. What was the word for this thing which killed the women?' And he turned to me with a ragged expression. I perceived that he feared this period of lucidity might be fleeting, that he must glean as much information as possible while he could phrase questions and attend calmly to the answers.

'Puerperal sepsis.'

'Yes, that is it. I remember – *De Mulierum Morbis* – what is that?'

'Hippocrates.'

'Yes, that is right, and it says something, I must remember it.' The horrible gestures had resumed, intensified by his desperation. He had become more urgent about the washing of his hands and so he had set his chains jangling again.

151

We waited, with only the noise of the chains between us. Then he said, 'I have it . . . I think . . . "And so Thasus, the wife of Philinus, having been delivered of a daughter was seized with fever attended with shaking chills as well as pains in the abdomen and genital organs." It is that. Something of that nature. And Thasus suffers agonies for twenty days after the birth of her daughter, and then she dies. Puerperal sepsis is an illness which takes the form of a fever, with a chill. The majority of patients manifest signs of the disease on the third day after birth. They have a headache, and cold fits followed by extreme heat, perspiration and thirst. Abdominal pain begins as a mild symptom but becomes increasingly severe. The pulse increases in pace, and the patient tends to lie on her back and appear listless. She loses her appetite. The tongue is usually white, though it can become dark and furred as death approaches. Respiration becomes laboured due to abdominal pain and distention, and the patient is nauseous and prone to attacks of vomiting. The production of milk is suppressed, though lochia continues. A few particularly unfortunate patients lapse into delirium and mania. During an epidemic, so-called, the mortality rate might be as high as eighty per cent, as opposed to a normal rate of twenty-five to thirty per cent. It is a monstrous disease. And these are women who a few days earlier were young, beautiful, at the height of their strength, birthing a child in all their vigour. The birth might have been entirely routine. Yet in the First Division every woman in labour was examined several times by doctors and students, for the purposes of research and teaching, even if their labour hardly required it. The students were often inexperienced, and sometimes they would push their hands clumsily into the women, hurting them even as they writhed in the usual agony. Students and doctors would delve deep inside these women, and then the women would become ill.

'They would complain of feeling a little flushed and faint, and the doctors would aim to reassure them, but often we would know anyway that the worst would soon be upon them. Every woman knew precisely the symptoms of childbed fever, and the look in their eyes when they realised they had succumbed was dreadful to behold. And beside them were their babies – these desperate tiny creatures, so plaintive and powerless, who just hours earlier the mothers had held and loved and been so delighted to see – but now in their illness these women would cry out when the babies were placed upon their abdomens, and they would speak of a pain in their bellies, and then they would vomit horribly and shudder, and cry about their babies and how they must feed them, and their temperatures would fly up the scale, and higher and higher, and the babies would cry because the mothers could not suckle them or hold them, oh these poor babies, these poor mothers – it was terrible to witness the decline of these mothers, just when they had performed this most vital act, summoning life, and when these new lives were crying out for them – yet despite this they were shivering with cold, their teeth chattering, and then they were hot and flushed, and they perspired and stank. That was when you knew their agony would soon be over – when the stink emanated from them, a smell of decay, coming from this womb which had so recently sustained life. The womb was infected, with vile particles, and these women were destroyed from within. They slipped away, no longer recognising the babies they had loved so briefly and intensely. And when they died, the babies were often left orphaned, their lives ruined too by the horrible demise of their mothers. If no relative came, these helpless creatures were sent to the orphanage, and half of them died within the first year.'

I sat there in silence for a moment, wondering at the change in this man. You must perceive it, Professor Wilson, even through my flawed account. Indeed to witness it first-hand was most disturbing, so stark did it seem. I had no understanding of how it might have occurred. It was rather as if Professor Semmelweis had been replaced by another man; as if the morning had presented me with an interloper, or perhaps the interloper was before me and the real, more confused and desperate Professor Semmelweis had been vanished through the twisted ministrations of Herr Meyer. Of course his appearance was the same, but the character was so very different, it was hard to understand what had occurred. I had not believed him absolutely lost to reason before, and had rather imagined – as I mentioned – that he was poised between the world we recognise and another psychic realm we generally regard as beyond our concerns, or only of concern in so far as we seek to police and restrain those who occupy this world. Yet now, as he described these unfortunate women, Professor Semmelweis was upset – the man was trembling in his grief and self-blame – and he was not eloquent in the ordinary way, but he might have passed for little more than agitated and eccentric. He would have been heeded at a supper party, though people might have said he ran on a little, lacked a sense of when to pause. And the hand-wringing, perhaps that would have attracted notice. It is true, his gestures were overblown and distracting, but, relative to the state of nerves in which I had previously found him, he was greatly changed. And though his memory was still betraying him constantly, he was picking a way through its blanks, eking out dreams and recollections. His general demeanour made me suspect his condition was one of fits and regressions, and that he might sink into an episode and then later appear relatively recovered, before descending once more. I had not previously seen an inmate who presented so dramatic an oscillation between lucidity and stupor, between his regressions and his advances, but thus I found him.

'You are remembering women you treated?' I said.

'I killed many of them. Before I knew about the way the contagion spread. I was one of the arch murderers in the Vienna General Hospital, because I was young and eager to learn my profession and so I performed an unusual number of autopsies. In the mornings I would always attend the autopsies of women who had died of childbed fever, and then I would hurry to the lying-in wards, and examine the living. And they would grow feverish, and often they would die. Personally I infected innumerable women, and deprived innumerable babies of their mothers' love.'

'Is this what you have been trying to forget?'

'I do not forget it,' he said, sharply. 'It torments me. Besides I think there are other crimes upon my head. These are the gravest, I confess. These must be the gravest, the successive murders I have committed. But you see, I have done something else, I know.'

'Tell me of your theory that puerperal sepsis is conveyed by the hands of doctors,' I said, aiming to move the discussion away from these themes which merely distressed him. But he had found his motif, and did not yet want to discard it. He said, 'I understand now why my former colleagues have banished me.'

'No one has banished . . .' I began, but he said, 'They fear me, because I remind them of their guilt. My very presence accuses them. These are feted men. They are accustomed to praise. And I offer them only condemnation. This is anomalous and they despise it. Fortunately for them, they are the majority, they are the respectable keepers of orthodoxies, applauded for their efforts to maintain everything, to conserve untruth and protect fiction, and so it is perfectly easy for them to dismiss me. They dismiss me powerfully, even with anger in their voices, and everyone follows them. In a sense, their anger is absurd, because how could I ever really damage their great reputations, the names they are so proud of, when I am a single voice and they form a chiming chorus? How?' He stopped at this, and looked at me.

I said, 'Perhaps you have worried them.'

'They are not worried. That is their gravest crime. They are not worried at all,' he said bitterly.

'Tell me of your theory,' I said again.

'I perceive quite clearly now that I was once a fool and because of my foolishness thousands of women died. I failed to convince my colleagues. Here in Vienna, I proved my theory, but then I was secretive and reluctant to present my findings. For years I failed to communicate what I had discovered, and during these years thousands of women died.'

'But I am told you wrote a book,' I said.

'Who told you that?' And now there was his former suspicion, his tone hoarse and abrasive. I said, 'A friend, no one you need be concerned about,' and he seemed to accept this response. 'I did write a book. I worked hard on it, thinking it would finally convince my opponents. And yet they massed to condemn it. The reviews were monstrous. They vandalised my argument, just to save themselves. And I became angry and lost the argument altogether. So you might say my crime is twofold. I am a murderer because of my reluctance, my secrecy. Then I am a murderer because of my anger.'

'But I do not yet understand your theory. I would be glad if you could explain it to me.'

He said, 'Are you a doctor?' – by this remark he revealed that however much he had regained a sense of his own past, his awareness of his immediate environment was tenuous indeed, and I was but a shade, a presence beside him, hardly an individual at all.

'I am not,' I said, again.

'Well, you may know that it is not yet accepted in Austria that puerperal sepsis is contagious, that this deadly infection can be prevented by something as simple as washing the hands. Simply washing the hands.' And now he splashed his hands frantically in the basin of water, so that most of it spilled over the sides, and he held up his hands to me. 'A little chlorinated lime solution. A thorough wash. That is all that is required. In my native land, this theory of mine has been generally adopted for some years now. There at least my conscience is clear. But Austria and the world in general have defeated me. I have failed entirely to convince anyone beyond my own land.'

'How do you know you failed to convince anyone?'

At that he leaned towards me, as far as he could. There was a rancid stink coming from him. Something like decay, the decay of the faculties naturally, and also a general bodily decline. The man reeked of stale blood, from the various wounds on his head and hands. He was leaning towards me, emanating these smells of disorder, as he said, 'We must remember, it is far too late for Frau Engel, murdered by Dr Fuchs. And it is too late for Frau Adler, murdered by my esteemed colleague Dr Kuhn. Though perhaps she was murdered by his student, Herr Hirsch. Then it is too late for Frau ... oh I cannot remember her name. It is in my mind but I cannot summon it. This woman was most certainly murdered by Dr Roth. You must know him. He is one of my most vehement critics, and one of the biggest murderers of them all. He moves from ward to ward, snuffing out lives. That man is Death, death to mothers. All these women, let us remember, and hundreds like them, thousands like them, had been delivered of healthy babies. So we must consider the hundreds of motherless children. The hundreds of mothers denied their destiny, to love and nurture their young.'

He was staring at me with awful intensity again, the dead and lonely gaze, more unpleasant to behold even than his hand-wringing and sudden surges of violent energy. Yet he did not see me, I now perceived, he saw merely the past and perhaps these ranks of women, reproaching him, but nonetheless his expression discomfited me, and I turned to my notebook, and began once more to write.

'Surely you should consider all the women you have saved?' I said, after a pause.

'I have forgotten the statistics. I must remember them. If you would only let me think I will remember them. Your questions are so incessant, I cannot think.'

Thus castigated, I fell silent, and eventually he said, 'I believe there was a colleague of mine. There was a colleague

. . . the details are clouded by my fetid brain. He was called Kolletschka, that was his name. His first name I am trying to remember . . . he was a good colleague, even a friend. And what was his first name? He has been dead now many years. I was a youth when he died. How long ago is it that Kolletschka died?'

'I do not know, I am afraid,' I said.

'Why? Why do you not know?' Again the anger, the sudden flash of aggression. 'My friend – I have forgotten his name . . .'

'Kolletschka.'

' . . . was performing an autopsy on a woman who had died of . . . of this disease . . . you know what I am referring to . . . and in the course of this he cut his hand with a scalpel and fell ill. The nature of his illness was similar to the sufferings of those women, even unto his horrible death. So after he died – I was most shocked and dismayed, naturally, and thought much about why he had died – I realised that he had clearly caught his infection from the direct contact of his blood with the infected blood of the dead woman. Or with some particles that came from her body, and went straight into my friend's blood.'

'So this is how you came to believe that these fevers, or distempers of the blood, were in fact transferred somehow from one person to another?'

'By the hand,' he said, and again he held up his raw and grimy hand. 'By these doctor's hands, infected with poisons from the dead, or from others who were dying, and then thrust into the wombs of mothers.'

'So it was not merely the dead, it was anyone who had the disease?'

'No, my friend. More even than that. And no one understood this. They thought I meant only the dead. But I meant any fetid or decayed tissue, any infected rancid tissue within any body. So there was a doctor who treated a woman with an infected cancerous breast, and then his next patient developed childbed fever. Anything! A corpse was not required! But the fools misunderstood that too.'

'That is most unfortunate.'

'They were too foolish to understand. And I was too foolish to explain it clearly. But I did something. I did a few small things. For a while in Vienna, before I was banished back to Budapest, I forced my colleagues to wash their hands in chlorinated lime solution, and instantly the cases of childbed fever were significantly reduced. For a full six months we had no deaths at all from the disease, an extraordinary, unprecedented statistic.'

'But with such success, why did no one believe you?'

Well, that made him rage. This simple question converted him from a lucid melancholic into a frothing maniac. He lashed out wildly, and for some minutes he was bestial and appalling, shuddering and pouring his rage into the room, so it crashed against me like a sea in storm. He slammed his hands on his face, on his knees, anywhere they would fall, raving and grinding his teeth. I stood up, and perhaps I was even a little afraid. Not for my own person, rather there was something distressing about the sight itself, the spectacle of a personality unravelling, inner chaos released. For I believe that we all contain within us these unbridled forces, and yet we marshal them in our minds, somehow, and sometimes we enslave and contain them too rigidly, and either they wither and die or they burst forth like the eruption of a volcano. They are ancient phenomena of nature, these forces that course through us, and here was this man, like a tempest raging in a single human frame; it was compelling and awful to view. Indeed I merely observed him for a time, while he raged and frothed and seemed likely to be overcome altogether. Yet then, almost as suddenly as he had begun, he stopped his bellowing, and paused. He rubbed his eyes, as if he had awoken from a deep sleep. He was exhausted by his labours; his voice was trembling, and at first he could not phrase a sentence. He was trying to summon his lucid state again, I thought. 'I . . . I . . .' he said, 'I . . . believe they have always found my proofs inadequate . . . Even though they were as clear as day . . .' He looked weak now, ashen-faced, his mouth filmy with saliva and his skin glistening, and he wheezed as he said, 'They have always talked to me about proof. Where is your proof of the real nature of contagion? How can you physically demonstrate the transference of disease from one body to another? I tell them – if they have not already turned away, which most often they have – that they must look at the women I saved. Aware as I was that my colleague, Koll . . .'

'Kolletschka . . .' I said.

' . . . died of contagion, I proposed the washing of hands in chlorinated lime solution, especially after my colleagues had performed autopsies. Instantly, the rate of childbed fever was reduced. It went down to one per cent that died. Only one per cent, from the previous heights of thirty per cent. A remarkable decrease. Palpable, I thought. So when they asked me for proof, I said I had none of the real nature of the infection but I had eradicated childbed fever from my section of the hospital. Even the midwives – who you know always had lower rates of childbed fever – I had even improved on their ratio. Had they allowed me to continue,

161

the hospital would no longer have been so greatly dreaded by pregnant women; they would have come to the First Division gladly and without foreboding. Perhaps I might have expiated my own guilt that way, so I would not now have to suffer . . .'

'It is clear you have worked hard to convince others,' I said.

'For a time I worked hard to convince my colleagues in Vienna, but then I was banished.'

'And why was that?'

'I forget the circumstances of my banishment. It is a terrible thing, but they will not return to me. Perhaps there is someone who can tell me. But I know I had not resided many years in Vienna, when I was forced home again. I fled, I remember that. I had so many enemies. They conspired against me. I was weary of their conspiracies, and so I fled, perhaps that was it. Cowardice and a yearning for my home.'

'It is a grave shame.'

He was angry once more, so his face was livid with a sort of rash, and his eyes were darting around the room, as if he was hunting out his tormentors. As if they even appeared to him – perhaps they did. I do not know what this man saw, but his thoughts were shattered once more. When he spoke again, he thrust his hands towards me, and he said, 'I killed a woman, once, with my hands. I remember she was a very young, very frightened woman. She had blonde hair. She was very frightened and said, "Doctor, I have six children and I must get home soon to them." And I assured her she would. But I murdered her all the same. She died screaming for her children. She was unusual, she did not forget herself. Her baby died a few months later. I murdered her and

162

her baby. I see her in my dreams and she berates me. She accuses me.'

'She is perhaps the woman you mentioned earlier?'

'I see her and then in her I see the others. There are so many. They were in grave pain as I examined them. Their bodies in the grip of childbirth. And I pushed my hands inside them' – and he made the horrible delving action of earlier – 'and sometimes I ripped the placenta from their wombs, at the time saving their lives, yet a few days later they were dead anyway.'

'But, sir, how can you be so certain you caused their deaths?'

'Oh do not torment me with your foolish questions!' he cried, and then sank into furious silence.

His thoughts were extreme; his accusations were extreme; yet there was a logic to his arguments. If his theory were true, then it was certain the actions of Professor Semmelweis and his colleagues had indeed killed many women. The accusation of murder was extreme, yet when he came to the matter of those colleagues who had refused his suggestions altogether and insisted on proceeding as before, one might suggest they bore a grave guilt. If his suggestions were as trivial as hand-washing then it seemed they might have simply entertained them, just in case he was correct. What did they stand to lose, by occasionally dipping their hands in a solution? I am ignorant of the discipline of obstetrics, yet I feel I might have, in their position, been moved to try this technique. If the epidemic was as relentless and inexplicable as Semmelweis proposed, then why were they not prepared to try anything, simply to ameliorate matters? As we are uncertain about the true causes of everything under the sun, why should we not experiment with theories we find outlandish at first?

History is full of theories which have been proffered, and self-appointed experts who have rejected them, simply because they were novel, or threatening of a general ortho-doxy. Those religious beliefs which dominate in my coun-try, and equally in yours, Professor Wilson, such as the divinity of Christ, and the truth of the Gospels, have at vari-ous points been regarded as madness and heresy and the mere expression of them has caused individuals to be slaughtered. Indeed history is a series of rising and falling so-called truths, each generation directed by certain absolutes which are most often cast off by the next. All my studies in early religions and all that I have read of scientific debate throughout the ages have caused me to become con-vinced that one of the most curious elements of human existence is the naivety with which we assume that now, now and never before, we have all the answers. For did we not, for centuries, believe that the sun followed the earth? And who was the crazed madman who proposed that it did not, that instead the earth ran like a child after the sun? And this man Galileo was tormented and told to abandon his claims, and he recanted in order to save his life. Yet he was right all the same, as we now know. The priests were dog-matic in their refusal of him, and punished him, just as Semmelweis's colleagues had been dogmatic in their refusal of him. And thus suffering continues. Dear Professor Wilson, perhaps we might say the great unacknowledged evil of our civilisation is dogmatism. Perhaps this is the canker we bear within us, which taints every society we fos-ter. But you will most likely disagree with me; I am merely rambling from my theme, to which I shall confine myself henceforth.

For the reasons I have advanced above, it did not concern me that Professor Semmelweis had been generally dismissed. I mean by this, that the censure of his peers did not convince me of the falsity of his proposals. I had no real knowledge of his field, and so I had no great opinion on whether he was right or not. Semmelweis himself was convinced of his rightness, and in this he was another dynamic zealot, driven to justify himself at every turn. Had he been more measured, he might have won more supporters. Yet it was also his unmeasured determination that led him to the theory, and thus his failure to disseminate it was bound up entirely in the attributes that had generated it in the first place.

Thinking to divert his thoughts, which I believed had festered, I said to him, 'Professor Semmelweis, I must ask if you now recall your wife and children?'

He raised his head at this, and perhaps his anger diminished a little. He said, curtly, but more continently than before, 'Yes, I think I have a wife and children. I do not remember them.'

'You only remember your time in Vienna?'

'I remember the period I spent in the Vienna General Hospital.'

'That is only a matter of a few years, Professor Semmelweis.'

'What is your meaning?'

'I mean that it is a pity, that you can only regain your memories of a very brief period in your life. Your memories of this period are very clear. But the rest is lost to you, at present.'

He said nothing in reply.

It was strange indeed. He had been discoursing fluently on matters concerning puerperal sepsis and his attempts to disseminate his theory. He ran on, unstoppably, when he sighted this theme. But the rest of his life, the fundaments of his existence as a father and husband, had departed from him. It was as if his theory of puerperal sepsis, his struggle to achieve its general acceptance, had so dominated his mind that it returned to him when everything else had fled or faded. He was left with a single theme, an intellectual argument, yet deprived of all his ties of love and friendship.

At that moment – quite the worst moment for such an interruption, when everything was so precarious – we were disturbed by Herr Meyer, who had sneaked along the corridor and gained the cell before I noticed him. He stared around, in his proprietorial way, as if this was his kingdom and I was nothing more than a base trespasser. He twitched nastily and seemed to be trying to persuade me to leave then, but I stood my ground. I turned to him and said, 'Herr Meyer, I desire a little more time with this patient.'

'You are of course welcome to pursue your enquiries,' he said, trying to smile, but it was a furious little grimace that made him look like a fox. 'I merely wondered if you required assistance.'

'That is most kind. But I have everything I need,' I replied, casting an ironic gesture at the dank cell and its unhappy resident.

That made him bite his lip, and nod reluctantly, and then once again he greased a path towards the door.

Professor Semmelweis was much disturbed by the intrusion, and would not speak for some time. Indeed I feared he would return to his previous inertia. When I could tolerate the suspense no more, I said, loudly, 'We were speaking of your work at the General Hospital, Professor Semmelweis.' Perhaps the stridency of my tone retrieved him, for he turned towards me once more, and said, 'Yes, I believe we were.'

'You were telling me about the advances you made.'

'I was telling you how I sought to atone for the slaughter over which I presided.'

'You accuse yourself too vehemently, Professor Semmelweis,' I said.

Herr Meyer was forgotten, as he said, his ire rising, 'You shall not be the judge of that, however you presume to assess me. Yet I was telling you about a period of many months, during which no woman died of childbed fever. Elsewhere the disease raged. Only our ward was an oasis. The women there smiled and were glad. They held up their babies, kissed them, suckled them without fear. They were not stricken by sweats and grinding pains and the obscene devastation that puerperal sepsis inflicts. They were not drained of life, life was not drawn out of them in blood. The patients were safe. However my colleagues, instead of applauding and celebrating my achievements, accused me of missing the point entirely. They informed me that we simply needed better ventilation. That there was no proof of the beneficial properties of chlorinated lime solution. That my methods were not scientific. They despised me because I was an outsider and thought I had no place proposing such a significant adjustment to their rules. Dr Roth called me unprofessional. Simply because I proposed a theory which was not his own! Simply because I did not sit worshipfully at his feet! These doctors claim to be devoted to the pursuit of knowledge but really they are vain and seek to be revered. They want nothing more than the reverence of those they regard as their inferiors. They are boulders in the river, preventing the flow of knowledge. I sought to drag a few of them out! I tried to blast open the dam! I was unequal to the task but I laboured to blast it open anyway. They stood firm and they condemned me. Dr Schneider suggested I was inexperienced! And by then I had two years in Vienna on my record. Two years in which scarcely a woman died.'

'It is most unfortunate,' I said, because he was staring so plainly and desperately at me, clearly hoping for such a remark. You will notice, Professor Wilson, that by now our conversation had become circuitous, and though I found the recurrences of his thoughts rather frustrating I felt I must allow him to continue with his wild arcs, in case something new materialised. Besides, I was genuinely transfixed by his energy and distress, by the horrible eloquence of his recollections.

'It is unfortunate, yes,' Semmelweis said, 'that I was insulted and dismissed. It is unfortunate, yes, that thousands of women have died. It is unfortunate, yes, that thousands more will die. All of this is most unfortunate, simply because of some stubborn old fools who call themselves doctors.'

'It is most unfortunate you have become ill,' I said.

'Ultimately,' he said, in a lower tone, 'I do not matter. It does not matter what happens to me. I plead for mercy for my wife and children, but not for myself. I deserve to be punished. I was the messenger and failed. I did not transmit my message. Perhaps to the few, but not to the many. What becomes of the failed messenger? It is right, in the end, that he should be consigned to such a place as this,' and he waved a hand, in disgust, at the cell.

'But surely you would like to leave, and see your family again?'

'I long to see them. I long so much . . .' He stopped for a moment, overwhelmed. Then he muttered, 'yet it is right that I should be punished. It is one thing that makes me glad, this fact that I am being punished. No doubt my family is disgraced, but then it is a disgrace to be the child of a murderer, or the wife of one. You are tainted by the murderer's sin. It is quite right. I am not complaining of my punishment. I merely propose that some of my colleagues should be in here too. There is a professor, I forget his name. He has been murdering women for a good forty years longer than I. Before and after. Before I made my proposals and after. I only have a couple of years of active murder on my conscience and then I have all the murders committed by those I could not convince. But this man said that no doctor could spare the time to wash his hands. An imposition on a busy man! And then he said I was a disgusting fellow anyway, for proposing that a doctor would be dirty in the first place. What was I saying about my colleagues? An appalling slur on a gentleman's reputation. Appalling arrogance, to tell a gentleman to wash his hands! He explained it all to me, one afternoon. He told me I couldn't go around insulting other fellows like that. He told me it was arrogant and rude. I lacked decorum, you see, in my outrageous suggestions that the medical profession might – for an hour, for a day – stop murdering mothers.'

'Perhaps because women had always died in this way, they assumed it was inevitable.'

'But they had not always died in this way. They had begun to die in great numbers, in numbers which would be categorised as an epidemic, only when the lying-in hospitals were established, in the last century. Prior to that, there had been incidences, naturally, but nothing on this sort of scale, nothing so catastrophic. Doctors had passed from one house to another, and infected their patients, but they had not conducted autopsies and through this procedure infect-ed dozens of women in the same day.'

'But women have always suffered from the fear of death, as they approached childbirth,' I said. 'There have always been grave dangers associated with birthing a child. Does the Bible not say that woman must bring forth children in suffering and affliction, as punishment for the sin of Eve? It is regarded as the natural state of women, to endure this torment in childbirth.'

'Yes, it is true. And the hospitals were established to end such fear and suffering. Their aims were virtuous. These aims were thwarted by the individuals who came to control them, by the murderers who called themselves doctors.'

He paused once more, and then he said, 'Let them wash the blood from their own hands.'

And with an angry jerk of his hand, he accidentally spilled the last of the water from the basin onto his lap.

'My God,' he said, suddenly fearful. 'And what shall we do now?'

'Professor Semmelweis, it is quite all right,' I said. 'I will send for some more water. Do not distress yourself.'

But he was staring in dismay at the empty basin, and he began to mutter, so quietly and rapidly I could not distinguish the words at first. And then I distinctly heard him saying, 'Behold I am behind thee I am thy mother for ever and ever,' and he repeated this several times. I was not sure where this derived from, or what it meant. Then he said, 'The woman who torments me, who comes to me and reveals to me the true nature of my sin, I believe her name was Birgit Vogel.'

'She was a patient of yours?'

'Yes, I think it was at a time when I was not quite certain of my theory. I could have been careful and I was not. I did not bother to wash my hands thoroughly, I merely dipped them in the solution and she became very ill with puerperal sepsis and died a few days later. I think it is that . . . And because of the death of Birgit Vogel, my own mother died.'

'What do you mean by this?'

'No sooner had Birgit Vogel died – and she died in horrible agony, and her little baby – a beautiful blond-haired boy – was taken from her as she shivered and screamed, and his wails were drowned out by her own – than I received news from Budapest that my poor mother had died. For the death of Birgit Vogel, I was summoned to account. So in a sense, I am also responsible for the death of my mother.'

This seemed to me highly significant. Not that there was any provable truth in his sense of causality, but rather it was significant because Professor Semmelweis had created his own symbolic universe and in this symbolic universe he was guilty of matricide and therefore he was condemned to eternal suffering. And yet also, he was the wounded god, rising from the corpse of his mother. He was sinner and divine king, combined into one person, and the confusion of these roles was probably the cause of much of his perceived insanity. For if we regard such mysteries with a literal mind, then they will indeed perplex us, and Professor Semmelweis was a doctor and thereby, originally, an empiricist. No doubt he had resisted, at the time, any sort of symbolic interpretation of the death of his mother, and had instead marked it down to awful timing, fundamental bad luck, and had suppressed his fears and the irrational terror the bereavement had caused him to feel. And it had festered, for years it had festered, even as he was ostracised by his former allies, and indeed I suspect he, in one sense, wanted them to ostracise them. He incited them to annihilate him, so he might atone for the death of his mother and so he might rise reborn, like the Phoenix from the ashes, Christ from the tomb, Osiris from the casket. Professor Semmelweis had become tormented by these suppressed symbolical demons, and all his endeavours had been undermined by the confusion he refused to acknowledge. He had destroyed himself, I was quite sure of that, in order to rid himself of guilt. Yet in so doing, he had burdened himself with a further form of guilt, for all those women he had failed to save. In casting himself and his theory onto the pyre, hoping the flames would be purgatorial, he had dragged thousands of women with him, suttee-like, and it was only now that he realised what he had done.

I was rather revising my theories, as I perceived that it was convenient for Professor Semmelweis to see himself as the innocent victim of a conspiracy, as the genius who had been ignored. Because he had denied the reality of his urges for so many years, he had persuaded himself – he had been obliged to believe this, for the reality was so much more disturbing – that his colleagues had waged a war against him, and after many years destroyed him. Rather, I was beginning to surmise that in two years, from the death of his mother, which was almost the same time that he developed the theory, to the point that he fled from Vienna – and he was confused about the circumstances of this flight, and could not remember anything after it – he set about ruining himself. As I was able to assemble a sense of chronology, from his words and those earlier of Professor Zurbruck, he had refused for many years to publish on his theory; he had published nothing of significance at all from the late 1840s when he developed the principle of hand-washing until recently when he had finally written his rambling account, an account he hardly thought – I suspected – would convince anyone. He cast off his supporters. He ran back to his native land. He ran back to the motherland, though his mother was no longer there. Everything was in turmoil for this man, who had been taught to believe that reason must prevail. He tried for years to reason through his actions, and because they were driven entirely by the unreasoning elements of the psyche and were unknowable by reason itself, he drove himself into a collapse. His reason had frantically rejected everything it could not assimilate, and he had slipped into a state classified as lunatic. He had placed himself beyond the understanding of his family and friends. He had exiled himself, so he might die alone. Birgit Vogel haunted him through his lunacy, because he had locked her away for so many years, he had confined her to a dusty recess of his thoughts, and now she had burst out and consumed him.

I am meandering once more, Professor Wilson – I fear this will be what you are thinking. To be plain about the matter at hand, to strip it of my theoretical ornamentation, it would seem that Professor Semmelweis developed an idea about the causes of puerperal sepsis and though by proceeding in line with his theory he reduced incidences of the disease significantly, his colleagues did not support him for one reason or another. It may be that they were ashamed of themselves and conspired to destroy him for this reason. Or it may be that he goaded them and goaded them, for his own psychic reasons, and this, combined with their own shame, caused them to reject him. There, that is as simple as I can make it, and now I will leave you to reach your own conclusion.

We had little more conversation, I am sorry to report. I asked him if there was anything I could do to help him, but he shook his head. Sadly and slowly. He was losing energy, that was evident. He had raged luminously, like a star in its final burst of glory, before it is consumed by darkness.

'Could I not contact your wife? Perhaps she does not know you are here?' I said.

He did not respond.

'Are there friends you remember? Could I contact any of them? Surely you would like to leave this place?'

'Like any prisoner, I dream of liberty. But I do not deserve it,' he said.

And he would not speak again, and sat there rubbing his hands. I stayed for some considerable time, but I could not rouse him at all. I lingered, even after Herr Meyer slithered along to fetch me. I stood there – under the disapproving gaze of Herr Meyer – and watched poor Professor Semmelweis muttering to himself or to the shades that accused him. Yet he had his head down and he did not acknowledge me again.

The Empress

'Hello, Margaret,' Patrick was saying to Brigid's mother. 'Hi there big guy,' he said to Calumn, kneeling to kiss him.

'Did you get delayed in the traffic?' said Brigid's mother.

'It was pretty gruesome, as usual.'

'Dadadada,' said Calumn, rubbing Patrick's face, pressing his cheek to his.

'Where's Brigid?'

'In the garden,' said Brigid's mother. She screwed her mouth up and whispered through her teeth, 'Very bad.' Then she turned to Calumn with a vivid smile and said, 'Now, darling, do you want to come and read a book with Grandma?'

Calumn was shaking his head, reaching for his father's hand. So Patrick took it, like leading a pet monkey, he thought, his adored heir and pet monkey, and they walked together, father and son, through the kitchen.

Naturally it was very bad, he thought. Brigid was in labour. The pain was shocking, he remembered. Last time she raved and talked about her dying father. Would this time be worse? He had been the helpless witness to her agony, dismayed by his impotence and later disturbed – though he never told her – by the viscera, and the violence of it all. He had been impressed by his wife's endurance, he wondered how she was able to stand it at all. Yet, he had acknowledged – guiltily he had acknowledged the fear he felt, the sense that reality was being overturned. He didn't like it. He was moved but he didn't like it all the same, the bizarre vision of a miniature human emerging from the body of his wife, followed by a stream of blood, as if Brigid was being disembowelled in the process. He had been mesmerised and disturbed, and afterwards he banished it all from his mind, gladly, thinking it might never happen – to them – again.

Patrick walked through the kitchen to the back door, his son trotting alongside him, despite Brigid's mother's cries. 'Oh Calumn darling stay with me, stay with your gran,' she said, but Calumn went along behind his father anyway.

'Euuurssschkkkad,' he said.

'Yes, absolutely,' said Patrick. 'Just today and possibly for the next couple of days, we have to remember that Mummy's having a bit of a difficult time. She's very tired because of all the work she's doing, to make your new brother or sister. You know, she's been making a new brother or sister for you, and this is the final part, where it gets to be very hard work. It's not terrible in any way, it's all good, but it's hard work. Like running very fast, like when we run in the park. We get tired and we have to sit down. Do you know what I mean?'

'Mamammam,' said Calumn, and nodded his head. Who knows what he understands, thought Patrick. They had been trying to prepare him. Reading him appropriate books, at one point they had even tried to interest him in a doll. But how could you really prepare a child for the shock of finding a new baby in his home? For himself, it had been different. He was the last child of three. There had always been others, and he had never – that he could remember – questioned the presence of his brother and sister. But Calumn, they had always treated Calumn as a miracle child, as if he was the only child Brigid would be able to conceive. When she became pregnant for a second time, they were overjoyed but stunned; they hadn't expected it at all. Poor kid, you just don't know what is going on, thought Patrick, looking down at the shuffling sweetness of his son, his chubby hands, his long eyelashes, his unruly hair. An amazing little boy, he thought. My little boy.

Through the window he made out the lumbering form of Brigid. She was standing in the rain, her clothes soaked and clinging to her great belly. She was turning slow circles, holding her belly as if that would help her. Then she would stop and breathe, gulping down air. It was moving to see her there, stooped under the rain, nearly broken with the weight of their child and the pain of labour. All day he had been dogged by a sense of guilt, that he wasn't with her, that he was indentured and had to stay at his desk. Brigid had told him she would try to cope without him. 'Perhaps the labour will go on for hours,' she had said, and he heard the strain in her voice. 'My mother's here,' she said. 'I can call the midwife. Stay if you have to.' So he had stayed, but everything was shadowed by this image of her, in pain and waiting for him to return. He had been unable to concentrate. He spoke on the phone, he smiled and shook people by the hand but he could only think of his wife. He had scarcely attended to the talk around him. Now he stood silently for a moment, held by the graveness of her struggle, as if he shouldn't disturb her. Then he saw she was grimacing as she breathed, and that made him open the door. Calumn wanted to run out-side, but he tried to hold him back. 'It's raining sweetie,' he said. 'You don't want to run out in the rain.' But he couldn't stop him anyway. So he held his hand and they went slowly down the steps.

'Brigid,' he said, more loudly. 'What should I do?'

She was grimacing horribly and then she saw Calumn. 'Oh good, you're here,' she said, brightly, but it was forced. She was trying to sound matter-of-fact, because Calumn was running towards her. 'Mamamama,' Calumn said, squeal-ing his delight, and she smiled down at him. 'Hello darling boy. Have you been having fun with Grandma?' Calumn nodded, doubtfully. 'Good, how good. Well, and now Daddy is here, isn't that nice?'

'Dah,' said Calumn.

Brigid turned away, pulled her lips into a silent howl, tried to breathe, and Calumn stared up at her back, looking uncertain and slightly sad. Naturally he knew something was happening, thought Patrick. He was still a baby, still bound up with Brigid's emotions, her shifts of mood. And this was far more than a mood shift, it was like colliding with something enormous and unyielding, and this gar-den was full of pain, and violence scarcely controlled; even Patrick felt it. Calumn made a tentative move towards his mother, patted her leg a little, and she – with a tight smile – leaned towards him and kissed his hair. She said, 'Darling, Mummy's very sorry she's so tired and can't pick you up. Mummy loves you very much. Daddy's here now and Daddy is going to get you some juice. Aren't you

Daddy?' Then she said, speaking quickly so Calumn wouldn't understand, 'Where the hell have you been?'

'You said you'd call if . . .'

'I thought you'd come back anyway, once I said . . .'

'I didn't know . . .'

She smiled again at Calumn, not wanting to disturb him. 'Never mind,' she said, firmly. 'Could you sort out Calumn's dinner?'

'Of course,' said Patrick. 'Just tell me what to do.'

'Mum brought some food, speak to her.'

'Yes.'

'It must be late. Is it late?'

'It's not very late. I'll ask her if she can stay. She can deal with Calumn while I help you.'

Brigid nodded quickly, and tried to kiss Calumn again, but the attempt was clumsy, hindered by her vastness and her pain, and Calumn was turning back to gaze at her as Patrick drew him inside. 'It's all wet,' he said to his son, aiming to distract him. 'All wet outside isn't it? How funny that Mummy is standing in the wet.'

But Calumn was silent, confusion in his eyes; it was impossible to know what he was thinking, impossible even to imagine how his semi-verbal brain marshalled events. Something was wrong, that might have been the thought, had he possessed the words to formulate it. He was uneasy and he clung to Patrick's hand, following along because he was thirsty and wanted some juice. 'And then Daddy must get you some dinner,' said Patrick. 'It's dinnertime now isn't it Calumn? Soon be time for bed.'

Determinedly, Calumn shook his head.

Brigid watched her son and husband going inside, into the ordinary world of the kitchen which had somehow repelled her, so she had fled into the garden. She was an outcast, excluded from normality by the tearing pains within her. She had been raging at Patrick, focusing all her rage on him, and now he was here – she watched him bitterly, as he opened the fridge, and she imagined Calumn below him, too small for her to see, trying to grab at some fruit, or holding out his eager hands for a packet of juice. She felt cast down, by something like mingled concern for her son and the mounting unstoppable pain. Calumn seemed so lost and small and deprived of her – she was troubled by a premonition that this scene would become habitual, once she had a newborn to deal with. Calumn would be the mournful interloper, escorted away from her by helpful adults. And their relationship would never be the same. Brigid was thinking how sad it was, that she and Calumn would no longer be so closely bonded, so nearly sealed off from the rest of the world, when the pain began again and she turned and started walking slowly round the garden, smoothing back her hair, the rain falling hard upon her.

Breathe, breathe, breathe. You must breathe. This new surge of pain was rising within her. The pains began slowly, just a suggestion, a dark promise. They rumbled faintly, and then the progress began, the relentless escalation, until you thought something must break, it should break, but now this pain was growing greater and more violent every second, and every second still stronger, and she gasped and tried to breathe.

Breathe, breathe breathe. Reeeeee-lax . . . Reeeeee-lax. Reeeeee-lax. That was something she had read. In one of those cheerful and now redundant pregnancy books. Never mind, that was all it really said. Nothing bad will happen. Reeee-lax. The body responds to thoughts. Think positively. Never mind the pain, never mind. Yet she was compelled to mind. The pain rose and all she thought was pain, pain and I am pierced by pain, and she was rigid with agony and no longer breathing in the advised way, rather holding her breath and far from relaxed, until it broke. The wave broke – she imagined it curdling and frothing onto the shore.

At the door, there was Patrick again.

'Everything OK?' she said, tersely.

'Everything's fine in here,' he said. 'You just worry about yourself.'

She nodded. Grim-faced, thought Patrick. She looked drawn and pale, as if she was shocked all over again. He wanted to hold her, but she looked somehow contained by her state, distinct and apart from him. He couldn't understand her, so he smiled at her, said, 'Let me know as soon as you need me,' and she nodded and turned away. And he went inside and didn't know what to do. There was Calumn, expectant and uncertain. His son, holding a cup of juice and waiting for his father to reassure him.

'Sweetie, drink your juice,' said Patrick.

'Uuughaughhhhh,' said Calumn.

'I agree. That's absolutely true, but you should still drink it.'

'Bhaltabish.'

'Yes, that's quite right. Your point is well made. Now let's have a swig. Can Daddy have some juice?' And Calumn offered him the cup with a baby swing of his arm.

'I can make dinner,' said Brigid's mother, in the background. She was hovering, in that way she had. 'Let me help.'

'Well, if you don't mind, that would be great,' said Patrick. 'Then I could go and give Brigid some support.'

'Of course. I made some pasta sauce. It just needs heating up. And there's homemade bread, and soup.'

'Well that sounds perfect. Of course, have whatever you'd like yourself. There's white wine in the fridge. Open some red if you'd prefer it.'

'What about you and Brigid?'

'I'll ask Brigid what she wants, if she wants to eat. Don't worry about me, I'll eat later.'

'You should keep your strength up.'

'Really, I'm fine.'

'OK little Calumn my darling, we're going to have a lovely dinner, aren't we, aren't we going to have a delicious scrummy dinner?' said Brigid's mother.

'Neaaaar,' said Calumn, shaking his head.

A mixed blessing, thought Patrick, grabbing a handful of peanuts from a bag in the cupboard. Hiding them from Calumn, who coveted foods he couldn't have. Yes, Brigid's mother could make dinner and maybe even put Calumn to bed. But later, what would they do later? Surely she wouldn't stay to the end? The final gore? Last time Brigid refused even to tell her mother she was in labour. She refused to tell anyone. 'Our private affair.' Her private pain. Now her mother was here, in the kitchen. Helpful, of course. Irreproachably helpful. It was unfortunate, but he didn't want her there. With her, he had to play the part, the

184

courteous son-in-law. It was quite impossible to relax with her; she was so determinedly remote herself. Remote from him, not from Calumn, and certainly not from Brigid. It was just with him she was so formal and polite. Perhaps he had just never tested her, and she, too, had been trapped in her guise. But he shook his head, because he didn't want to think about her.

In the garden he stood in front of his wife, and she placed her hands on her hips and leaned forward, so her head was almost touching his chest. He recognised this as a sort of reconciliation. She needed him, however hopeless he was, it was that sort of weary acknowledgement.

'How bad is it?' he said, putting his arms around her.

'Quite bad. It'll get worse.'

'How often do they come?'

'Quite often. But not so I need to count.'

'Let me know when you want to count.'

'I will.'

'I love you. You're doing brilliantly.'

She didn't reply. Her face was twisted and he thought another contraction must be starting. She lowered her head and breathed. She breathed like an asthmatic, gasping for air.

For a minute they stood, Brigid drawing in air and Patrick trying to think what it must be like for her. A deep pain in the centre of your body. He had been in pain in his life, but he had no real recollection of it. He once broke his leg skiing and he told everyone that the pain had been monstrous, as if something was gouging a hole in his thigh. Yet he remembered only the words he had used to describe it, not the pain itself. His body had rejected the real memory of the pain, as soon as he recovered. Just as you couldn't really remember the precise sensation of sexual ecstasy, once it had passed. You knew you had enjoyed it, acutely, just as you had acutely despised intense pain. But all the real sensation was gone, there was something you couldn't quite regain.

He was kissing Brigid's forehead as she stood there, trying to protect her. The silence extended around them, until she sighed deeply and said, 'That was a bad one.'

'It's very wet in the garden,' he said.

'It is wet,' she said.

'Do you like it?'

'I did but it's getting a bit cold now.'

He took her arm and began to lead her along. She was elephantine and fragile, a great round egg cracking open.

They both went inside and Brigid kissed Calumn as she passed him. 'Darling boy,' she said. He raised his hands to her, he wanted her to hold him. She kissed him as he sat in his high chair, her mother spooning food into his little mouth. He babbled into her ear. 'Eeeerrrrrugggcscckkkbelowbleoble.'

'I know sweetie, I know,' she whispered. 'Mummy loves you. What delicious food you have! What a lovely dinner!' And she nodded towards the bits of pasta, laid out before him. It was bad, she thought. She was being stretched, drawn out on a rack. She pulled her hand away from her son's clutching fingers, because she could feel a contraction rising. She kissed him again, 'Mummy loves you, darling boy,' and turned away. She was forced to ignore his protests, the way he held out his arms to her. Trying to bring her back. In the living room she sat on a rocking chair. Patrick had put Bach on the iPod, hoping it would calm her. Brigid was aiming to focus on the soft arpeggios, and perhaps as she focused the music calmed her a little. Not enough really; she needed much more than Bach.

In the background she could hear Calumn and her mother, Calumn still whining a little, not entirely placated, and she remembered how it had been with Calumn, how finally after all the false alarms she had fallen ill, a horrible stomach virus which made her feverish, and she had been stricken with anxiety because she assumed this would hurt the baby. So she agreed to everything, when they said she must be induced. They took her into the hospital and controlled the contractions with a chemical drip, oxytocin she thought it was, so when they wanted them stronger they poured more oxytocin into her, and when that became too much to bear they stuck a needle deep into her spine and numbed her entirely. Chemicals were flushed through her system, and her body was subdued by them, her responses dulled. And there was a graph beside her, constantly monitoring the baby's heart rate – she could hear the scrape of a pen on paper, and something beeping regularly, a falsetto pulse – she was rigged up to lots of machines, and the midwife told her she had done the right thing, 'for you and baby', she said.

Perhaps that was true, even though she was numb and powerless. She had to grab her legs to move them at all. When she wanted to piss, she had to be helped onto a bedpan, and then she barely squatted, could hardly keep herself in position, as she tried to eke out some piss. She was moved – briskly, practically – from side to side by the midwife, and some doctors came and peered inside her. She couldn't feel their hands at all. They broke the membranes with a hook, 'a big bag of membranes, hanging down', they told her, and she couldn't imagine what it must look like. When the membranes broke, the bed was soaked. So much fluid – the midwife had to change all the sheets, drop them in a sodden pile onto a trolley. She only felt the dampness when it reached her lower legs. The rest of her body was unfeeling, unknowing. Even so, she didn't think of it as a bad birth. She wasn't traumatised. She didn't really understand when friends talked about being disappointed by their birthing experience, as if they had hoped for something else. Everything had been managed, and she had been flooded with chemicals, and all the machines had whirred and beeped efficiently and in very little time, her baby had come. She didn't even know he was coming, she was still pretending to be pushing. The first she knew about him was when they landed him on her belly – a great – it seemed to her – wet thing, his mouth wide open in a scream. 'Fine set of lungs,' said someone – a nurse, or maybe the midwife. 'A beautiful big boy,' said another.

Now Brigid was rocking herself in the living room. She had been determined this time to experience the birth – this phrase she and her friends bandied around, meaning to experience it with a minimum of interventions, or chemicals. This time she wanted to stay at home, to avoid the bleeping and lights and the midwives moving her body around. She wanted to be active, to control the pain herself. She had all these phrases in her head, and she wondered if they would help. She was trapped between two forms of fear; she feared pain, of course, but then she was afraid of those long days and nights in hospital – once you were in there, you had to stay, and more and more things happened to you – and she thought perhaps it was better to endure the finite horrible pain of labour if that meant she escaped all the stitches and scars and bruising which last time made her limp for weeks. Last time the really insidious pain had come after labour, when the drugs left her system and her body finally realised what had happened to it. She was in agony for weeks, and then it took months before she felt anything like normal again. Perhaps this would be better; she hoped it would be better. Pregnancy was an exercise in optimism; having children was an eager assertion of optimism against all the dangers inherent in life, the tragedy which lurked constantly, at the edge of joy. So now she was trying to sustain this perilous optimism, clinging to a sense that things should be well.

She was swinging backwards and forwards, trying to focus her mind on this repetitive motion. When Patrick came in and said, 'What would you like?' she said she wanted a hot-water bottle and her TENS machine. Before, the rain had helped but now she needed warmth around her lower body; she wanted to be wrapped in warmth. He made her take off her clothes, and dressed her in things he had found in her labour bag. Even as he pulled a sweatshirt over her belly, she felt another contraction rising within her, this questioning, insistent pain. Her body was signalling to her, in these surges. Had she been more instinctive, she might have understood them better. They were becoming more regular and she thought she should time them. 'Can you get me my phone?' she said to Patrick, who was gathering up her wet things. When he gave it to her, she fiddled around to find the stopwatch setting, and pressed Go. She kept her eyes on the seconds passing, as the pain gripped her. It was like a crocodile, tumbling her in a death roll. It had trapped her, it was her. There was no escape, until these pains forced out the child. The seconds were moving, time was passing, and still the pain rolled through her, and she saw a minute had elapsed. Then she pressed Stop.

'Every five minutes, lasting a minute,' she said to Patrick when he came back. He was fixing pads on her back, for the TENS machine. She was wired up to a little box; it was something about an electrical pulse which clouded the brain. The brain couldn't recognise the real pain beneath the prickling discomfort caused by the TENS machine. It was better to be pricked by a thousand tiny needles, that was what it felt like, this electronic buzzing on her back, than to feel the pure delving stab of her contractions. Voluntarily, she pricked herself, it was strange. It was counter-intuitive, but this dancing of needles on her back started to help. Underneath, she could feel the pain, as another contraction surged and broke. She timed it again. 'Another one the same,' she said. 'Or perhaps a little shorter.'

'I'll time them too,' said Patrick. 'You just tell me when they start.'

It was a different enterprise altogether. A nervous experiment. They were amateurs at this; Patrick with his stopwatch, timing her to the finish. Perhaps they could stay like this until the baby came, she thought. It was consoling to be at home. Around her, the ordinary objects of their existence. The corner of the room, filled with toys. Some plastic trucks. A pile of wooden bricks. A drum and a xylophone. Her mother had tidied, of course. She had stacked things in her own way, so everything looked slightly different from usual. There were books on the coffee table; Brigid couldn't imagine she'd ever read them. It seemed impossible that she, in this immense pain-filled body, had once sat quietly. Yesterday, though she could barely remember it, she had been sitting in this room, in relative comfort, drinking a cup of tea, smiling at her son as he pushed a plastic truck around. It seemed impossible that she had been sitting there with a book and flicking through the pages, idly and as if she had infinite time. Now she was being seared by the minutes and seconds. She had four minutes to recover. To breathe deeply. She thought she should try to focus on something, a point in the room – the glare of the lights above her, halogen bulbs twinkling from the ceiling. She stared at a point and watched light fill it and dissolve when she blinked, then fill it again. The pain sounded its first notes. She said, 'Start now.' A minute of pain. It was possible to endure. And then she was busy with the TENS machine and the rocking chair, feeling the warmth at the base of her spine from the hot-water bottle, and the crackling of electricity on her back. Patrick was staring at the phone. He looked crazy, like a workaholic, unable to take his eyes off the job. For a moment she tried to focus on that, but this thought too was dispersed by the mounting severity of the pain. There was a blank, filled only with pain and her desperate attempts to neutralise it, until finally it receded again. Dwindled and died. 'Stop,' she said.

'A minute, after five minutes,' said Patrick.

'Quite regular then.'

'Do you think they're strong enough to get the midwife?'

'They said only call the midwife when you're not coping with the pain.'

'Do you think you're coping?'

'Do you think I'm coping?'

'I don't know. It has to be your call.'

From the kitchen, there was a wail, an escalating cry from Calumn. Thwarted or genuinely upset, Brigid couldn't tell. The wail was too muffled, and there was the sound of Bach above it.

'What's going on with Calumn?' she said. In the intervals between the contractions she was comfortable. During those intervals she could hardly accept that she would soon have to bow her head again, that the pain would once more come to ransack her body and she would be able to think only of the TENS machine in her hand and the prickling on her back, and how many seconds more until she was released.

'Shall I go and check?' said Patrick.

'Yes.'

So Patrick went out, as the cries became more desperate. She heard his voice in the kitchen. The higher pitch he adopted with Calumn. He was an affectionate, patient man. Her friends told her so, and she knew it anyway. He tried hard, though Calumn usually wanted her, would even push his father away when she approached. She knew that hurt Patrick, but it had been going on for so long now, it seemed impossible to change. She couldn't remember when it had started, because at first they had been allies, equally shell-shocked and excited, taking turns to rock Calumn when he cried, changing nappies, laughing together about the debris and chaos of it all. Slowly things had shifted. They needed money, one of them had to work fulltime. Brigid could claim maternity pay, so she stayed with Calumn, while Patrick trudged back to the office. He had been sad about it, she knew; he called her up, wanting news from home. Gradually Brigid became the one who consoled Calumn, who woke with him, fed him, bathed him; the one who was always there. When Calumn was ill, when he was feverish at night and could not settle, it was Brigid who went to him. Patrick tried to help, but Calumn wouldn't stop crying until Brigid came. And because he worked on the other side of London, because they could not afford to move, Patrick could never take Calumn to the crèche. So Brigid drove there two mornings a week, watched Calumn cry inconsolably in the arms of his 'key carer', then she dragged herself away and went home. Often she was in tears in the car. When she got back she had three hours to work and she sat there determinedly at her desk but really her work suffered and she was inefficient, slowed by a sense of heaviness and mental fog. She knew things weren't easy for Patrick either. He was hardly having a luxury time of it, commuting in London and sitting out the hours in his office. Sometimes she longed to trade places with him, and yet she knew he envied her, on the days when he returned and found her and Calumn huddled together over a book, content in their enclosed world. Another relentless rising pain and she could hear Patrick's high-pitched comforting voice, though she couldn't distinguish the words. The crying stopped. She imagined him holding their son, stroking his hair. The pain and breathe breathe breathe. The TENS machine buzzing at her back. The buzzing was superficial, but somehow it heated her belly. It heated her through and slightly assuaged a pain she felt mostly at the front of her body. She thought of her confused brain, tricked by this electrical buzzing. Then she breathed more easily as the pain crashed and dwindled again. Patrick was constantly loving and patient with his son. She should be more grateful and praise him. With the second child, she would be more realistic. She was taking three months off. She would try not to work at all during this time. She would simply enjoy her children. Patrick would go back to work after two weeks, and she would get to know her new baby, and help Calumn to adjust.

That was if the baby came, she thought, gripped by superstition and not wanting to plan. She heard Calumn crying again and assumed Patrick was trying to leave the room. He wanted reassurance. Naturally he couldn't understand why they were closeted together. Something he couldn't see. She heard the voice of her mother. Then Patrick came in again.

'He's fine,' he said. 'Just a bit tired. He's got some milk now. He ate a good dinner.'

'Did he? Lots of pasta?'

'Yes. An entire bowl, and then he had nearly a punnet of blueberries.'

'Good.'

How much time passed like this, Brigid wasn't sure. Perhaps an hour. Nothing changed except the pain. The pain was developing, aiming to surge beyond her attempts to contain it. She had grown accustomed to one sort of severity, but it – this presence, moving within her body and precipitating every surge of pain – wanted more. It wanted her raging, blind with agony. It seemed to Brigid as she rocked herself that a TENS machine and a hot-water bottle would soon fail against this pain. She would have to submit in the end; she would be torn apart. She did feel angry too, now that the pain was mounting constantly, with so little regard for the bounds of her strength. Always Patrick was at her side, timing everything, and they were mostly silent together. She would say 'Now' when a contraction started and 'Stop' when it ended, and he would tell her how long it had been. And there were dark intervals when he went to find her food, or water, or something else he thought she might need. She would hear him in the other room, talking to her mother, or was it Calumn, and now she remembered Calumn was in bed. Patrick had taken him, because he wouldn't go upstairs with her mother. She thought of her son, asleep in his little room, wearing pyjamas with birds on them. Small and beautiful and made from her. That had to console her, though she was growing desperate with the pain.

She was rocking herself quite dementedly now, because it helped a little. Patrick renewed her hot-water bottle, pressed it against her back. The heat made her wince, but it was soon eclipsed by another contraction. The buzzing of the TENS machine. She needed to be constantly inventive, to find new ways to evade the pain. 'Perhaps you could massage my back,' she said, and Patrick went off to get some oils. Obligingly, he kneaded her skin. That diverted her briefly, but not as much as she had hoped. 'Would you like a bath?' he said. 'Isn't that meant to help?' but she couldn't imagine lowering herself into a bath, wallowing there as the water cooled around her. 'I think I'll stay here,' she said, and then another contraction came.

Patrick saw his wife and wondered what it was to be her, gripped by this agony, which had to be endured, and for some reason – he couldn't understand – she was embracing agony, clutching it to her, though there was a hospital nearby, with a cache of analgesics. They had argued about that, because he didn't understand her decision to stay at home. He thought it was arbitrary masochism, but she said she was being pragmatic, because her body took so long to heal last time and she had learned from her experiences. She couldn't cope with Calumn and a new baby, in the state she was in last time, she had argued. And it was true, her recovery had been torturously slow; he remembered it well enough. This time, she said, she would annihilate herself during labour, in order to improve her chances of a quick return to health. It seemed a crazy gamble, but he didn't know. In all of this, he was adrift, seeking guidance from her, her instincts. He believed there must be something within her, telling her what to do.

Brigid heard her mother at the door, and wondered how much more time had passed. 'Can I do anything?' said her mother.

'No, but thanks so much for looking after Calumn,' she said. 'If you don't mind, perhaps you could stay here tonight. Just in case we're in the middle of things and Calumn wakes up.' It was such a funny euphemism. The middle of things. The splitting of the body. They called it parturition but really it was blood and wreckage. Just in case we're drowning in blood, she thought, that would be closer to the truth. Her mother was agreeing. 'Of course, I'm glad to be useful,' she was saying. 'I might just pop back for my night things.'

'Yes of course. We'll be fine for a couple of hours, I'm sure,' said Patrick. 'The midwife is coming, and Calumn is fast asleep.'

The midwife was coming soon, said Patrick when Brigid asked again. But it seemed a long time had passed. The evening had been fractured, and she understood minutes only in terms of focused agony or fleeting respite. She waited – urgently – through the pain and then she waited for the next surge to begin. 'Where is the midwife?' she said again. She wanted someone to tell her what the pain meant. It was too lonely now, this amateur divining with their mobile phone stopwatches and their nervous scraps of paper.

5 minutes then a contraction 1 minute
4 minutes then a contraction 55 seconds
5 minutes then a contraction 1 minute 10 seconds
6 minutes then a contraction 45 seconds
4 minutes then a contraction 60 seconds
4 minutes then a contraction 60 seconds
3 minutes then a contraction 1 minute 10 seconds

Hours they had annotated in this way. But she wasn't sure what it meant, despite the care they had taken, marking it all down.

'On her way,' said Patrick. Then there was another span of time, just pain and then a respite, and then pure pain again. Over and over. Her mouth was dry, but Patrick was there, holding a glass to her lips. It was the interval that made each contraction bearable, she thought. Without the knowledge that it would soon end, you couldn't endure it. At its height it was as if she was being run through with a spear. A terrible delving stab, so she thought it must destroy her, and then it receded again.

The midwife had arrived, with her practised manner. She was called Gina, and she said, 'Haven't you been doing well? Decided to stay at home, did you?' and then she sat on the sofa near to Brigid's chair. 'Do you want to try some positions?' she said. 'They'll help with the pain,' but Brigid didn't want to move. 'I want to stay on the chair,' she said. 'I'm so tired.'

'Of course you are,' said the midwife. 'You just do what works for you. Would you like a cup of tea?' and that sounded so incredibly quotidian and reassuring that Brigid said yes, even though when the tea came she found she couldn't drink it.

'Let's have a listen to baby's heart rate,' said the midwife, putting a machine to Brigid's belly. In the room, suddenly, the eager sound of the baby's heart. Gina smiled and said that was all normal. Then she fixed Brigid up with a gas pipe, and Brigid was so grateful for the relief it offered that she found she was breathing in desperately, ravenous for gas. For some time she simply inhaled gas. She knew she was meant to inhale before the contraction, then take her mouth away and breathe normally, but she was too afraid of missing her cue, leaving herself gas-free for the next surge of pain, so she just kept her mouth over the pipe and breathed in nothing but gas. The sickly sweet taste didn't bother her, she just wanted to reduce the pain. She was rocking frantically and in one hand she had the TENS machine – her fingers still desperately twiddling the dial – and in the other she had the gas pipe. She hardly spoke any more; she was too fixed on breathing in gas. And breathe, and breathe, she was inhaling as much as she could, gulping down clouds of gas. She imagined it as yellow, a yellow cloud moving into her lungs. It was amazing how quickly it became a prop. Sometimes she dropped the mouthpiece and then there was a desperate rush, Patrick and the midwife fumbling around to get it back to her.

Breathe breathe breathe, she thought, and the gas made her dizzy. After a while she felt as if she was very drunk and in a room full of sober people, trying desperately to conceal her state.

'How are you feeling now?' said the midwife, and Brigid muttered something. 'I feel as if I am at a cocktail party and I just want to take my clothes off,' she said, or something like that. 'Are you too hot, darling?' said Patrick, not really understanding her, and Brigid said, 'No no, not too hot. A bit cold, in a way.'

He went to get her some socks. She was still wearing her tracksuit and her T-shirt. Perhaps she was still wet from the rain, or was it sweat? She wasn't sure. Then she remembered Patrick had changed her clothes. So she had sweated her clothes damp. 'My son is called Calumn,' she was saying to the midwife. 'How lovely,' said Gina.

'You know, he's just upstairs. It's so strange he's just upstairs. Asleep through all of this,' and then the pain began again so she became disciplined, serious, her lips tight around the gas pipe, breathing in hard, trying to draw down gas.

Rock rock rock, breathe breathe breathe, and her head was swirling and the rocking was making her sick, or was it the gas, certainly she felt nauseous to a degree, and when Patrick came back with the socks she found she couldn't bear him fiddling with her feet, though she had to submit because she was cold. 'Breathe,' he said to her, though that was all she could do anyway. She had her head down, because she was trying to turn the dial on the TENS machine and hold the gas pipe. She had them both constantly in view, she moved her eyes from one to the other, in case anything happened to them. Without both of them, she thought, she wouldn't survive. She would be consumed by pain and fear. And beyond her, beyond her oversized form, rocking insanely and puffing and breathing, were two people who felt no pain at all, lived in a parallel world in which they could move freely and without agony.

'Just keep breathing, darling,' said Patrick. 'You're doing wonderfully well,' and she thought how odd it was, that he felt this urge to keep talking, to fill in the silence of her pain. When he wasn't talking to her he was aiming words at the midwife, making awkward small talk, as if they really were at a cocktail party and Brigid had been taken ill, and he was obliged to chat away to someone while he looked after her. Brigid wondered if it would help if she thought of herself as someone who had become drunk and disorderly, who had been confined to a room upstairs, with her husband and someone else looking after her. And that's what they call visualisation, she thought – but she decided it wouldn't help her much. Her imagination was not forceful enough to counter the insistent agony of her body. Always it was insisting. It was terrible how shrill her body was, how it sought to overwhelm her spirit, or mind, or whatever she possessed that wasn't her body – and she wasn't sure if there was much left; her body had taken everything over. Now she tried to think of Calumn, and wondered what this second child would be like. She pictured her son peacefully asleep, she knew precisely how he liked to sleep, curled on his side, one arm flung across the other, and he would be holding his elephant, and perhaps Patrick had given him a dummy, because although they were trying to wean him off such things they had failed entirely. She thought of him breathing in his soft way, making his sweet little moans, and all the time she was trying to birth this other, this child she had no sense of at all, no real love for yet. It was undergoing its own unknowable process, a relentless tightening of the walls around it, something which might seem as bewildering as labour on the outside, labour in the world. She hoped this baby wasn't too uncomfortable, too frightened, in this dark womb with the walls tightening around it.

There was some more pain and then Brigid found she was lying on her back on the sofa, the midwife's fingers deep inside her. 'Dilation,' the midwife was saying, and Brigid clung to the word while she endured a vicious contraction, one which tore at her, and she said 'Oh no, oh no.'

She wanted to push the midwife away, but then she wanted to know how much longer she had to endure, so she submitted and tensed her muscles and tried not to cry out, and the midwife finished what she was doing and said that the labour was progressing. 'You're five centimetres dilated, so you've done very well.' But Brigid wanted to cry. Only five centimetres! She wanted to rage at someone, though she couldn't think who was responsible for her state. She had been too inert. She had been sitting down for hours. She should have moved around more, but then it hurt to move. 'But that's only halfway,' she said to Gina.

'Yes, well the later stages should go a bit faster than the earlier stages did. If we can just move things along then we'll see some progress. You will have to climb the stairs, for example. And a few other tricks of the trade. But I'll be here all the time and so will Patrick.'

'I don't want to climb the stairs.'

'Just one at a time. If it will make things go faster,' said the midwife.

'Will it really make a difference?'

'It certainly will. Come on you brave girl. Let's get you climbing those stairs.'

She saw Patrick nodding reluctantly, and he put out his arms and lifted her from the chair.

Slowly, she gained the length of the hall. There were the stairs before her. This was a vile pain. Perhaps the worst she had ever known. She had been forced to relinquish the gas pipe, so now all she had was her TENS machine, the pads curling away from her sweaty skin. When she put a foot down, she felt as if a spike had been rammed up her leg. With each movement she demolished herself. And within her, she could hardly imagine what it was within her, what made the pain so horrible.

'One step at a time. Just think you have one step to do, and focus on that single step,' said Gina. Patrick was behind her, and Brigid knew he would be hating it all. She couldn't see him, but she knew he would be anxious and wanting it to end. So she raised a foot, and placed it on the first step.

'Good girl.'

Her belly was aflame, it felt as if she was burning inside. There was a fire in her belly, and she had been spiked and held in the flames. The spike had stopped her, she couldn't lift her leg again, because the spike was holding her down. She stood with one foot on the step and found she couldn't move the other. It was absurd, at one level she knew it was absurd that she couldn't move, because she was so afraid of pain. It is only pain, she thought. A bodily sensation. Transient. It was not fatal. She would not die of pain, surely. Not in this century. Anyway the body was designed to endure it. For millions of years, perhaps, humans had given birth without gas, without epidurals; they had given birth screaming and writhing, but they had managed to do it. She had been making these arguments for months, to herself or Patrick, or anyone else who cared to discuss it. The body was meant to withstand the pain of childbirth. It was designed for the trial. So why was she standing there, unable to move? If she lifted her left foot she would run down the spike altogether and hang there, she thought. She would be hanging there as the midwife said, 'Good girl.'

'Come on Brigid, the faster you do it, the quicker it will all be over, and then you are all the closer to meeting your lovely baby,' said the midwife.

So Brigid moved her left foot. That rearranged the pain, drove it further inside her. Trying to gain momentum, she forced herself onto the next step. Two steps, she thought. And there were – she counted them quickly – ten more. A sixth of the way. How she was trying to calibrate her agony, to make it scientific and thereby acceptable.

'And another one,' said the midwife.

'Well done, Brigid,' said Patrick. 'You're doing really well.'

But he hated it anyway, she knew.

'The sooner we get this moving along, the sooner you can start to push,' said the midwife. That just filled her with further dread, the thought of having to flex her muscles through this pain. She was trapped. If she didn't move, she would just prolong it all; she would be in labour tomorrow and perhaps beyond that. It was unimaginable. Yet her body was stubborn and rebellious. And there was her hopeless sense of outrage, that she alone was in pain and the others were just pretending to her, claiming a sympathy they didn't really feel. They congratulated her, but it was hollow. They couldn't understand what was happening to her.

Brigid lifted her leg again, dragged it off the spike. And then she held it in mid air for a moment, unable to force it down again.

'Go on, Brigid, put your foot down,' said the midwife. Brisk and practical. A sadist, thought Brigid. A deep dark ravenous sadist, trying to torture them all. She put her foot down, surrendered to the agony, and then moved her other foot. Another step gained. Another. She was on the sixth step, in tears now, but they were desperate solitary tears, so she wasn't sure Patrick or the midwife – behind her, exhorting her all the way – noticed them at all. And even if they did, there was nothing they could do. She had to impale herself over and over again. She was battling onto the eighth step, crying quietly as she moved, when she looked up and saw the moon through the landing window. It was a full moon, so huge it was barely contained within the window frame. She looked up at it and paused. It was so round and large. It was somehow comforting, though she didn't know why. It looked solid, though it was an immeasurable distance away. Immeasurable to her. For a moment she just looked at this moon, and then she moved again.

Down onto the spike she went. Impaled thoroughly. She cried out, and she heard Patrick saying, 'Does she have to do this?'

She wanted to wail now, though she was trying to be quiet because of Calumn. Still, in some weary smashed-up portion of her brain, there was the image of her son, peacefully sleeping. Then the contraction came and she bent over and gripped the banisters. Nothing could help her now. She had lost the gas and she hardly bothered to turn on the TENS machine. She just bowed to the agony, let it rage through her, and she opened her mouth wide as if to scream, though no sound came.

'Can't she go back to the chair?' Patrick was saying. 'This is ridiculous.'

'Just a couple more stairs,' said the midwife. 'Let her get through this contraction.'

She was bent double and clutching onto the stairs and her mouth was hanging open. Her body demanded certain postures. It had an idea of how to minimise the pain, though it was only a faint improvement. She clung to this anyway. She had her mouth open and she was trying to breathe, though all she wanted to do was rail against the midwife and tell her to go. She wanted to blame her.

When the pain receded she moved up two more steps, because she didn't care how much worse things got. 'Well done, excellent,' said the midwife. 'That's really wonderful, Brigid. Can you do just one more?'

'Hasn't she done enough?' She could hear from this that Patrick had already condemned the midwife. As if to show him it was OK, she lifted her leg again. It was the shrillness of the pain which was so shocking. You could only think, how shrill. How I have never felt pain like this. How I never will, unless I give birth again. How I must not. How I must never do this again.

'Well done,' the midwife was saying, patting Brigid gently on the back. 'You did brilliantly. You were very brave. Patrick, can you carry Brigid downstairs?'

And Patrick, glad to be able to do something, took Brigid in his arms, and kissed her. 'Was that horrible?' he said.

'Yes.'

He was wiping tears from her cheeks.

'My poor darling. I'm very proud of you.'

The next hour was confused. There was a sort of acceleration. She lost control altogether. She was back in the rocking chair, and the gas had drawn her under. She felt as if she was dying, with the gas pipe in her mouth. She imagined this must be what it was like to die. This merging of the mind and body, this realisation that the two were inextricably bound together. The mind dwindled as the body faded, she had a sense of that, and she imagined her eyes must be glassy already. And then the gas made everything like a vision, or a nightmare.

So she shut her eyes and thought for a moment that she was running through her house, trying to find Calumn or her newborn child. In this imagining, or hallucination, whatever it was, she had already birthed the baby, and yet she couldn't find it. She kept flinging open doors, and each one would open onto the same scene – a woman squatting in childbirth, semi-naked, screaming out her pain. And each time the woman would stop screaming and look at her. Brigid would stand there for a moment, held by this stare, then the door would slam shut. All these rooms, with women squatting in them, crying and screaming. Some would die, perhaps, and some of their babies would perhaps die with them. That made her shake, and she opened her eyes again, but she couldn't focus on the faces of the midwife or Patrick; they were too remote from her, contained entirely apart from her, and she breathed in gas and murmured – Patrick bent down, but couldn't understand her – and she saw the women again.

The midwife examined her, and her fingers were like shards of glass, and Brigid imagined her interior as a ragged hole, ripped apart by all the pain. The midwife was grave now, something had changed. Six centimetres dilated, she said. Six centimetres was nothing, for all these hours of pain. They had told her the second time was easier, and yet they had lied, or she was the exception. Hours and hours; it must be late, and she was lost and fumbling in the dark. Patrick was beside her. She was holding his hand; his skin was very damp and warm. She was sweating and she had heated his hand. Escalation, that was what was happening. Something she couldn't control. She no longer tried to breathe deeply. The contractions seemed to be constant, or the intervals were too brief for her to recover from the lancing pain. There was no respite. She felt water at her lips, and she realised she was thirsty. But she couldn't swallow.

'You must drink,' said the midwife. 'You mustn't get dehydrated.'

A cold flannel on her face. That helped briefly. And she had forgotten to twist the TENS machine. She had forgotten but it didn't matter any more. She ripped off the pads, scrabbling with her fingers at her back. Her back was burning, she felt as if she had been branded.

'You want to take it off?' said Patrick.

She couldn't reply, she just scrabbled with her fingers, and so he helped her. He ripped off the pads and rubbed the sore skin.

Into this nightmare of gas and pain came the voice of the midwife. As if from very far away. She was infinitely far away, in the world of non-pain. Patrick was there too, and Calumn and her mother were in the house but elsewhere and she could hardly remember them now. This too was death, losing any sense of your family, finding they had faded from your mind. She heard a voice, the measured tone of the midwife, and now she tried to turn her head towards it. It was saying, 'There are things we can do to help the labour along, but you will have to move again.'

'I don't want to move,' said Brigid.

'I am afraid you will have to. We will have to change your position. It's simply not going to happen other-wise.'

'I can't move any more,' said Brigid. Her voice was only a whine. She shook her head. She thought of the hospital, the tower across the river, and how she had wanted to avoid it. 'It's too much.'

'You must keep trying,' said the midwife.

She had been defeated, that seemed clear. Flayed and torn, and now she was searching for an escape route, or if not escape then something she could endure. 'I want to go to hospital,' she said, because she knew it was the only way she could reduce the pain. The pain was the unbearable constant, and her body was piteous and amoral, desperate for a release. 'I want an epidural,' she heard herself saying, and she was trying not to cry.

'Are you sure?' said the midwife. She sounded disap-pointed. 'It's your choice of course, but equally I can sit down with you and your husband and discuss some other options.'

'No,' said Brigid, and though she was weeping now she was quite resolute. 'I want to go to hospital.'

'Shall I drive her?' said Patrick.

'No, she should go by ambulance,' said the midwife. 'At this stage, she can't go by car.'

Now Brigid stopped rocking herself, she just let wave after wave of pain grip her and toss her around, as if she was driftwood on an endless ocean, while Patrick stroked her hair and kissed her, said kind words she could hardly disentangle. Her face was greased with tears. She could barely lift her head and take a breath before the next contraction came. And she was weak from trying to stay afloat, from trying to 'manage her pain'. 'Manage your pain.' 'Stay in control of your pain.' Well, she had failed in all of that.

'Fine,' she said, not caring any more, and then she bowed her head as another contraction swept her under.

She was under for a long time, and her thoughts were just of blackness.

'Darling.' That was Patrick's voice. Somewhere else. She heard it above her, or maybe she was above it and he was trying to call her back. 'The midwife has called for an ambulance. It will be here very soon.' There was a why in her mind, but she couldn't express it. She didn't understand. She could hardly even think of the baby, she was just thinking of her body and how she was drowning in pain and how pointless this pain was – she had forgotten it had a reason. It was her natural state – she had always been in pain, would always be – she was in a new world, in which pain was continuous and unceasing and there would only ever be pain. Patrick said to her, 'Darling it will be OK,' and she thought he meant the pain, and that he was lying anyway, the pain wouldn't end.

'They say we will be picked up very soon,' said Patrick.

Patrick watched his wife, he saw her neck drenched in sweat and her body hunched, and the terrible fear in her eyes when a contraction came. Mostly he wanted to be sick. He was in a vile state of panic; he understood how powerless he was, to help her or their unborn child. Even the midwife seemed worried. On the phone to the hospital, she sounded urgent, not professional at all. 'Come as soon as you can, she is no longer coping with the pain,' she said, but softly so Brigid wouldn't hear. Brigid had her eyes shut and he couldn't imagine what she was thinking. Everything had failed, all their optimistic plans, and he felt a grave sense of pity for her, that she had been trying so hard and yet it had stalled anyway. The midwife was gathering things together. Her gas pipe. Her birthing ball and her aromatherapy oils. Redundant, all of them. It was unfair to blame her, this benevolent practical woman, with her short brown hair and her open face. It wasn't her fault, he tried to think. They were unlucky, that was all. But he was too panicked to be clear at all.

'You've done everything right,' the midwife said to him. 'Brigid is just very tired. I suspect baby is in an awkward position. So labour has been particularly slow and difficult.'

'What would happen if there wasn't a hospital, if no hospital existed?' said Patrick back to her, when Brigid was distracted, clenching her teeth and writhing through another contraction.

'Well, that's hardly relevant,' said the midwife, and for a moment she looked irritated.

'But just can you speculate? Just out of interest?'

'No, I don't think I can,' said the midwife, and Patrick

had to desist. He couldn't interrogate her. He was angry with himself too, because he had failed Brigid.

'I just want to see her before she goes,' Brigid's mother was saying, and Brigid looked up to see her mother in the doorway.

'Where's Calumn?' she said to her, she thought she said something like that, though her words were slurred.

'He's fast asleep. He's been such a good little boy.'

'OK. Is he OK?'

'He's fine, dear. We'll be fine until you get back. I hope it all goes well for you,' and her mother came over and kissed the sweaty brow of her daughter, and stroked her gently on the cheek.

Brigid waited until her mother left the room and then she began to cry again. She couldn't restrain herself at all, she sobbed and Patrick put his arms around her.

As they took her into the ambulance, Brigid, prostrate and no longer able to care about her state, perfectly supine, looked up and saw directly above her, hanging above her, like an improbable stage prop, the moon. This full moon, so vast and white; she was mesmerised as she lay there. As they adjusted elements around her, clipped one thing and unclasped another, smoothed blankets over her, as Patrick held her hand and stroked her hair, Brigid stared up at the moon.

The Hermit

The moon hung above Michael Stone as he stood in the garden of a Hampstead house. It was a handsome garden, abundant in flowers and gnarled old trees, candles sputtering on the terrace. 'This is Lucy-Rose Simpson, editor of the *Weekly Review*, and her partner, James McIntyre, whose poetry you have doubtless read,' Sally had said, as they arrived. 'Thank you for inviting me,' he said, and they laughed generously, as if he had been witty. Lucy-Rose was saying to him now, 'Do you have everything you need?'

'Oh yes,' he said, gesturing with his glass at nothing. 'Thank you.'

'My pleasure,' she said. Her voice – husky and compassionate – was familiar; he had heard her often on the radio. She reviewed books of the hour; she was decisive, but seldom rude. In the flickering light, Michael noted her round eyes, her cropped hair, stained bronze, and into the round-eyed compassion of Lucy-Rose, he said, 'An amazing moon.'

She looked up and said, 'Of course, you like moons.' She laughed towards him. 'It's very full isn't it? You can almost imagine you're standing on the shore of the Sea of Tranquillity.'

'Yes.'

'I'm so glad we're all out in the garden,' said Lucy-Rose. 'It rained so hard earlier, I thought we'd be shut up inside.

So much nicer, in the summer, to stand in the garden, even when everything is wet to the touch.'

Then there was another person beside them. A poet, saying how much he admired the book – 'the book' – that was how they flattered him – and Michael said, 'Thank you very much. I appreciate your support.'

They had introduced him earlier, this man, Dougie Ascherson, that was his name. Winner of the Hodgkinson-Healey prize, they added, and Michael murmured his congratulations. The *Weekly Review* was all poets, Sally had said. 'Bad breath and horrible clothes,' she laughed. But they weren't like that at all. Everyone was smooth-skinned and charming, far from seedy.

'I'm just glad it's seen the light of day,' said Lucy-Rose. 'That we can raise a glass to your published work.'

Michael had been drunk after lunch, and in his drunkenness he had become aware that the hours were passing slowly, that his mood had tottered and then descended still further. Sally had arranged this launch party, a robust celebration, and so the evening was shaded in, everything was planned. During the intervening hours, he had tried to stay busy. He read through the reviews, received their barbs. Now he had their phrases in his head, despite Sally's exhortations. All afternoon he watched the clock slide onwards, as he drank one Irish coffee after another, until his throat was dry. The working day dwindled towards its close. It was an anti-climax. He had been expectant for months, because this was the day he would be judged. He had imagined it would be swift and decisive. But still everything hung in the balance. It would be weeks before the reviews all came in, Sally told him. She added, 'Anyway, it really shouldn't matter to you. The important thing, for you, was to get your work published. And you did.'

He couldn't believe her. Instead he drank coffee and thought of his errors, the things he should have revised while he had the chance. That narrator, why did I let him run on so much? Why did I allow him to be so muddled, so vague in his assertions? He had sacrificed so much and even then he had written a bad book, and if he had the chance again he would destroy it. He never had much of a sense of loyalty to his books. He finished them with pride, thought them perfect for a day, a week perhaps. Then he lost faith, by degrees. And yet this book – he had hoped this book was his best, and Sally had said so too. He had called it *The Moon*, thinking this was a clever title at the time, but now he wanted to tear his book to pieces, because of what they had said.

At 3.00 p.m. the phone rang, and Sally said, 'I forgot to remind you about the radio programme tomorrow. At 9.00 a.m. sharp. You might want to get everything ready before you come tonight. It'll be live.' That made Michael feel quite sick; he swallowed carefully.

'I'm not sure . . . I don't think I really should . . .'

'Michael, I know. You are very reserved. But this is the only radio interview the publicity people could arrange for you. Katherine Miller is the presenter, and she's terribly good. She'll just ask you a few gentle questions about your book. It would help enormously with gaining an audience.'

'But . . .' he said.

'Now, let's think about this evening. You should come up to Hampstead for around 7.00 p.m. The launch is a bit of fun. No need to worry about it.'

'Perhaps I should just stay here, prepare myself for the radio . . .'

She dismissed his words, before he could finish.

'Nonsense. There's something very irritating about writers who don't go to their own launches. Come out, just for an hour. It'll cheer you up.'

So Sally and good sense had prevailed, and Michael put the reviews on his desk, covered them with a piece of paper, and then he showered and found another shirt. He opened a bottle of wine because he was afraid of sobering up. Standing in his boxer shorts so as not to further crease his suit he gazed out of the window at the current far below and the current seemed more furious and driven than before. He was dependent on the judgement of strangers, on their opinions about him. He would be consigned to something or other, and then they would all forget him. The flood was passing, even as he watched it from his window.

He was drunk and calmer than before, when the phone rang. He assumed it would be Sally, or perhaps the publicity woman who had said she would call. Yet it was James again.

'Ah, you're still at home,' he said, in his clipped and chilly way.

'No, no, back at home,' said Michael. 'I was out earlier at a . . .' but that sounded defensive, so he stopped.

'I won't keep you,' said James. 'I wanted to speak to you

because I have just been to see our mother. I told her that you were launching your book. One speaks even though she doesn't really understand. Normally she says very little, or what she says is incoherent. Yet today' – his brother's voice was softening a little, registering surprise, or something else – 'well, she nodded a little as I spoke. A reflex, perhaps. When it was time for me to go, she scrabbled with her hands, she wanted to write something. I couldn't find a pen, so she said I must wish you luck. Then something else, which was garbled. About a story you once wrote for her. He is always writing little things for me, she said – because of course she is confused, she is half in the past, more sometimes, and she asked where you were . . .'

The taxi was outside, and Michael had to go.

So she clawed his day apart. His small moment, torn to shreds. It was melodrama, possibly, but he was trembling as the taxi conveyed him through the streets, as the driver turned the wheel and spoke loudly on his phone. When they pulled up outside the house he lingered by the door of the cab, unable to shut it. The driver looked at his watch, trying to hurry him away. Yet Michael was thinking, if he got back in, told the driver to take him to King's Cross, he could be there in a few minutes. He could press his lips against her dusty hand, beg her forgiveness. He could say he was sorry, even if he wasn't sure he really meant it.

But he paid the driver, and slammed the car door.

At the house he knew it had been a terrible mistake to come. He was welcomed by Lucy-Rose, Sally hovering in the background, trying to orchestrate his entrance, conducting him through the kindly nodding hordes and into the garden. His coat was removed, and someone brought him a glass of wine. He admired the walls covered in elegant prints, the shelves full of interesting books. He thanked everyone; he was indiscriminate.

Standing in the garden he saw them assembled. He wasn't sure who had rallied them, but here they were, vivid in the dusk. Lucy-Rose was saying, 'A few people couldn't come, but they said they had heard good things about your book.'

Michael nodded and then, to change the subject, said, 'Is that an aspidistra?' and pointed at the flowerbed.

'Yes,' said Lucy-Rose. 'We have a man who does the garden. He cultivates the most extraordinary flowers.'

'It's very fine.'

'Michael, I have to leave in a second, but I wanted to say a brief hello before I went.' There was a publisher at his shoulder. Martha Williams. She had once rejected a book of his, but now she was here.

'I do hope things go well for you,' she said, briskly. When she rejected his book she had written to Sally: 'Dear Sally, further to our conversation on the phone I wanted to repeat how sorry we are that we could not accept Michael Stone's novel. We are happy to take commercial risks if we really believe in the quality of the work but somehow we didn't believe enough. I wish you and Mr Stone all the best in finding a suitable publisher.' She had dashed that off in a second or two, to soften the blow, or to avoid offending Sally who had been at Cambridge with her. He had read it once and thrown it away. Still he remembered every word. Now she was speaking, in her brisk and terrifying way, her hands moving, her form shapeless within a billowing coat; but he couldn't follow her words. He nodded as she said something about how she hadn't had a chance to read his book but she looked forward to doing so, how she had heard something and something else, and he nodded and said, 'Yes, it has all been . . . very . . . surprising.'

She shook his hand suddenly, before he had time to wipe it, said, 'I wish you the best.' Then she swept away, silk flowing from her ample shoulders. She had a coat the colour of the moon, he thought.

Here were more people he didn't know. They were different from the lunchtime people, different in their particulars, though they were just as bold and loquacious, just as able to hammer out glinting phrases. To him they seemed perfect, some of them in shirts and slacks, and some wearing suits, recently arrived from their offices. The women well into attractive middle age, elegantly dressed, smelling of perfume. They mingled, the perfumed women with their flowing skirts, and the men in their slacks, and they smiled and kissed each other on the cheeks.

'More wine?' said someone, and he held out his glass.

'Michael Stone,' said someone else. 'I just wanted to say how much I admire your book. I was trying to review it, but alas they had already sent it out.'

'That's a shame,' said Michael. 'But thank you.'

'I'm Paul Ardache. I've written a few novels.' And the man held out his hand. Perhaps he was forty, perhaps older. He had thick black hair, but his face was creased and folded. Like a much-used handkerchief. He was lean and he looked as if he smoked. And he was producing a cigarette packet now, offering it to Michael.

'No thank you.'

'How disciplined of you,' said Paul Ardache.

There was a pause while the flame was kindled. Paul Ardache breathed in deeply, exhaled. 'Ah God, I always chain-smoke my way through the launch of a book. But I lack self-control. Anyway,' he began again, 'I liked the way you wrote about this solitary man. Furious that he had been forgotten. Railing against everyone.'

'Thank you.'

'And I was moved by the story of those poor women, their sacrifice.'

'You're most kind.'

'Then there were these strange moments, when I felt something else was coming through. Were you conscious of it, I wonder? I am fascinated by the elements we cannot control, the narratorial elements which somehow inveigle their way onto the page, seem inevitable to us but then strike others as peculiar and intriguing. Do you know what I mean?'

'I am not sure.'

'Well, for example, that ghost-woman Semmelweis saw. Is that documented, did he really see her?'

'No, I must confess it isn't a fact. I imagined he might . . .'

'And what was her name again?'

'Birgit Vogel.'

'Of course, that's it, Vogel the bird. A bird of peace, or a bird of prey, one wonders?'

'I just wanted a German name. And not Busch or Fischer.'

'Yes, well, that is interesting isn't it? Still, of all the other names you could have chosen, you chose Vogel. The pecking beak. Like something from a Freudian nightmare, do you not think?'

'I . . . I don't know . . .' He was stumbling, he wasn't sure he liked what the man was saying to him. But Ardache was courteous and insistent.

'You mean you do not know, or you are not sure this has any relevance to your work?' he said.

'I think . . . perhaps . . . such questions . . . these things . . . should remain unanswered . . . If we are not to delude ourselves . . .'

'Of course, these matters are ultimately beyond our power to comprehend. The mind falters, and so on. I just wondered what you really thought. One thing I felt about your book was that you were a veiled presence. You were holding your cards close to your chest. What does the author actually feel about all of this, I kept thinking. The narrator is a study in irresolution, of course. He mustn't become an ideological tyrant himself, that would defeat the purpose of your book. Sometimes he gets carried away, but he always tries to check himself. "Professor Wilson, I'm rambling on," he says, and what he really means is, "I must squash my inner ideologue," does he not? But what about the author, I thought. I felt you wanted to conceal yourself. You were modest, or like Joyce's conception of the artist, you were indifferent to your creations. Paring your fingernails.'

'No . . . it wasn't that . . . I wasn't aloof . . . At least, I didn't intend to be . . .' said Michael.

'Perhaps you were forcing your emotions down,' said Paul Ardache. 'As if you thought that, unrestrained, they might carry you off.' And now he inhaled again. He was not aware of the significance of his words. How he was making Michael want to cry and shake. Ardache was simply trying to find something to say, to show he had read the book, engaged with it. Yet suddenly it was very clear to Michael that his book was tactless, quite appalling – he had not thought carefully enough, had been in such a hurry to finish it – but he had inadvertently revealed the fury that drove him on. Ardache was saying, 'Anyway, perhaps you are just a Blakean at heart. A Blakean trapped in modernity. The birthing of life – the human form divine. The terrible divinity of nature.'

'I don't really think . . . in the way you are proposing,' said Michael. He was aiming at a lie, while he tried to calm his nerves, slow his heart. 'I don't think very clearly . . . I am not clear at all . . . But even then, isn't it rather that we never really get to the heart of any matter, in the end? We get captured by convenient metaphors, or clichés, by other people's modes of expression . . . Our real intentions, or thoughts, are lost . . .'

'I don't agree,' said Paul Ardache. 'I think it's amazing how frequently we do manage to say what we mean, or something roughly commensurate. Somehow our words resonate to others, even though they are inaccurate. Something gets through, for all the static and distortions. I find it quite moving, how people do understand, despite our flawed efforts.'

'In that case, they know it anyway . . . they don't need my rambling prose to tell them.'

'Ah, so are you the narrator? His rambling prose is your rambling prose?'

'Oh, no, I'm not half as . . . determined as he is,' said Michael. He thought he felt better now. When someone poured more wine into his glass, he gulped it down.

'You mean you are even more rambling?'

'Quite possibly.' They were smiling vaguely at each other.

'Ah, you see, you are an archetype yourself. The humble man,' said Paul Ardache, flicking the end of his cigarette into a nearby shrub.

'No, no, but I am not humble . . . No no, not it at all . . . I don't believe . . . well, no writer is humble, surely.'

'Well, I know I'm not. But I am handing you the accolade,' said Paul Ardache.

'That's kind of you . . . But it isn't true at all.'

They were looking at each other with a kindling of interest; perhaps they might even become friends later, thought Michael. He was wondering if it might be possible, to befriend this interesting man, and then someone else arrived.

'Mr Stone,' said this someone else. A boy, not more than twenty-five. Perhaps he was an apprentice, or a prodigy. He was so young, wearing a jacket that looked too big for him, and he said his name was Alistair Madden. 'I designed the cover for your book. I hope you liked it.'

Michael, who had not particularly liked the cover, smiled and said, 'I liked it very much. Thank you.'

Behind the boy, he saw Paul Ardache grimacing towards him. Michael had a sense that Paul Ardache perceived his discomfort, and his desire to be grateful nonetheless. He didn't want to look churlish so he said thank you again. And Paul Ardache nodded towards him, and lit another cigarette.

It wasn't much later, but Michael found he was leaning

against a wall. He had felt his way towards it, and rested against its solidity. Still he had the stem of a wine glass between his fingers, as if it was attached to his body, the surgical addition of recent days. He was thinking about what Ardache had said, and how he had put his mother in his book, without realising. He had convinced himself he never thought of her and yet she was there, plain for all to view – and he wondered if it could be true, that she was mortal and afraid, that she would die.

'Are you feeling ill?' Sally was saying into his ear. He realised he had bowed his head, screwed up his eyes.

'I think . . . perhaps . . . I think I should go.' If he went now, he could be there in an hour. He could go to her and say . . .

'Now? Already? But you've hardly arrived.'

'A taxi,' he said. 'Perhaps I could . . .' He felt as if a weight was pressing on his lungs.

'Naturally, if you are ill, I will drive you home,' said Sally, sternly.

'Is Michael ill?' said someone, overhearing and looking concerned.

'No no, not ill,' Michael was trying to say. 'Please, I don't want to inconvenience anyone . . . I just need a taxi.'

Is Michael going to leave?

The party had heard he was leaving early. After all the rain it was such a beautiful clear evening, with the lovely garden glistening and the daylight ceding to this lustrous moon. Lucy-Rose had just been remarking to herself on the success of her gathering when she received the rumour.

'Already?' she said.

'He's exhausted, apparently. Looked quite ill, said Maggie.'

'Poor man,' said Lucy-Rose, feeling irritated nonetheless.

'Has no wife or family.'

'An eternal bachelor, says Sally. Very nervous.'

'But can't we persuade him to stay?' said Lucy-Rose.

From his corner, Michael heard the general murmur. He imagined what he could not hear, and anyway phrases kept floating towards him, like petals. The garden was full of drifting petals, and each one was about him. 'A sudden turn . . . Too much strain . . . Impossible . . . But really . . . ill? Did someone get a doctor . . .?'

Then Sally was saying, 'The thing is, Lucy-Rose invited the literary editor of the *Observer*. And she may be coming. It's surely worth waiting if you possibly can.' She was standing very close to him, nearly whispering in his ear. 'Perhaps – I know it's a big ask, but these people have gone to a lot of effort. Lucy-Rose has gone to a lot of effort. Perhaps you could lie down in the conservatory for a short while, then you might feel better by the time she arrives. You just need a rest.'

'But I think it might be better just to go,' said Michael. 'Though I don't want to make a fuss.'

'Michael,' Sally whispered. 'Don't be absurd. This party is for your benefit. It's your party. You are quite entitled to make a fuss.'

'Then I think, much as I appreciate all the . . .'

'Perhaps the best thing to do would be to lie down briefly. Take it from me. I'm an old hand at this game. You'll feel much better when you've had a little lie down.'

'Of course,' said Lucy-Rose, stricken with relief. She almost put an arm round the author, but she sensed he was one of those who dreaded social touching, however well-intentioned; so she held back and said, 'You're welcome to lie anywhere. Anywhere you like. Go into one of the spare rooms, have a sleep. We can wake you in a while.'

'Just a quick rest in the conservatory,' Sally was saying. 'That would be fine.'

Defeated by them all, a hostage to their kindness, Michael lay in the conservatory, a pitcher of water on the table beside him, and a copy of Dougie Ascherson's latest collection of verse by his arm. A blanket over his legs, though the evening was still warm. Below he could hear the rise and fall of voices, undulating tones; the drift of petals.

'Naturally reclusive . . .'
   'Did he leave?'
   'I don't know . . .'
   'No, he's just upstairs, lying down.'
   'Sally says he'll come back later . . .'

He was in here, as they cast petals on him from the garden. The drowned man in the conservatory, he thought. What came after death by water? He couldn't think. They would come later, perhaps if the literary editor arrived, and they would fish him out. They would get him on a hook, and then they would reel him in.

He should fling open the window and issue a general announcement. Thank you all. Thank you. Thank you for everything. But I simply have to go. Goodbye.

There was a bellow of laughter. Staccato hoots. Inside the conservatory it was cool and quiet. In a corner, ivy climbing a trellis. Some gardenias in a long pot. He had always wanted a garden. Or a conservatory. The concrete tower he called his home was one of a formidable series, standing like battlements, defending the north from the south. From his outpost he could see the river like a silver serpent and the miles and miles of sprawl. At the base of his concrete tower was a concrete yard, with space for parking. A wall around it, to repel burglars, then a main road and the Victorian terraces, squat and defeated. No room for a garden.

It was important to remember, thought Michael, that no one had begged him to do this. No one had approached him on bended knee, pleading with him to become a writer. No divinity had alighted from a cloud and commanded him to go forth and write. His parents had certainly condemned him – severely, for his own failings and by comparison with his gainfully employed, affluent brother. It seemed absurd now, that he had persisted, all these years, in hating them. He had worked so hard to prove them wrong. And yet now . . .

The moon was shining through the glass. In the moonlit room, Michael knew that it would pass; things – everything – would change and change again. There would be a point when this would be long gone, a past he no longer had to consider.

Time passed.

Lucy-Rose, in her serene vitality, would pass.

Roger Annais, Peter Kennedy, Arthur Grey, Martha Williams, would all pass. Sally Blanchefleur would pass.

And the people who had discouraged him, over many years, and those committed people who had been forced – briefly – to consider him; they too would pass. Even these ideas they were debating, their beliefs in a certain sort of world, all this would most likely pass, as so much before had passed and faded altogether. For who worshipped Ishtar any more, or Attis? Who quaked at the thought of Zeus or the judgements of Osiris? Who invoked the virtues of Cybele or Artemis?

Yes, it was quite certain Lucy-Rose would pass, and so would her garden. Her garden would stand neglected, the wind ruffling the aspidistras, the sun cultivating weeds in the once-manicured flowerbeds. The walls of her house would crumble though tonight they looked sturdy and imposing, and earlier he had leaned against them.

He would pass too. And the mother who had birthed him. Paul Ardache was right: he had untied himself from every knot of obligation or necessity. He would have no wife, no lover, no family. He had fled from so many people who had approached him. Prospective wives, prospective friends, people who simply stopped to pass the time of day; he had fled from them all. He had been left cut off from everything and mistaking this detachment for strength. And what was it he had feared? That someone would need him, that his purpose would be diluted by the demands of others. He had feared all his life that someone would make a claim on him, ask him to live for them as well as for himself.

So he had come to despise his parents, perhaps because they offered him complexity, the confusing array of emotions he experienced when he saw them, love and bitterness and even pity sometimes, as they grew older and more shambolic. He had been dutiful but entirely distant and his mother had set herself against him, told him he had failed, that he was wasting his life. Her questioning of his life, her anger at what he had not done, had seemed to him a dreadful liberty, an intrusion on his immaculate retreat. Really he had failed her, not even because he had been rude, not even because he had hated her, but because he rebuffed her every attempt to know him.

Then he fled from every woman who approached him, when all they offered was love or friendship. He thought of these kindly women, shyly proposing dinner and finding him tickets for concerts and trying to involve him. He thanked them for their labours, perhaps he had gone to a concert or two – but then he departed. With a wave, politely but firmly.

'Are you actually happy?' his mother once said. He thought she was judging him again, finding him wanting in some further way. But he had not seen the truth behind her words. He had hazy images of her, smiling down at him, benign and loving. Showing him dinosaur skeletons in a museum or taking him to play in a park. Lifting him in her arms and kissing him when he cried. Holding his hand as they walked, telling him to mind where he stepped. And when he became an adult and his happiness was no longer within her jurisdiction, she merely asked – had the life she created for him been a good one?

He had turned away as if she had offended him, and he had established his hiding hole, his flat, four walls between him and the mass of desire and love and hatred and confusion. Monastic and – he thought – safe. And he wrote his pompous little books – now he thought they were pompous, as he sat there tracing patterns on the blanket, the moon shining on his hands – they were pompous because they were so preciously sterile, they were the products of his determined sterility. He generated nothing, caused not a ripple, except in writing his books.

All of this sequestering, for his art – as he had called it – and now Michael saw what a flimsy thing that was anyway. Why had he thought he must be pure, untrammelled, in order to create it? How could you communicate meaningfully with others, if you understood nothing of their fears and desires anyway? Because the conditions of life were so unclear to him, he decided to refuse them. He would not muddy his hands until he understood all things, the meaning of all things. The world had found him out, and come to rave at him. They had scaled his fortress and flung open the gates. For if thou openest not the gate to let me enter, I will wrench the lock, I will smash the doorposts, I will force the doors. So said Ishtar, thought Michael, and he shivered, though he was warm under the blanket.

In the garden, the rise and fall. The literary editor had called to say she could not come. Michael heard the murmur, and now Lucy-Rose was saying, 'She's just rather busy with the Lamott story . . .'

In the balance, Michael thought, the things I have done weigh heavily against me. Or the things I have not done. The love I have failed to return. The approaches I have fled. The four white walls of my monastic cell. The locks on my door. Now he was standing in the open air, deprived of his bolthole. And he thought that the years behind him, the years yet to come were inconsequential, in balance with this moment, this moment when the world – in all its imperfection and madness – had turned its eyes upon him. He had been observing it, surreptitiously, secretively, peering out from his hiding place. And now he had been forced to show himself.

Tomorrow, he thought, I must go to her. I will not tremble and complain. I will meet her eyes. Really had I done this earlier, things would have been easier. I would have been less unhappy, and more grateful to those who have tried to help me. Perhaps it was not my brother who ruined this day, perhaps I ruined it myself. Because he saw that the unease he felt about Arthur Grey and Sally Blanchefleur and Lucy-Rose was a response to their engagement, the fact they cared so much about things including him. He could only squint at them through his own personal fog, struggling to discern them.

I have been wrong, he thought.

He should go back into the garden and he should say to them all, 'You must understand in a sense I am guilty. In a sense I am guilty of a crime . . .'

The Tower

Transcripts of interviews with members of the anti-species conspiracy of Lofoten 4a, Arctic Circle sector 111424

Part 2, 1.45–2.45 p.m. 15 August 2153
Interview with Prisoner 730005

At time of commencement the prisoner will not disclose his real name.

Prisoner 730005, your co-conspirator Prisoner 730004 has confessed to everything. She has supplied a very full account of your activities. You will understand that we want to verify her account and to ask you some further questions. For your own protection and that of the species. Your other co-conspirators will shortly be interviewed too.

I have no co-conspirators.

Prisoner 730005, you are aware that, with your co-conspirators, you stand accused of the capital crime of conspiring against the Genetix and thus against the survival of humanity?

I have not conspired against anything or anyone.

You are not here to express your opinions about the justice of the Protectors, Prisoner 730005. The Protectors are very disappointed in you. They fear you have behaved in a manner dangerous to all. What do you say to this?

It hardly matters what I say.

They regret to inform you that while they seek to assess all matters reasonably and dispassionately, your case – and that of your associates – must be considered a crime. We are appointed to discuss with you the precise nature of this crime and to relay information to the Protectors. Do you understand?

It hardly matters if I understand.

It matters to the Protectors, Prisoner 730005. And it matters to us, on behalf of the Protectors. Can you firstly explain to us how you came to be living in the Restricted Area?

I went there when I left Darwin C.

Why did you leave Darwin C?

I can barely remember what I thought at the time. My life in Darwin C has faded from my mind, like a malevolent dream. I only really have clear memories of life on the island.

Correction, Lofoten 4a, Arctic Circle sector 111424. We do not believe that you have no recollection of your life in Darwin C, Prisoner 730005. Please apply yourself to the question.

It's something about . . . I think it was boredom, in the end, a lack of anything – meaningful or joyful. I think the years I spent in Darwin C were so lacking in love, or despair, or any extremity that makes you feel you are actually here, on the planet . . . that they have been effaced by my experiences since then. I just see myself as this distant figure, a nervous man, running through the glass tunnels, processed from place to place, breathing in processed air, glancing up at the dangerous blue skies from time to time. It is as if I am seeing myself from a great distance.

How did you leave Darwin C?

We all left Darwin C. We were a group of friends and we left together.

Who were your co-conspirators?

I told you already, I have no co-conspirators. I am not part of a conspiracy.

Prisoner 730005, we must explain to you on behalf of the Protectors that you are advised to co-operate with our questions.

I will co-operate, but I am not telling you who my friends are.

Ah yes, the pact. Prisoner 730005, we must advise you that your co-conspirator Prisoner 730004 has not been so mindful of the pact and so withholding further information is irrational and futile.

In that case, if this poor prisoner has not been mindful of the pact then you do not need me to tell you who the others are. You can allow me to maintain my sentimental allegiance to our pact.

There is no place for sentimentality here, Prisoner 730005. We will return to this question later. What was your allocated role in Darwin C?

I was an engineer, dealing with environment conditioning units.

Your sector?

Sector 1127.

How did you meet this woman they call Birgitta?

When we were in the crate, leaving Darwin C. I met her then.

You had not met her before?

No, I had only heard of her.

You had heard what about her?

That she would be a mother.

Correction, egg donor. You also adhere to this delusion that Birgitta was carrying a progeny of the species?

It is not a delusion.

On behalf of the Protectors we are obliged to advise you that such words constitute a grave threat to the survival of the species and cannot, for the common good, despite the generosity and forbearance of the Protectors, be permitted.

I do not mean to threaten the species. I am merely telling the truth.

This selfish anti-species delusion was shared by all of your group?

They all saw Birgitta give birth, with their own eyes, yes.

Prisoner 730005, we must warn you again.

I understand your warning. Yet you have also told me to co-operate. So I am trying to co-operate by telling you what I saw.

Are you claiming that you left Darwin C, risking everything you had, casting away the life that the Protectors in their infinite generosity had bestowed upon you, just because you heard a story, a mere myth? This is not logical, Prisoner 730005.

It is not logical, I agree. I was not behaving logically at the time. I had found that logic only worked up to a point. But there were some other factors too. Though I don't think they were very logical either.

What were these other reasons?

Well, the most significant among them was that I had a dream. I dreamed of blood, and drinking blood. Swimming in blood. That is one of the few things I remember clearly from Darwin C. When I woke I realised I had to leave the city.

You attached significance to this random twitching of neurons?

Yes.

You did not seek chemical therapy?

No.

Were you regularly seeking sexual release?

Occasionally.

Not regularly?

I don't really remember. Such loveless liaisons seem tawdry and irrelevant now.

Did you go to the same Sexual Release Centre as Birgitta?

Yes, I went to the Sexual Release Centre where she worked.

Did you seek sexual release with her?

No, I did not.

We will check the logbook, Prisoner 730005, so you should be honest.

As I said, my recollection of Darwin C is tenuous, but I am quite sure about matters concerning Birgitta.

How did you find out about the conspiracy to leave Darwin C?

There was just a morning. A wonderful, extraordinary morning. A friend told me that something had changed and we could never be the same again. I did not understand at first. Then I heard someone talking about an old, neglected idea, the Magna Mater.

What do you mean by this?

We are not entirely sure. But it is a force flowing within everything there is.

Everything there is where?

Everywhere.

You will explain yourself in plain speak, Prisoner 730005.

It is not my place to explain the life force.

What do you mean by the phrase you have just produced?

Which one?

You know precisely what we mean, Prisoner 730005.

I'm really not sure I do.

On behalf of the Protectors, we must warn you against such refusal to co-operate with our inquiry. Do you admit you have desired the ruination of the species? That you have favourably contemplated societal collapse?

I do not desire the ruination of the species.

By leaving Darwin C and going to the Restricted Area, are you saying that you did not desire the ruination of the species?

I did not. I think life is an extraordinary thing. Even in our despairing times, I am grateful to have lived. But my thoughts and desires are not important anyway.

Who is Birgitta?

I do not really know who she is.

You have already confessed that you met this woman. Do not try to deny this now.

I am not trying to deny it. I met Birgitta. I was on the island . . .

Correction, Lofoten 4a, Arctic Circle sector 111424.

. . . with her for many seasons. I know her. But I do not entirely understand who she is.

Prisoner 730005, you will explain yourself in plain speak.

I cannot be plainer, I am afraid.

Do you know this woman called Birgitta?

Yes, in some ways I do.

Who is she?

I cannot tell you precisely.

Why not?

Because it is beyond my powers to comprehend.

Prisoner 730005, you are not co-operating and this will only worsen your position. For your own protection, let us try to understand matters more thoroughly. Your co-conspirator tells us this Birgitta worked at the Sexual Release Centre. There is no one called Birgitta on the data records of this centre. Several women disappeared from the Sexual Release Centre at the same time. We are happy to assume each one of these women is Birgitta and, as we find them, which we shall, deal with them accordingly. For their protection and for the protection of the species. But it will help us, and help these other women too, if you tell us now what Birgitta's real name was.

I only ever knew her as Birgitta.

You are saying you left Darwin C for a woman you had never met and whose real name you did not know?

Yes.

You clearly do not understand how grave the situation is. We are trying to help you, on behalf of the Protectors. But you must be more forthcoming. Tell us about your departure from Darwin C.

I just remember a long journey, and everyone very silent and afraid, and then the sea. The sea, I remember that very clearly. The smell of salt and air.

Who was directing you to Lofoten 4a, Arctic Circle sector 111424?

Our guides.

Who were they?

I do not know.

What did they look like?

I cannot remember. I never saw their faces.

How many of them were there?

There seemed to be many. But perhaps there were not so many after all. It was a very small boat.

Can you be more precise, Prisoner 730005?

I am afraid I cannot.

The Protectors, via us, assure you that it is categorically in your interests to co-operate fully.

I understand that is one way of looking at it.

What do you mean by this?

If I wished to survive and go back to Darwin C, then I suppose it would be in my interests to co-operate. Otherwise, it is not in my interests.

The Protectors will decide what your interests are, and how best to protect you and more importantly the species.

I am sure they will decide for themselves. But I think my interests must be very different from those they decide for me.

Prisoner 730005, we must warn you that such remarks are not appropriate.

I am sure you think they are not.

We know they are not. Where are your co-conspirators?

If you mean my friends, then I do not know. Are they not all here? Have some escaped?

You are not permitted to ask questions. Why will you not tell us, and thereby the Protectors, precisely who was living in the Restricted Area?

I cannot. I promised.

Yes, your pact again. This counterproductive allegiance to an obsolete agreement.

I do not understand what you are saying.

Who was Birgitta's egg donor?

I do not understand this term.

You understand it clearly, Prisoner 730005. Who was Birgitta's egg donor?

I do not know what you mean.

What did you do on Lofoten 4a, Arctic Circle sector 111424?

We lived. We worked. We waited for the birth.

Some of your number died?

Yes, they did.

Who were they?

I cannot tell you.

On behalf of the Protectors we are obliged to warn you again that such a failure to co-operate will stand against you in the ultimate verdict.

I understand. As I said, I am not sure it matters much to me.

We think you will find it does. How did you live?

Those of us that lived, farmed and foraged. It was a hard life but a better one, infinitely better, than the lives we had in Darwin C.

Your egg and sperm donor were from Lofoten 4a, Arctic Circle sector 111424?

My parents, yes.

When did your egg and sperm donor leave?

When they were forcibly taken away.

No one was forced. The arguments for the necessary action to save the species were compelling, Prisoner 730005. You know this, you have had it explained to you many times.

It is what I was told when I lived in Darwin C, yes.

Who is Birgitta?

I already said, I do not know. She is an ordinary woman but then she must be something else besides. Or there is something else working within her. There may be some who have more developed notions of what she is but I do not.

Who are these people who know who she is?

They do not know. They simply have their notions. No one on the island told anyone else what to think or feel. There were no laws that governed our thoughts.

You are mistaken. We live in a universe governed by laws.

The Protectors marshal these laws for the protection of the species. Without these laws, we perish. Will you tell us who Birgitta is?

I can tell you she is a woman from Darwin C. I never knew her real name. I can tell you she has long hair. Or she did, I don't know if she still does. I can tell you she sings beautifully. I can tell you she raises her hands when she laughs. I can tell you her skin is pale and threaded with delicate blue veins. I can tell you I love her. Is this what you want to know?

On Lofoten 4a, Arctic Circle sector 111424, was Birgitta one of your partners in sexual release, Prisoner 730005?

No.

Then why do you speak of her in this way?

Because I miss her. Because I cannot believe it is all over. It is destroyed utterly. The community we established, which we worked so hard to establish, which was founded on love and solidarity, has been burned to the ground. I will never see it again.

Where is Birgitta now?

I do not know. I lost sight of her, among the flames. I cried out to her. But she was gone, and then they seized me. They smashed me around the head and I knew nothing else, until I woke up here, in a cell.

Do you believe that Birgitta escaped?

I only hope she did.

On behalf of the Protectors we must ask you if you want to

be allocated another role in the struggle for the survival of the species, Prisoner 730005.

It is not important whether I live or die.

Take Prisoner 730005 back to his cell.

Transcripts of interviews with members of the anti-species conspiracy of Lofoten 4a, Arctic Circle sector 111424

Part 3, 3.30–4.30 p.m. 15 August 2153
Interview with Prisoner 730006

At time of commencement the prisoner will not disclose her real name.

Prisoner 730006, you are aware you stand accused of the capital crime of conspiring against the Genetix and thus against the survival of humanity?

Yes.

The Protectors are very disappointed in you. They fear you have behaved in a reckless manner, dangerous to all. What do you say to this?

I hope they will one day find true understanding and this miasma that surrounds us will be banished. I hope this for them as I hope for it myself.

They regret to inform you that while they seek to assess all matters reasonably and dispassionately, your case – and that of your associates – must be considered a crime. We are appointed to discuss with you the precise nature of this

245

crime and to relay information to the Protectors. Do you understand?

I understand the plane of existence you are summoning me to recognise and I recoil from its every element.

Your co-conspirators have made full confessions. They have pleaded for clemency from the Protectors. There is a chance this clemency may be granted to them, and to you also, if you all co-operate. Do you understand?

I understand this is what you are saying to me. Whether it has any relation to the truth, to the reality of all things, I do not know.

You will find that we speak truth, for the protection of the species, Prisoner 730006. Can you explain firstly how you came to be living in the Restricted Area?

I was sent there.

Sent there? By whom?

By a force beyond my comprehension.

What force?

I do not know precisely what it is but I believe it drove me out of Darwin C.

You had lived in Darwin C all your life?

Yes, my parents . . .

Correction, sperm and egg donors.

. . . were sent there from their home.

Correction, Lofoten 4a, Arctic Circle sector 111424. How

did it come to pass that you left Darwin C?

I was driven out of the city. My longing for something else –
I was not entirely sure what it might be precisely, but I
sensed I must search for it – caused me to leave. I began to
realise that we had fallen somehow, that we had lost everything that mattered. But I did not know whether I might
regain anything; I just felt I had to get out.

How did this so-called realisation happen?

I do not know. There was a day – I was working as usual . . .

Your allotted role, Prisoner 730006?

The nurture grounds, sector 1127.

You worked with Prisoner 730004?

I do not know anyone of this name.

Your area of specialisation?

I cared for babies.

Correct 'babies' in the usual way for the record. Had you
been harvested as legally required?

Yes. At the age of eighteen like everyone of my generation I
was stripped of my biological right and deprived of joy.

Correction, the Prisoner was harvested and her womb was
closed. How did you meet the other members of your anti-
species conspiracy?

The process was very slow. Of course, we had been taught
to think in an entirely different way, and so we had to unlearn
the previous ways and gradually intuit another sort of understanding. At first we did not really know what we craved. We

were only able to define our desires negatively. We knew what we did not want. That was everything around us, everything we had ever known, and so it was hard to imagine what we did want. If it even existed on the planet. If it remained to us – some of us remembered aspects of our early childhoods, and they were a source of inspiration, these shared memories of something else. But we were fumbling in the dark.

You had been taking the advised doses of hormone re-adjustment?

Of course. No one has any choice about this.

You are arguing that you felt like this despite taking the advised daily dose?

Yes.

We assume you attended Species Survival Courses A, B and C?

Naturally. No one has any choice about that either.

So you were fully aware that your thoughts and subsequent actions worked directly against all the emergency measures currently in place to protect the species?

I was aware that if I was found out I would be condemned, yes.

And you understood that it was necessary for you to be housed in Darwin C in order for as much land as possible to be used for mass-scale farming to support the species?

Yes, that is what I had been told.

And yet you continued with your course of action anyway?

It was as if I was being directed by something beyond me. Stronger than me. I could not resist this direction.

How was your group formed?

Somehow we were drawn together. There was never a point at which we were a group. We were not a society, there was nothing formal. We never met together until we were in the crate. First there was someone and then another, and then someone else and then another. We recognised something in each other. It was an accumulation, a burgeoning of spirits.

How many were you?

I cannot tell you.

Why not?

Numbers no longer hold any meaning for me.

You all had a tenuous link to Lofoten 4a, Arctic Circle sector 111424?

It was our home, yes.

You felt this, though you had never seen it?

Yes.

Who was it that devised the plan to abandon your posts and desert to the Restricted Area?

No single one of us. As I explained, we were drawn into this course of action, by this unfathomable power, this force around us.

You are not being honest, Prisoner 730006. On behalf of the Protectors, we must remind you how important it is that you are honest and precise.

I am telling you the truth as I experienced it. We did not have a leader. No one directed us. Gradually we found a way. We came to understand that we would do these things, that we would risk our lives. As I said, it was as if a greater something was directing our behaviour. It is not precise and certainly it is not like anything I was taught in Darwin C. It was not provable by experiment and it did not conform to any of the established scientific arguments. I am afraid it was all irrational and perhaps absurd, if you subscribe to the world-view of Darwin C and the Protected Area. But that was the thing. We no longer subscribed to this worldview. I cannot be more precise than that.

Prisoner 730006, who is the Magna Mater? Is she this woman you call Birgitta?

The Great Mother . . .

Correction, egg donor.

. . . of the world.

Prisoner 730006, can you answer the question clearly?

She is . . . Well, there is something I remember. A song the guides sang. When we took the boat across the sea. I remember it so vividly, though events of that day are otherwise confused in my mind. Somehow the song imprinted itself on our memories of that strange day and then later we sang it on the island.

Correction, Lofoten 4a, Arctic Circle sector 111424.

Then a storm arose in fury,
From the East a mighty tempest,
And the sea was wildly foaming

And the waves dashed ever higher.

Thus the tempest rocked the virgin,
And the billows drove the maiden,
O'er the ocean's azure surface,
On the crest of foaming billows,
Till the wind that blew around her
And the sea woke life within her.
And the sea woke life within her . . .

What do you mean by this, Prisoner 730006?

It is an old song. I do not know how old.

Where does it come from?

I do not know. As I said, our guides sang it as we crossed, and then we remembered it and sang it later.

Who were your guides?

Well, they seemed to be people, ordinary people wearing rags or tattered clothes but there was something luminous about them, as if they were possessed with unusual grace. I could not see their features because their faces shone. But perhaps I was unaccustomed to the sunshine, the broadness of the sky, the wide-open sea.

Prisoner 730006, we advise you for your own protection not to insult the Protectors with such responses. How did you get from Darwin C to Lofoten 4a, Arctic Circle sector 111424? Please be very careful about how you answer this question, Prisoner 730006.

The mechanisms were not important. The momentum was incredible. When I saw the sea I understood it more clearly.

It was like being washed by a tidal surge. A surge of energy and love.

Once more your answer is meaningless. You understand our questions, we assume?

I understand the individual words but somehow the way they are combined is obscure to me.

What do you mean by this song you sang?

All I can express to you is ambiguity. Gaps and the unknowable. The ancient beauty of things. For me, the song explained some things I had been unable to understand for some time. Or not really explained, perhaps that is overstating it. I never had a sense that anything was truly explained to me. It was all vague inference, suggestion, half-heard harmonies, resonating within me. Something chiming with something else.

This is not a clear answer.

I fear I have lost all this so-called clarity you admire.

What do you mean by this, Prisoner 730006?

Life is very mysterious, to me.

Life is not mysterious. We understand very well how life is generated. This knowledge is central in the struggle to protect the species.

You are wiser than I am.

Of course we are. We speak on behalf of the Protectors, who are most just and wise. Do you also adhere to the delusion of your group, that this woman Birgitta birthed a progeny of the species?

Birgitta brought life onto the planet, yes. It was magical to behold. Impossible, but there before us. Defying everything we had been taught.

You are all deluded. You are suffering from a collective delusion.

Perhaps you are right. It is true, we have no proof, except the evidence of our eyes and our shared experience. And the beautiful miraculous baby who was born to her.

Correction, progeny of the species. There was no such thing, Prisoner 730006. How long has your state of delusion lasted?

My state of joy has lasted for many phases of the moon.

How many years and months?

I do not know.

How long were you living on Lofoten 4a, Arctic Circle sector 111424?

I do not know. I no longer thought in hours or even days or months. The moon waxed and waned. Then again and again. The tides rose and fell. There were hot phases and less hot phases. Occasionally a cooling breeze, those were the most wonderful times of all.

What did you do there?

We lived naturally and so sometimes this stripped us of dignity and hope, as the natural world does, and sometimes we railed against elements we could not control. A storm which ravaged our crops. Rain so hard and thick it swamped the soil. Or the blistering sun, which threatened everything we had worked so hard to cultivate. We suffered, but we were permitted to survive. Something perhaps took pity on us. A reprieve was granted to us, a sort of desperate victory. Imperfect as we were, we were allowed to exist on this beautiful island, and the soil sustained us. Even now, though I know I will never see that island . . .

Correction, Lofoten 4a, Arctic Circle sector 111424.

. . . again, I spend each night looking up at the sky and thinking that it is the same sky, or nearly enough, that hangs above us all. That the ancient rocks and trees, the beautiful mountains sliding into the sea, the fragile mosses and the swirling birds, are all still there, under the sky. That the land will endure, somehow, even as the species fades from the planet.

Prisoner 730006, you are aware that it is a crime to predict the destruction of the species and on behalf of the Protectors we must warn you instantly to desist from such remarks.

I am aware that we are not permitted to contemplate the natural end of the human race.

Prisoner 730006, do you accept that your actions are reprehensible? That such selfish resource abuse cannot be permitted if the species is to survive?

I can be certain of no such thing. I live out my small allocation of years. I love the planet and the circling progress of darkness and light. But I have no knowledge of how my actions will affect anything.

Then you must be guided by the Protectors who act to protect you and the species.

I understand that I must be punished. Within the system established in Darwin C I am a criminal.

Correction, you must be allocated a new role in the struggle for the survival of the species.

I do not mind that. I do not mind dying. Perhaps I wish I was dying among friends and not in this place. But I have lived more fully than I could ever have imagined in Darwin C. Even now I know I have been fortunate. I saw the birth of Birgitta's child.

Correct 'child' for the record. Why do you maintain this delusion that Birgitta produced a progeny of the species?

I saw the birth.

On behalf of the Protectors we must advise you to struggle against these delusions and overpower them.

Why must I?

You are not permitted to ask questions.

Then I cannot understand why I must try to convince myself that something I saw was not the truth.

You did not see it.

You were not there.

We do not need to have been there. It is not possible for a closed womb to be fertilised. We are certain of this.

I do not know what is possible in your world. It is possible in mine.

Our world is your world, Prisoner 730006.

I know that is not true.

It is true. On behalf of the Protectors we ask you again, who is the Great Egg Donor?

From the sea her head she lifted,
And her forehead she uplifted,
And she then began Creation,
And she brought the world to order
On the open ocean's surface,
On the far extending waters.

Wheresoe'er her hand she pointed
There she formed the jutting headlands;
Wheresoe'er her feet she rested,
There she formed the caves for fishes;
When she dived beneath the water
There she formed the depths of ocean;
When towards the land she turned,
There the . . .

Prisoner 730006, you are insulting the Protectors with this nonsense. Will you answer the question plainly?

I am sorry but I can be no plainer.

Why are you singing?

Because my heart is full of life. Even in here, my heart is full of life and my head is full of memories of what I have seen.

Prisoner 730006, we repeat so you understand. You are accused of the capital crime of conspiring against the Genetix and thus against the survival of humanity. You are aware of this?

Yes.

And yet you are singing?

Yes.

Do you want to be protected?

It is not important what happens to me.

Are you a member of a primitive death cult which despises the species and wants to destroy it?

I would never consider myself in this way, though I perceive this is the charge you will use to condemn me.

Once more we must caution you, Prisoner 730006. The Protectors hope to understand your actions more thoroughly. However we cannot afford to be sentimental in our dealings with cases such as yours, lest we imperil the majority. This is a question of billions of lives.

Billions and billions of lives. You are right. There are so many living on the planet. And yet is it not strange that lives commingle, that patterns form, that humans love each other even now, even here. I find this so wonderful. It fills my heart with this absurd and incongruous joy, I cannot suppress it.

You insult the Protectors and all who work to save the species with your words.

Perhaps humanity will cease. Perhaps all the species of animals and plants currently existing on the planet will cease. Yet I believe that life continues. The life of the planet. The life of the universe we still know so little about, for all your assertions. Generation and growth. Whatever you do, something will resist, something will not go to plan, and thereby the cycle begins again . . .

Prisoner 730006, you must be aware that your words constitute a capital crime. We cannot let you continue, for your own protection. Can you answer directly, who is Birgitta?

She is the mother . . .

Correction, egg donor.

. . . of a son . . .

Correction, progeny of the species.

The power is everywhere. That is what the guides said. And they sang:

Any leaf swallowed, any nut,
or even the breath of a breeze,
may be enough to fertilise
the ready mother . . .

Prisoner 730006, why were you on Lofoten 4a, Arctic Circle sector 111424?

Because of Birgitta. Because I could not have been elsewhere. Because even in this world you have tried to strip of mystery, something occurred that was inexplicable and I was drawn to follow it. Because I longed for a true home, a place I could feel – well, like a human, a true, flawed, ravaged, urgent, desiring human. I think that is why but there may be other reasons I cannot comprehend.

Prisoner 730006 will be taken back to her cell. She needs the attention of the Corporeal Scientists.

They can drug me all they like but they cannot change what I have seen.

You are not able to judge your state, Prisoner 730006. On behalf of the Protectors we assess you as mentally incapacitated and in need of treatment. Take her back to her cell.

Transcripts of interviews with members of the anti-species conspiracy of Lofoten 4a, Arctic Circle sector 111424

Part 4, 4.45–6.00 p.m. 15 August 2153
Second interview with Prisoner 730004, after first phase of rehabilitation treatment

Prisoner 730004, we hope you are feeling better after your treatment.

My mind is deadened and I cannot think clearly. I trust this is the intended effect.

We are working to ascertain your real names and identity numbers and soon we will also know the true identity of Birgitta. With these facts we can better protect you and protect the species from the consequences of your selfish species-endangering activities.

I cannot entirely understand what you are saying. My head is swimming in chemical filth. You have poisoned me. Before – there was a before, I know, before this place. Something before – fresh air. The sea. The great ocean. I remember that. There was something – the island . . .

Correction, Lofoten 4a, Arctic Circle sector 111424.

Yes, that is what you call it, isn't it? As if by categorising everything, giving it a number, you can erase the destruction of the planet. It is too late. The Arctic is destroyed,

259

however you number it.

You are wrong, Prisoner 730004. You are ill and tired. You have been starved for some time. During the time you existed in your primitive death cult, you were starving.

I was not starving. I had an abundance of things to eat. My body was enriched by my existence on the island . . .

Correction, Lofoten 4a, Arctic Circle sector 111424.

I am sick now, it is true. They have dosed me so I cannot think. If I could only think – what was it?

Prisoner 730004, do you want to live?

On the island . . .

Correction, Lofoten 4a, Arctic Circle sector 111424.

. . . Yes, if you call it that. On this island you name and number . . .

Lofoten 4a, Arctic Circle sector 111424.

Will you never let me finish?

We are interested in anything you say.

On this island . . .

Lofoten 4a, Arctic Circle sector 111424.

It is impossible to speak! It is impossible to think. My brain is doused. This is what I escaped from! I escaped this deadening of the brain. I did escape, didn't I? Or did I dream? I dreamed of so many things. Was everything a dream? Was Birgitta merely a dream? I think this was her name.

She was not a dream but a real woman who was bound up

260

with your delusions. Birgitta is not her real name but we will shortly trace her and then she will be captured.

My memories are fading in this fog. Where will I be sent now?

You are not entitled to ask questions, Prisoner 730004.

Entitled? What does that mean?

You are not entitled to ask questions. Now we ask you, who was on Lofoten 4a, Arctic Circle sector 111424?

I told you, I would not – I cannot.

You are sick. We accept your words earlier were a product of your sickness. Now we are healing you. It will be better for you if you co-operate.

But you told me you knew. You already know. Did you tell me that? My head is . . .

We will soon know. We are offering you the opportunity to be helpful. The Protectors are inclined to favour those who acknowledge their mistakes and seek to rectify them.

The Protectors. The Protectors are inclined. The Sexual Release Centre, I remember it said, 'The Protectors offer you sexual release.' The Protectors themselves, I used to think. I went there sometimes, when I was young. Of course I did. Everyone goes there. And everywhere, 'The Protectors offer you food and drink' at the dining centre, and 'The Protectors offer you a good night's sleep' above your bed and 'The Protectors offer you an allocated role' above your desk and 'The Protectors offer you a crucial role in the battle for species survival' when you were harvested and closed.

Once again on behalf of the Protectors we must explain that such digressions are not required. Now tell us clearly, who is Birgitta?

In Darwin C she worked in the Sexual Release Centre. She was fucked twenty times a day. Twenty-five-minute sessions, five minutes to wash herself between each person, ten-hour days. A rest day every week. One hundred and twenty fucks a week. No one must see her more than ten times consecutively, lest an attachment develop. She had been working there all her adult life. Her routine was very precise.

Why are you using these base terms, Prisoner 730004?

I was not aware they were offensive to anyone. This is what she did.

We are aware of the procedure at the Sexual Release Centres and how some individuals are allocated roles in this aspect of the struggle for the survival of the human species. We do not require your explanation, unscientific and deliberately emotive as it is.

When we took her away and gradually as she opened up and told us about her work, it became apparent that she was subjected to what – in the old days – might have been called horrible degradation and assaults. That anything was permitted, so long as the client felt sexually relieved by the end. That she was often torn and beaten. That she was not permitted to set any limits at all, because everything was justified as necessary for the survival of the species. For the heightening of morale through sexual release. An important role to be allocated, I believe.

These are lies. The workers at the Sexual Release Centre

find their work fulfilling. This has been extensively proven and calibrated. They are aware that the sexual instinct is a basic human urge, and that if it is not required for procreative purposes then it must be fulfilled somehow, and the Protectors in their generosity understand this. The suppliers of sexual release are performing a useful function in our battle against species extinction, as they know. This enriches their work.

I am sure you are right. Perhaps Birgitta secretly enjoyed being ritually raped and abused . . .

Correction, deployed in the battle against species extinction.

. . . Perhaps she felt that way she supplied more sexual release than in other ways. Perhaps she felt that way she could best serve the Protectors. Anyway that's all I know about Birgitta before we escaped together. That she was raped many times a day.

Correction, supplied sexual release.

We do not know which of the rapists . . .

Correction, seekers after sexual release.

. . . impregnated her.

Prisoner 730004, it is unfortunate that your delusions have proved so resistant to treatment.

You will not find the drugs to rid me of this conviction.

What is Birgitta's real name?

I do not know.

You are aware however that Birgitta is not her real name?

Yes.

But you do not know her real name?

No, I do not.

Why was she given the name Birgitta?

She took it from an ancestor of hers. Her great-great-great-grandmother . . .

Correction, egg donor.

. . . was a woman called Brigid. So she became Birgitta, to us. Brigid was the earliest ancestor she knew of. Those who lived before are no longer known to us. The name of her great-great-great-grandfather, Brigid's husband, has been lost.

Correction, sperm donor. Where was this DNA relative Brigid from?

I believe she lived in the former city of London, but that is all I know.

So how did this egg donor's DNA relatives end up in Lofoten 4a, Arctic Circle sector 111424?

Birgitta's great-great-grandfather, who was I believe called Calumn, went to the Arctic sector when the climate evacuation protocol was announced in London. He was one of the last to leave the city, before the borders were closed. He was an old man by that stage, and Birgitta's mother remembered him weeping quietly as they left the house, which they knew would soon be destroyed. He had lived in the house when he was young, and had moved back in there after the death of his parents. Birgitta's mother told us many stories of how it was to leave London – she was only a small child when they left, but she said the experience was scored across her memory . . .

We are not interested in these stories. Correct instances of 'parents', 'great-great-grandfather', 'mother', 'child' for the record. Once more on behalf of the Protectors we ask you to confine yourself to the facts, Prisoner 730004.

Who are the Protectors?

You are not entitled to ask questions.

I am confused and ill but now I wonder – who are the Protectors?

As we said, the nature of your position makes it entirely inappropriate for you to ask such a question.

But if I had another position?

Your meaning is unclear.

What sort of position would I need . . . my head . . . I wish I could clear my head . . . What position would I need before I could ask such a question?

As before, we must emphasise that the nature of your position makes it entirely inappropriate for you to ask such a question.

But I cannot understand. Why are we all here, you too? When we have passions and old desires and once we had lovers . . .

Correction, partners in sexual release.

... and families ...

Correction, DNA relatives.

... parents ...

Corrrection, sperm and egg donors.

... we loved, children ...

Correction, progeny of the species.

... we loved – we were protected by our parents ...

Correction, sperm and egg donors.

... and we protected our children ...

Correction, progeny of the species.

... we would have died to protect our children ...

Correction, progeny of the species.

... and now we are dependent for protection on – I cannot think it through, it is too clouded ... These drugs make me spill out words, and some of them I do not want to say, some of them are drawn from me by your drugs, but others – these others – what is it you are so afraid of, that we must speak your language? That everything must be processed in these phrases. 'Sperm and egg donors'. What are you afraid of? What menace do the old words hold for you? Why will you not let me use them?

Prisoner 730004, we have explained to you that you are ill and delusional and we are trying, on behalf of the Protectors, to help you, but we cannot permit you to ask questions.

I am merely wondering, though my head hurts and I think they have killed me, have they not poisoned me fatally, it feels as if something is slowly stopping my heart, but I am wondering just why we have to look for protection to these Protectors we do not know and cannot see, who do not hold us or kiss us or tell us they love us they simply offer us protection and a place in the battle and sexual release and food and drink and this is our life this is meant to be a life. Who are they?

On behalf of the Protectors, we assure you that such questions are not appropriate and will not be answered.

Cannot be answered. You do not know. I begin to think you do not know who these Protectors are you work for. You have never seen them? I think – yes, I think it must be true that even you have never seen them. Have they seen each other? Are they bodies and humans or something else? My head, I think you must have killed me. Am I dying and is this where I must die?

On behalf of the Protectors and for the protection of the species, we must advise you that unless you cease such unscientific talk we will be forced to commit you to an Institution for the Improvement of the Reason.

But I have never thought more clearly. Suddenly I see it. All this, everything you believe, it is just a gauze, a film separating you from the real forms of things, and if you could only see, like I am seeing . . . I am seeing something, I am not sure, but it is so beautiful . . . If you could only see it . . . You would understand . . . You would understand you are deluded and you have never thought clearly yourselves. And perhaps you would despise these Protectors, whoever they are. Whatever they are . . . You would understand that there was a time when love was the generating spirit of humanity – I believe it, though you have changed everything – that children were birthed in – through – this prevailing love. And you would perceive what is at least clear to me, that the Genetix is an atrocity because it cannot love and deprives every human born on the planet of this love . . .

Prisoner 730004, for your own protection and on behalf of the Protectors, you must be returned to the medical section and treated.

I no longer care what you do because though I am dying my head is finally clear and . . .

Take her for her treatment. She will be returned later for sentencing. We do not need to speak to her again.

... Look through the Earth ...

Throughout the night, Prisoner 730004 cannot sleep. She paces the floor of her solitary cell and she thinks of how it was on the island, when every night she was lulled to sleep by the waves and every morning she woke to the sound of birds. Simple sounds, which she thrilled to; something within her was stirred by these sounds. And Prisoner 730004 remembers the glowering mutable sky, and the salt sea, and the beautiful wreckage of nature.

Now, she is in a city; perhaps she is back in Darwin C, or somewhere else she has never been before. She can hear the whirrs and grinding of the transport system, and the air-processing units throbbing, expending precious energy in their mission to keep the city habitable, and she thinks she hears landing craft whining above. Beyond, the inhabitants are sleeping and at the allotted hour they will rise and begin the day. Through the covered tunnels they will move, from one sun-protection zone to another, and all the time their lungs will be filled with generated air. And their bodies will cry out at the madness of it all, but the cries will be lost, in the pulsing hum of the city.

Surely their bodies must cry out, thinks Prisoner 730004. And she is drugged, she knows, and her mind will not work properly, so although she cannot sleep she drifts in and out of lucidity, and sometimes she thinks she is on the island, listening to the sound of waves, the wind gusting through the grasses. Then the coldness of the cell recalls her again.

Michael Stone finds he cannot sleep, because his mouth is dry from all the wine he drank, and his head aches. So he rises from his bed, walks into the kitchen, pours himself a glass of water. And he thinks that it does not matter, the dawn will come, he only has to wait. He draws the blinds and sees the city beneath him, the lights shining from successive cars, and the street lights with their sallow glow, and all the diminished motion of the pre-dawn hours.

Michael sips the water and thinks of his heart beating. Below he traces ribbons of light and motion spanning from one stone building to the next. He hears the sirens and the hum of the night. He breathes deeply and thinks of the planet turning in space and time creeping onwards.

Time will creep, and then it will spring the dawn upon him.

Robert von Lucius wakes with a start, and finds he is thinking, 'But what if it is really true?' This theory of Semmelweis, he realises he means. He has considered it until now only as an element in the case of Semmelweis's so-called madness, not as significant in itself. But now he is bolt upright in his bed, thinking, 'What if he is right, and no one believes him?' This thought grips him by the throat, so he feels he cannot breathe, and he rises from his bed and walks through the corridors of his house, his footsteps echoing around the panelled walls. To one side his grandfather gazes down at him, a bastion of propriety, a man who attracted neither censure nor praise. Further along, in another portrait, the judgemental stare of his father, a man with a straight back and a chest full of medals. A fine man, a military man, who once saved the life of a fellow officer. Admired by his troops; by thirty-five he had been decked in glory at the battle of – but Robert von Lucius stops himself from considering the battle honours of his father. His thoughts slide once again towards the asylum and the hunched figure of the doctor. The candle flickers as he hurries along. The corridor is draughty, and he draws his collar up. He does not know where to walk, and for a while he meanders, thinking of what he should do. What can he do for this man, he thinks? Then some time has passed; he finds he is in his study, and he takes a sheet of paper and begins to write . . .

Brigid is awake, though she was promised sleep; after the epidural she would be able to sleep, they told her. They took her in a lift to the sixteenth floor, and she lay on the stretcher, merely relieved that she was here. She was rattled on a trolley, along corridors, and she kept her eyes on the ceiling and breathed. The soft tones of the doctors were reassuring to her. She longed so much for release that she didn't mind the needle at all; she turned her back to the anaesthetist and waited for him to save her. He told her she must be very still when he injected her, and he was about to insert the needle when she felt a contraction beginning. 'Stop stop,' she said, quickly, and he said, 'Just in time, well done.' They waited – the midwife and the anaesthetist, and Patrick with his hand on hers – while Brigid lay on the bed and groaned – a weary, horrible groan which perplexed her though she couldn't stop it – and when the surge diminished she made herself very taut and still, and the needle went in. She remembered the sensation from last time – ice-cold liquid coursing down her spine; like last time it was as if she could feel it trickling along, and then she willed the minutes down – ten to fifteen minutes said the anaesthetist and, though that seemed limitless at first, she willed them down. The contractions faded furiously, she didn't think they would ever submit to the epidural, until finally there was a contraction she only partly felt, and then she found she could breathe normally again. She emerged into an exquisite numbness, her body dulled. The midwife – a new midwife, not Gina, this one in hospital scrubs and with a short bob, less intimate than the other, but kindly all the same – said to her, 'Now you can get some sleep. If you sleep, you'll find you get through transition unconscious, which is a very nice way to do it, and then we'll wake you when we think it might be time for an examination.' She was eager; she lay on her back and waited, but the epidural sent her into spasms; she began trembling uncontrollably, and every time she thought she might sleep she was awoken again by the shuddering of her body. 'Nothing we can do, just a side-effect,' said the midwife, so Brigid stayed on her back, shuddering but not minding it so much. She was simply grateful they had taken away the pain.

For hours she has been lying there, still relishing this absence of pain, despite the violence of her trembling. The night has moved slowly along. Every couple of minutes she feels the distant rumbling of contractions through her body, palpable but not agonising and that is all she cares about. Patrick is asleep in the corner, on a mattress. Brigid can see his arm slung out to one side, and the rise and fall of his body. 'Let him get his rest,' said the midwife, as she covered him with a blanket, patted it down. 'He'll need his strength tomorrow.'

After watching her husband for a while, Brigid closes her eyes. Her body reaches urgently towards sleep but then the shivering begins again. She is shuddered awake by one more spasm, then another, to confirm her body's self-thwarting, its confusion. The clock has moved, but only slightly. Brigid hears the sound of cars, tyres drumming across the bridge, and over the river she can see – if she turns her head she can just see the Houses of Parliament on the opposite bank, and boats moored for the night. Lights twinkling on the water. The city looks soft and tranquil; she has never seen the river before at this empty time of night.

She closes her eyes again, trying to sink into the stillness. The suspense is the worst part, being in the middle of something and knowing that it will end, somehow, but not knowing what the ending will be. The hours will flow along, but Brigid longs to escape them, to accelerate to the conclusion.

She only has to endure.

I must only endure, thinks Prisoner 730004, sitting on her thin bed, and rubbing her eyes. They have drugged her again, and everything is hazy and disturbing; her thoughts have been chemically addled, impaired by their drugs. She despises them, for invading her brain in this way, for pretending this is a cure. And she sits on her thin bed, not really caring to consider the time, because she has so little to gain from the dawn.

Not many more hours, thinks Michael, sitting on his sofa, having glanced too recently at the clock to permit himself to glance again. Today I will see her, after many years, and she will be much changed. She will be lying in her bed. The bed she lay in with my father, who is now dead. And when I have crouched beside her, I will be free to return to this solitary life, to do anything, to live or die, however I please. Only – and now he cannot stop himself, he looks at the clock – a few more hours, and it will be over.

Only a few more hours, says the midwife quietly, to Brigid – seeing that she is still awake – and I will examine you again.

In his study, Robert von Lucius is finishing a letter.

Dear Professor Wilson, it is early in the morning, and I find I cannot sleep. I have been so concerned about the case of Professor Semmelweis. You are a sage and certain man, and I hope you can tell me the answer to this question: what does it mean if Professor Semmelweis is right? I perceive that even if this question is answered it will not necessarily save him from his rages or determine how he should be treated – though that asylum is no place for him, of that I am sure. But what does it mean for the medical profession, for mothers who give birth in our modern hospitals, if Professor Semmelweis is correct, and if he is generally ignored? And what does it mean for our notion of sagacity, of the temperance and fairness of our sciences, if he is dis-missed so roundly, and it transpires he was correct all along? Surely the case must be reopened? Surely someone must conduct a study?

For myself, I find that I must act. As soon as morning comes I will go to the asylum, and talk more to Professor Semmelweis. I feel I must champion this theory because if there is the slightest vestige of truth in it, if adhering to its precepts might save the life of a single woman, then we must – someone must – bring it to general notice again. I will go to the asylum and make sure I understand very precisely what Professor Semmelweis has proposed. If only my library were a little more extensive, it would house a copy of his book. But I will procure one as soon as I can. However, it is more important to talk to the originator himself, as I am fortunate enough to have personal access to him.

Professor Wilson, I will write to you again very soon but in the interim I beg you – so far as your studies and work allow you – to make enquiries about the reputation of this theory in your own country, and to advise me of your opinion on the matter.

Yours ever,
Robert von Lucius.

Now Brigid notices that through the window dawn has broken, and the sky has turned pale blue. Robert von Lucius thinks, at last the morning, and now he can act. Prisoner 730004 sees the light at the high window changing, and understands the day has come. And Michael thinks at least now he can rise – he has recently made one last attempt to sleep, curled up on his sofa, but hopelessly alert and stricken by nerves – and he throws off the blanket and moves towards the kitchen. There, he switches on the kettle and he cuts a slice of bread. He puts that in the toaster and waits for the kettle to boil. Then he pours water into a cup and when the toast is ready he spreads it with butter and jam. Normality, he thinks. All this calms him slightly, though his hands are shaking.

Now I must act, thinks Robert von Lucius, as he hurries into the breakfast room. He pours himself some coffee and takes a bite of a roll. The newspaper has been neatly arranged beside his plate and he glances through it. It is full of news he cannot digest entirely, something about the Emperor on his annual retreat. There has been a scandal at court. Robert von Lucius drinks his coffee down, and feels the warmth in his belly.

Brigid finds she is hungry, her stomach growling a reproach, and she asks the midwife if she can have some toast. But the midwife says they must wait until the doctors have assessed her. 'There may be the need for surgical intervention,' she says, and Brigid feels only disbelief. On the mattress in the corner Patrick is stirring. When he turns towards her, she sees his eyes are bloodshot. He looks tired and as if he hasn't slept at all. But she must look far worse, she thinks, ravaged internally and still awaiting the final act.

Prisoner 730004 is given a bowl of nutri-meal, which she cannot eat. 'Am I to be moved today?' she says to the guard, but he doesn't answer. She has been trying not to think of her fellow islanders, in order that they may stay free of her misfortune and thereby happy, but now she allows herself to think of Oscar, and she hopes he is free, and she hopes that Birgitta and her son are not caught. She hopes they have fled into the mountains on the mainland, or the remaining forests along the coast. There is still land which no one uses, vast tracts of unusable land, of no interest to the Protectors. She hopes they have found the guides there, and can live quietly. Or die quietly, together, mother and son. And now Prisoner 730004 succumbs to tears, and she sits there for a time with her head in her hands, weeping as she has not in years, perhaps she has never wept in this abandoned way, because she thinks there is no real hope, not for her and perhaps not for them either.

This will pass, she thinks, but that does not console her.

Michael holds the phone to his ear, but Sally will not answer. He wants to tell her he cannot come. He must go to the studio, find her there, explain that he cannot speak on the radio. He will make his excuses and then he will catch a train. So he drinks his tea and finishes his toast. Beyond his window, London is rising into life. The streets are filling with cars. The traffic moves, slowly in the morning sun. In his flat, high above it all, Michael washes his plate and leaves his cup in the sink. He looks around his spartan room and does not know what he should take with him. So he takes nothing, except his wallet. He dresses in his suit, which looks a little shabby this morning. He was too drunk to hang it up the previous night, and now it is lightly wrinkled, the collar crooked. It doesn't matter, he thinks. His mother will scarcely notice him.

At the door he turns and surveys his flat, as if recording this ordinary scene: the coffee table strewn with newspapers, the sofa cushions flattened by his weight, the bed unmade in the adjoining room. At this moment Michael stands, in perfect ignorance of the future. He has no sense of foreboding. He puts the keys in his pocket and walks along the corridor to the lift. He presses the button and waits for the lift to ascend.

It is unfortunate, the midwife has told them, but they must wait a little longer. The doctors are on the ward, but they have a couple of other women to assess first. They are called women, not patients, Brigid notes, because of course they are not ill. Swollen and weary, mad with pain or shuddering as the epidural dulls their nerves, but they are not ill. This state is perfectly natural; its conclusion is the birth. Whatever happens, she thinks, it was meant to happen. She is wondering if this is true, as Patrick says to her, 'Is there anything you need?'

'I'm just so hungry,' she says. Patrick looks down at his empty plate. He has – before Brigid's eyes – consumed two pieces of toast, and drunk a cup of tea. Guiltily, he says, 'Hopefully you'll be able to eat something soon.'

'We'll have a better sense of what will happen when she's been assessed by the doctors,' says the midwife.

So Brigid waits. She waits, trembling on her regulation bed. Patrick washes his face in the sink. Cleans his teeth. He takes a book and tries to read. 'Let me know if you want anything,' he says to Brigid. He is sitting on a low chair, trying to read a thriller. Even now, thinks Brigid, as Patrick reads, and as the midwife tidies the room, and as she lies there, inert apart from the involuntary spasms, her labour is continuing, without her intervention or even awareness. Within her body, though she does not notice, everything is changing, the baby is preparing to leave.

She thinks of Calumn, waking in his little bed, wondering where she is. Crying, 'Mamamam.' She has only spent a few nights apart from him since his birth. She wonders if he woke in the night, and if he cried for her and found she had gone. Her mother would have been sleeping in the spare room – she imagines Calumn shuffling along the corridor, opening the door of the main bedroom, finding it empty, not knowing where else to look. Bemused and lonely in the corridor, in his little pyjamas. She should have told her mother to sleep in the main bedroom instead. She hadn't been thinking, at the time.

She says to Patrick, 'Can you call my mother?'

Patrick takes his phone and dials the house. There is a brief pause and then he is saying, 'Hello, yes, it's Patrick here. How was your night? Oh no, no news here. We're just waiting for the doctors to come in and assess Brigid. But she's fine. Well, she can tell you everything herself. Here she is.'

'Darling,' says her mother, as Brigid takes the phone. 'What on earth is happening? You can't still be in labour?'

'I had an epidural. So everything slowed down further but wasn't painful any more.'

'Oh, I'm so glad. That was sensible of you. But what's happening now?'

'The doctors are coming in a moment. Then they'll tell me what stage we're at.'

'How frustrating for you, dear. What bad luck.'

'Never mind. Anyway, how is Calumn?'

'Oh, he's fine. A little bit up and down in the night; I think he just knew something was going on.'

'Did he find you in your room?'

'No, I heard him crying in the corridor.'

'Was he upset we weren't there?'

'Oh, perhaps a little, at first, but then we had a fine old time of it. I took him back to bed and sang him a few lullabies, and he fell asleep soon enough. And then I slept on the sofa bed in his room. So I was there the next time he woke, and – oh Lord – the next. Reminded me of all the sleepless nights I had with you.'

'What's he doing now?'

'He's just having some milk. And we're reading a story.'

'So he's not too upset?'

'No no, he's fine. He's just here. He's a resilient little fellow, aren't you darling? We'll be absolutely fine here until you get back.'

'Can I speak to him?'

'Of course.'

And Brigid imagines her mother holding the phone to Calumn's ear, the phone touching his shining hair, and she says, 'Hello sweetie. How are you? It's Mummy here. I love you so much. And I'm coming back very soon, lovely little boy. I hope you're having a nice breakfast. Daddy is with me and he loves you very much too. We will be back very soon and then we will all sit down together and eat some food and read some books. Won't we sweetie? I love you very very much.'

'Is that everything?' says her mother.

'Did he smile?'

'Oh yes, he knows his mummy, don't you Calumn?'

'Patrick will call you and let you know what's happening, if I can't,' says Brigid.

'Of course, I understand. I've been through it myself. Don't worry about us at all.'

'Thanks Mum.'

'You look after yourself.'

Brigid hands the phone back to Patrick. Her mother, always good in a crisis. A coper, self-determinedly. And Brigid yearns for her son, and wants to hold him and kiss him and hear him babbling lovingly at her, and she worries – once again, once more after all the times she has worried about it already – that he will never recover from the arrival of the other child. But this other child – and she turns to the midwife and says, 'Will it be soon?'

'Oh yes, very soon.'

Michael is on the platform, and the train is delayed. Sally had offered to order him a taxi, of course she had offered, and almost insisted, but he said he wanted to take the Tube. 'Madness,' she said to him, the night before. 'You don't want to be jostled around and probably end up late, do you, really? Arrive puffed out and sweaty, hardly in the right frame of mind? When you could come along in an air-conditioned cab?'

'No no, it's quite all right,' he said to her. She was obliged to accept his whim. 'Whatever you prefer,' she said in the end. 'You're the one who'll be in the studio.'

So he is waiting for the Northern Line, and then he will have to change at Tottenham Court Road.

All around him, thousands of humans, passing through time. Moving at their own pace through the hours and days. Michael looks around at them – at the man with a bulging briefcase, and the woman with a grim fixed expression, as if she hoped for something better, and all those with grey hair and balding heads and potbellies and a few more of their infirmities revealed to the world. A few more hidden away. He knows nothing of their experience of time, though each one has woken to the sunshine and eaten breakfast and conducted their morning rituals, and each one, thinks Michael, lives – though perhaps they do not know it – governed by ancient impulses – a desire for human company, love, intimacy, family, a fear of darkness and the unknown, an aversion to pain, a curious sense of hope, despite everything. Perhaps some of them believe that this series of days – their series of days – will be infinite. Perhaps the repetition has deluded them, so they do not notice the years passing, or perhaps they look up from time to time and see that things have subtly changed, that something in their cycle of days has changed. But maybe they dismiss the thought. Ultimately, he thinks, we must all dismiss this thought, because otherwise how do we live? How do we live through our series of days?

The train is swinging towards the platform, and now it whirrs to a halt, and its doors open. In a swathe of people, a directed surge, Michael gains the entrance, and is deposited into a bright carriage. The train is crammed with bodies, and so he stands and holds onto a rail. All around him people are doing the same. The carriage is full of overheated humans, dressed in work clothes, shoulder to shoulder. But never, thinks Michael, face to face. Some of them are holding newspapers and struggling to read them. These people are hoping to differentiate themselves. But they are buffeted and jostled all the same.

'This is a Northern Line train for Mill Hill East. Stand clear of the closing doors.' It is foolish, thinks Michael, as he is buffeted and jostled in turn, to be too concerned about your own destiny, about the way the Fates toy with you, if they are toying indeed and not concerned with something else entirely. It is foolish to be too concerned, because in the end it is impossible to change things. Small elements might be rearranged, but the grand sweep, well, that is impossible to change. How could I have foreseen anything that has happened, all the events that have accumulated? All the mistakes I have made, the destruction even I have wrought? I was blind, as everyone is who lives within time.

To blame yourself for lacking foresight is perhaps like blaming yourself for being mortal, thinks Michael. You know nothing of the future. The past is unfathomable, stretching into darkness. The present is where you live. And the future – the future is simply the locale of your hope, the place where you deposit your expectations. And your fears too. But for some reason, today Michael feels more hope than fear. He thinks he may be redeemed. If he can go to her and say – something – what it is, he is not sure. When he is there, perhaps he will know.

It must or might be, thinks Michael, that – but now the train is pulling into Charing Cross and the carriage empties and fills again, and Michael is knocked on the back and turns his head round, though he is not angry at all. He just wants to see the person who has collided with him, and it is a woman wearing red, looking urgent and troubled as she leaves the train. She is hurrying down the platform, and now the train moves out of the station, and he can no longer see her.

Robert von Lucius walks through the streets of Vienna, his head bowed. The streets are crowded with people, and he hears the clatter of horses' hooves on the cobbles. Carriages pass him, in a continuous line. He steps aside to avoid a man, and the man nods his thanks. The shops are opening, and the market sellers are setting up their stalls in the square. Von Lucius is hurrying, and the crowds merely irritate him. They are an obstruction, so many people standing between him and the asylum on Lazarettgasse. Between anticipation and action. Though what he will do when he arrives, he is not sure. Much depends on the mood of Professor Semmelweis, on whether he is lucid or raging. Now the cathedral clock chimes above him – he checks his own clock against it – and it is 8.30 a.m.

'Brigid, I am Dr Gupta,' says one doctor, holding out his hand.

'I am Dr Witoszeck,' says the other, younger and less self-assured.

'We are going to examine you, if that is all right?' says Dr Gupta, though Brigid can hardly refuse. She says it is all right. They say, 'We are now beginning the examination,' and they push their hands inside her, one after the other, and then they jot down notes together.

They say things she cannot understand. They speak quickly, using medical terms. Then Dr Gupta addresses her. He sits down – on the chair Patrick has vacated for him – and says, 'The labour has progressed quite some way. You have done very well. However, the baby's head is stuck. It is the wrong way round and so this is making things very difficult for you. I think this is quite a large baby, larger than your first baby. This is why your contractions have been so unproductive, I suspect, because of the size and now the awkward position of the baby.'

'What can I do?' she says.

'We will see if some pushing turns the head. If that doesn't work then we will consider the other options. I'll leave you with the midwife.'

So her baby is stubbornly fixed. They are sending stronger waves of chemicals into her body, making the contractions more forceful even than before. Brigid is positioned; her numbed legs are moved. Upturned, stranded on her back, Brigid sees that her legs have been opened wide, and she becomes aware that she is naked below the waist. She observes this fact, though she no longer cares. Deprived of feeling, her body does not seem to be her own. The midwife says, 'An hour to push. Then the doctor will come back again.'

Outside, the hum of traffic. There are boats moving on the shining river. And the midwife says, 'Now! Push!'

With deadened nerves, Brigid aims to push. Her muscles are asleep, she thinks. The epidural has numbed her body and somehow it also seems to have detached her altogether from her surroundings. From what is really happening to her. She is obeying the midwife, but automatically, as if it doesn't matter any more. And the midwife says, 'That's it! Keep pushing!' and Patrick is there too, saying, 'Push! Brigid, keep going!'

She grits her teeth, only an hour she thinks, from some reserve she must produce a final burst of energy – and she thinks she is pushing though her body has been silenced and cannot tell her what it is doing at all. She hears a deep guttural growl, like an animal, and she knows, though it seems improbable enough, that this sound is coming from her. In her desperation, she is growling like a beast.

And Patrick says, 'Go on Brigid – that's great. Well done! Keep pushing!'

'You should rest for a moment,' says the midwife, and the growl stops. Brigid breathes, tries to understand her body; she listens but all the shrillness has been muffled. Patrick kisses her and says, 'You're doing really well.'

She is given a drink of water, tended to briskly, her brow is wiped, and then the midwife holds up the watch again and says, 'Now! Push again!'

Within her, Brigid feels the suppressed force of a contraction, still tearing her apart, but surreptitiously, so what she registers is something like an aftershock, not the real force and fury at all. She has her eyes on the ceiling, a great lamp is shining down on her, she is the illuminated centre of the room, and so she grimaces and makes grunting noises, as if that will help. She grunts to compensate for the muteness of her body, these silenced muscles she has been dutifully honing throughout the months of her pregnancy, with special yoga exercises. She has been training for the marathon of the birth, and now she is lying on her back, with Patrick and the midwife peering doubtfully inside her. And because there is nothing else she can do, Brigid growls like a beast and bares her teeth, and she hears Patrick saying, 'Come on Brigid, come on.'

She is pinioned by drugs. The midwife's hand is upon her knee, though Brigid can hardly feel it. And in the other hand she holds a watch.

'OK, now off we go again,' says the midwife. Brightly, as if it is a race.

The true horror, the horror I am not prepared for though I have already seen it once, is still to come, thinks Patrick, looking over at his wife, her face contorted, her jaw wide open in a snarl. He thinks of all the effort she has gone to, the months of pregnancy and hauling her belly around, and now this. He wants to put his hands on her, to comfort her, but she is engrossed in her state, and he holds back. Later blood will flow and then there will be the ruined and deflated belly, wrinkled as if aged prematurely, a flap of baggy skin. Patrick remembers this melancholy voided belly, which he loved because it had housed his son, because each silvery stretch mark reminded him of the months of suspense, the eventual birth. And then the gradual recovery, the body slowly regaining shape and definition, though never quite the same as before. But before that, they must pass through the terrifying beauty of the birth – the gory sundering. And now he says, because it is all he can do, and he is otherwise ineffective, redundant otherwise, 'Go on Brigid, push!'

Brigid thinks how impossible this is, how she fails to understand it, how her body is – even the second time, when they lied and told her things would be easy – refusing to release the child. She had never really considered that this birth might be worse than the first. In the midst of it, even as she strains and snarls, Brigid sees what is happening to her and knows it is worse than last time.

And though she can hardly imagine it, her thoughts turn to the child within her, contained in some bony unyielding place, its head trapped, and so she growls and wills her deadened muscles to work.

'Go on Brigid!' says Patrick. Like a nervous cheerleader. 'Go on, you can do it!'

She screams in her effort, a thin shrill scream, and Patrick says, 'Good girl, you're doing so well,' trying to make his voice sound warm and calm, and then the midwife says, 'OK, and relax now.' Brigid lets her head fall back, and she stares at the ceiling.

It hasn't worked. The midwife examines her and makes the pronouncement. None of it – the grunting and straining and even the final cry – has moved the baby.

'Unfortunately, we could be doing this for hours,' the midwife is saying. The allotted hour has elapsed. It is 9.30 a.m. and the baby has not arrived.

'No sign even of the head,' says Patrick.

'No sign at all?' says Brigid.

Dr Gupta returns again, and he feels inside her and says little has changed.

'For the sake of the baby, we cannot extend this any further,' he says.

'The head really hasn't turned?' says Brigid. Incredulously, because she hoped so much it would.

'No, I'm afraid it hasn't. At this point, the only real option you have is a Caesarean,' he says. Already she can see people moving around the room, making preparations. 'Anything else carries a greater risk for your baby.'

'You are certain?'

'Personally, I am certain that the risks of any other procedure are significant,' says Dr Gupta. 'A Caesarean is the safest course of action for your baby, and for you.'

Another doctor appears, with a form for her to sign. Consequences of a Caesarean may include . . . she doesn't read the list. She signs her name, hands the paper back to the doctor. Patrick is beside her, winding his fingers around hers. They have no choice. There is simply nothing else she can do, and now she must abandon her efforts, submit entirely. She is close to tears once more, but she is exhausted beyond measure, flushed with chemicals, hardly in her right mind. There is a distant voice saying, 'Why me?' and she manages to conjure the image of Stephanie, just yesterday, and how sorry she had felt for her, and how certain she had been that this wouldn't happen to her. But it is remote now, she can hardly remember yesterday. Patrick says, 'I'm so sorry, darling,' but he doesn't understand. He assumes she is devastated, he doesn't realise how far she has fallen. Because under it all, the confused pulsing of her thoughts and the insistent rhythmic beep of the monitor beside her, and the doctors murmuring at the door, she has tumbled into a dark secret sense of relief, that it is no longer her responsibility, that someone else will prise the baby out.

'It's over,' she says, and Patrick doesn't know what she means.

Prisoner 730004 is dragged roughly from her cell. 'We must move quickly for your protection,' says a guard. There is another guard beside him, both of them sinewy like trees, their faces wiped of everything except conviction. She sees them plainly before her, and then they open a door and the corridor is filled with light. Dazzled by the glare, she blinks and turns away. Now they are grappling with her, tying her hands.

'For your protection and that of the species,' one of them says.

She is walked along corridors, the doors tightly shut. Door after door, and she thinks that behind each door is another prisoner, and she wonders what they have all done, how they fell under the censure of the Protectors, and how they will be punished. She wonders if any of them will be freed – but that question seems absurd, when freedom is Darwin C. She feels sick and wants to pause, but the men lead her along. They will not look directly at her, they just march on, their boots hammering on the floor, a rhythmic thud, and she is dragged along beside them.

'Where are we going?' she says, after the hammering has gone on for a long time.

'You are not entitled to ask such questions.'
'Will I see my friends?'
'You are not entitled to ask such questions.'

The hammering begins again and the doors are all tightly shut and Prisoner 730004 falls silent, they will not answer her. She struggles on, her grey-faced captors flanking her, their arms rubbing against hers, and she remembers her parents and how they were sent to the mass-scale farms, and how she believed at the time this was a good place for them to go, a pleasant retirement, a gift from the Protectors, and it was only gradually that she pieced the rumours together. Then she was stricken and horrified for many years, because she had been so eager to believe a lie. Because she had waved them off, in her willing ignorance.

Her parents had believed it too; they had gone to the train as if they were embarking on an adventure, and she wonders when they realised – whether they began to suspect something on the train itself, as they were shunted into a carriage with dozens of others, all of them old and frail and clearly expendable – or whether they suppressed their fears until they saw the farm itself. She wonders when they knew they were being discarded, and how long it took them to die.

Prisoner 730004 understands more than her parents did about this world, the world of the Protectors. If they send her to the mass-scale farms, she knows what that will mean. She will be given a bunk in a vast barn, full of others like her, she will be dragged into the domes at daybreak, there to collect the harvest, she will work until the sun drops beneath the horizon, she will receive her allotted

293

ration of food. She will not be murdered, not precisely; she will be neglected and beaten when she fails to work, and her deprived body will protest, it will struggle for survival but it will decline nonetheless. She wonders what happens then – there are many rumours about what happens then – but now she does not want to think any more about the mass-scale farms. She is afraid, though she tries to tell herself that she must not show her fear. The drugs are making her afraid; they are conjuring these memories of her parents. The Protectors want her weak so she will beg for mercy. So she will tell them what they want to know.

But they will send her away whatever she says. Prisoner 730004 strives to remember that, despite the drugs they have fed her. Though the drugs are designed to make her cowardly and penitent, she tries to resist their effects. She must remember, she thinks, that she will not be saved.

The guards slam their feet on the cold floor. They slam their feet and she is dragged along beside them. The smell of the guards is thick and vile; she is repulsed by their bodies close beside her. They have walked for so long, it is a surprise to her when they stop. They come to a sudden halt outside a door. High and broad, and barred against her.

'Wait here,' say the guards.

In Lazarettgasse, Robert von Lucius hammers on the door of the asylum, and for a long time no one comes to meet him. He hears bells tolling in the distance. He hammers again, more loudly. There is another lengthy pause, and then, finally, the face of Herr Meyer appears, but he will only open the door a crack. He seems different today, all his oily charm is gone. It has seeped from him, and he is pale-faced and reluctant. He peers around the door with a sour pinched expression, and says, 'Herr von Lucius. You have returned again?'

'Yes, I wanted to see Professor Semmelweis.'

'I am afraid you cannot enter,' says Herr Meyer, holding up a hand.

'Why not?' Robert von Lucius is prepared to argue, to fight the man; he has come full of resolution and even excitement. He says, 'Come now Herr Meyer, I demand an appointment.'

Herr Meyer says, perhaps less sour now and merely frightened, though prepared to deny everything, 'Herr S is dead. He died in the night.'

And though his mind is suddenly blank, his thoughts erased by shock, Robert von Lucius hears himself saying, 'But how? How did he die?' He sees Herr Meyer working his mouth, forming a lie, he thinks. Even as Herr Meyer forms his lie, Robert von Lucius feels a great surge of rage as if he would like to strike him down.

'He clearly had a degenerate condition. It festered internally and finally killed him,' says Herr Meyer.

'I do not believe you,' says Robert von Lucius. His body is tensed with rage, and with the effort of suppressing it. Yet he tries to speak slowly and clearly. He says, 'Professor Semmelweis told me he had been beaten. He said he believed he had internal injuries. He was a doctor, an esteemed doctor. He diagnosed himself . . .'

'Herr S was insane. This means anything he said cannot be considered,' says Herr Meyer, abruptly.

'You are wrong. He died because he was savagely beaten. I am convinced of it. His death was avoidable. If you had treated him as a suffering human and not as an animal, he would have lived . . .'

Robert von Lucius stops talking. He understands that it is pointless to say anything to this man, this torturer, who thrives on pain and despair. And he is aware of something else, a horrified recognition that this is what he feared. He might have averted it, he thinks, if he had acted sooner, if he had allowed himself to act on his fears. So his rage is mingled with self-reproach, and he clenches his fists.

'He was a violent madman,' Herr Meyer is saying. He is puffed up with indignation. Robert von Lucius wonders if the man truly believes, if he believes and does not doubt himself, that he has done nothing wrong. 'We restrained him in the only way possible. Otherwise he would have been a danger to himself.'

'You are a murderer,' says Robert von Lucius. 'You have killed this innocent man, and thousands of women will die because of your actions.'

'You should leave now,' says Herr Meyer. 'Before I call the guards.' And now he slams the door, and will not open it again, though Robert von Lucius breaks his knuckles hammering on it.

When he finally realises that this door will not open, Robert von Lucius turns away, head bent, stricken with a terrible dark guilt, that he saw the suffering of Semmelweis and did nothing. The man is dead, he thinks, and I planned to speak to him today, to understand him further. I planned to help him, but I have arrived too late, and my plans do not matter now. The man is dead and we shall never speak again.

He thinks – though he tries not to, but he cannot repel the thought – of Semmelweis dying alone in his cell, the fetid dungeon they cast him into, dying in darkness, deprived even of the light of the moon.

Robert von Lucius turns with his head bent, and walks back down the hill.

Heads bent, the prisoners are pushed into the room. Prisoners 730004, 730005, 730006, 730007 are pushed into the room, and they nod their recognition quickly, not wanting to incriminate each other.

Prisoner 730004 lifts her head and sees before her the servants of the Protectors, called Protection Scientists. Half a dozen men, hard and vital, the beneficiaries of intensive courses of gene therapy. They are the elite guardians of this civilisation; they act to protect the species – their actions justified by this aim. Their lofty phrases, all those phrases they threaded around her, as they are threaded about Darwin C, woven across a thousand walls – they believe them all, coldly, rigidly. To Prisoner 730004, they look alike, as she glances at their faces one by one – her glance rushed and nervous, because she knows they have come to condemn her. Perhaps she thinks they are alike because their faces phrase the same attitude of mind, this absolute conviction. Nothing will shatter this conviction, she thinks, as she scans them with her weary eyes. They do not look at her. The Head Scientist – taller and sterner still – appears among them, wearing a grey robe. He is old, but he has been repeatedly rejuvenated, his cells replaced; he is a hybrid, an ageing body filled with borrowed life. Now one of the Scientists says, 'Line them up.' And the guards obey them. Prisoner 730004 can barely stand, fear has softened her limbs, but a guard grabs her and she is lined up anyway.

Another Protection Scientist says, 'We regret to inform you, Prisoners, that you have been found guilty of conspiring against the survival of the species, and therefore you will be processed and conveyed elsewhere.'

Involuntarily they gasp. Elsewhere means the mass-scale farms, or an Institution for the Improvement of the Reason. They will be dispersed; there are innumerable such places. Prisoner 730004 looks at Oscar, sees he has been numbered 730005, and she wants to fling her arms around him, weep with him – but her hands are tied. His eyes are on the floor; he looks too shocked and broken to raise his head.

'You should be grateful for the compassion and clemency of the Protectors,' a Protection Scientist is saying. 'In other, less advanced civilisations your crimes would be punishable by death.'

'There is something else,' says another of the Protection Scientists. Very slowly, enunciating his words clearly, so there can be no mistake, he says, 'Your co-conspirator, the egg donor you called Birgitta, has been found. The Protection Agents tried to protect her, but she died in the struggle.'

'She has been killed?' says Prisoner 730004, too horrified now to stay silent. She sees Oscar slump forward as if a weight has fallen on his back, and for a moment she closes her eyes. It is too much to imagine. The death of Birgitta and the destruction of everything they loved. It is too much and she no longer cares what comes, her fears have been drowned by a limitless wave of grief.

With her eyes shut she hears Prisoner 730006 saying, in a voice barely above a whisper, but somehow she is phrasing the words, 'You have done an abject and evil thing. You have committed a terrible crime.'

'Birgitta was the criminal,' says one of the Protection Scientists.

'You are all the criminals,' says another.

'You have killed an innocent woman, whose only crime was to birth a child,' says Prisoner 730006, in her frightened whisper.

'There was no progeny of the species,' says the Head Scientist, who has been silent until now.

'What do you mean?' says Prisoner 730007.

'Birgitta was found alone. There was no progeny of the species with her, nor anywhere in the vicinity.'

'There was a child. A beautiful boy child,' says Prisoner 730006. And now she is raising her voice, she is looking directly at them, these Protection Scientists who have discarded compassion. 'You are lying and you have killed Birgitta's son.'

'So both Birgitta and her son are dead,' says Prisoner 730005, and now he falls to his knees, and the guards raise him again roughly and force him to stand.

'We found no progeny of the species,' says the Head Scientist again. 'We found no progeny, because there was no progeny.'

'You are evil men, you have killed a mother and her son,' says Prisoner 730006.

'For the final time, we tell you there was no progeny.' The Head Scientist is emphatic. He is stating what he believes to be the empirical truth. There is no emotion in his voice; he does not need to persuade them.

His words hang in the silence, and then Prisoner 730004 says, slowly, 'You are right, there was no child.'

The other Prisoners turn to her, stunned by her words.

'What do you mean?' they all say to her. 'There was a child. You know there was.'

'No,' says Prisoner 730004, and now she looks at them urgently, willing them to understand. 'We were wrong. We were deluded. I see it now, now the true light of reason has shone upon my clouded thoughts. There was never a son.'

'What are you saying? Why are you denying everything that is true?' says Prisoner 730007.

'There was no son,' says Prisoner 730004, flatly, as if she has finally apprehended the truth. The facts, she thinks.

And Prisoner 730005, who understands, though the others do not, says, 'Perhaps you are right. Perhaps – now the fog is lifting – perhaps you are right. There was no son.'

'There was a son,' says Prisoner 730006, ravaged by despair and now believing they have betrayed her. She shakes her head towards them. 'You are both lying, and it is too late even to save yourselves. What is the purpose of your lie?'

Prisoner 730004 says again, 'There was no son.'

She bows her head. Within her bitterness and all her fear, there is something else, something like hope, fragile and perilous, but fluttering within her.

Brigid is being wheeled along a corridor, confused and prostrate. Lights pass above her, and she closes her eyes. Patrick has disappeared, she doesn't know where. They said he would come back soon. When she turned her head wildly, and asked where he was, they said she mustn't worry. 'You just lie back and everything will be taken care of,' someone said, though she couldn't see them. Now they are turning a corner, the doctor is hurrying past her. A nurse is at her side, saying, 'It's fine, dear, we're almost there,' and they are moving down another corridor – all these closed doors, thinks Brigid, and each door represents a mother in pain, birthing a new life – and then they are at the entrance.

'Here is the theatre,' says the nurse. 'We'll get you in and get you ready. There's nothing to worry about.' The doors swing open, and all Brigid can see is a new glare, a still more intense and burning light. It is going to happen here, in this over-lit white room – she can hardly see what is in there; she is screwing up her eyes against the light.

When Michael arrives, Sally Blanchefleur is standing outside the studio. He sees her before she notices him, and though she is angular and beautiful, tapping a long finger on her phone, he feels sorry for her, that she will have to make excuses for him once again.

'I was so worried, Michael, I thought you'd never arrive,' she says, quite sternly, and he knows he must be plain.

'I am so sorry,' he says. 'It is my mother. My mother is unwell. I have to go to her now. I cannot speak on the radio.'

She is staring at him in disbelief, now, her hand to her cheek. He sees her eyes, thinks there is pity in them, but anger too. 'Sally, I am sorry to have caused you so much trouble.'

'Michael, it is not that. Your mother, you say. I thought you never . . .'

'I will write to the producer myself. Say how very sorry I am, about it all. I know that doesn't really help . . .'

'They will understand. If only you'd told me – how long have you known?'

'Not long.'

He knows he has wasted her time. And she had come out to support him. 'Sally . . .' he says. But she puts her hand on his arm, strokes his sweaty shirt. She says, 'Michael, it really doesn't matter.' Though he has been a fool, he thinks, perhaps she has understood him anyway. He nods to acknowledge it, flushed and almost elated. 'Call me when you can,' whispers Sally, and turns away.

He sees that the sun is shining, that the day is fine and bright. The sky is a perfect brilliant blue.

Robert von Lucius stands in the sunshine thinking that it is a fine day – the richness of the light, a gentle breeze unfurling along the street – and he wonders what he should do with this fine day, marred so entirely by the news he bears. The guilt he must endure. He stands in the square with the cathedral clock chiming above his head. The noise of people all around him, and the ordinary clattering of horses' hooves on the cobbles. Something terrible has occurred, he thinks. And no one will acknowledge it.

Under the clock, Robert von Lucius thinks it is necessary to do something to repair the reputation of this man, as he failed so abjectly to help him when he lived. He was too hesitant, and now he has missed the chance to save a life. Yet something remains. The work is not lost. It is perfectly necessary, thinks von Lucius, with the breeze on his face, that I prove the theory of Professor Semmelweis, if I can. That I disseminate it more widely. For someone must believe it, he thinks. There will be someone who understands.

Patrick has come back, dressed in a surgical gown, and Brigid cannot look at him, because she is so afraid. He is like a figure seen in a nightmare; at one level familiar but troubling in his strange clothes. He holds her hand, standing beside her. He says, 'Are you OK? Brigid are you OK?' But she cannot speak to him. The doctor says, 'There will be an incision and then you may feel a tugging sensation. Everything will happen very quickly. The baby will be taken out and then he or she will be checked and warmed up a bit. Then you will be able to see your child.'

'Can Patrick hold the baby, until I can?' says Brigid. With the doctor she is trying to sound businesslike. She suppresses her fear and it is only when she feels Patrick's hand upon hers that she wants to beg them to change everything, to do something else.

'Of course he can. We'll just have a quick check, and then the baby will be handed over to its father,' says the doctor.

'Don't tell me what is happening as you go along,' says

Brigid. 'I don't want to think about it.'

She doesn't want to see the knife. Her skin, torn apart. She doesn't want to see them ripping through her flesh.

But Patrick, standing with a clear view of the naked body of his wife, sees it all. He sees the doctor holding the blade. With a practised movement of his hands, he presses it to the skin. The great belly is to be punctured, thinks Patrick. The knife sinks in, and blood begins to flow.

Michael has the money ready before the cab stops; as soon as he is out he starts to run. He thumps his feet upon the paving slabs, hears bells tolling in the distance. He feels free, now, as if he has been released from diffidence. He has not run this fast for years. At the station he rushes to buy a ticket, slaps money into the hand of a person he doesn't see. Everything is blurred around him, until he focuses on the train he must catch – it is not far from him, though the clock says it is about to leave. So he runs again, stalled by metal barriers, scuffling from side to side, and then he hurries up the steps to the door and turns the handle.

The door does not open. He twists the handle again, hammers on the glass. 'Let me in,' he says. 'Please can you open the door?'

He hammers still – he does not understand why the door will not open. Then he hears a whistle, and someone is saying, 'The train is about to leave, step down sir.' He turns towards the voice, says, 'Can you not open it?' Hammering still on the glass. 'Please. You must open the door . . .'

There is a pause, then Michael hears a sigh of frustration, and the guard hurriedly twists a key in the lock, pushes him onto the train.

'It's your lucky day, sir,' he grunts, and slams the door behind him.

A few people look up as Michael walks through the carriage. Perhaps they heard the commotion at the door. They look him up and down briefly, then turn back to their phones and papers. Staring out of the window at the receding girders of the station, Michael tries to catch his breath. He feels glad, simply because he made the train. Though he is breathing heavily, though his heart is pounding in his breast, he smiles to himself. He looks down at the moulded plastic of his tray table, thinks that he should get a coffee, something to eat. He has a couple of hours to kill, and then he will see her. James will be surprised that he has come so soon. His mother will be in her room, frail and wild-eyed, unkempt, half-mad with age.

He wonders what happened on the radio, how they explained his absence. It was fairly certain his book was going to dive anyway. It was falling like a wounded bird; the descent was making him ill. He thinks of how he spent his launch hiding in that conservatory, because the swiftness of the descent was giving him vertigo. Perhaps it was nothing more than that: a sort of dizziness, caused by the gulf between his dreams and the reality around him. His expectations, popping like balloons as he descended. Still they had been kind, they'd tried to cushion his crash landing. Sally especially – he must do something to make it up to Sally. He's feeling sick and slightly faint, but it must be the effects of that spiralling sense of vertigo. He has fled from the scene of his embarrassment, he's getting further away with each minute.

His imagination has failed him, and he can think of nothing he must say to his mother. No fine words, nothing to soften the anticlimax of his arrival. He will be obliged to repeat back to her what she said to him. Good luck. She needs it more than he does. 'Good luck,' he says, under his breath, so no one hears.

Torrents of blood, thinks Patrick. So much blood. It seems impossible that anyone could bleed this much, and not be dead.

'Is it OK?' says Brigid, so he swallows and says, 'Yes, all going fine.'

The doctor is grappling inside his wife. His hands are delving deep inside her. As if he is searching for something. And the blood is thick and red on his hands, viscous and strange. Extraordinary, thinks Patrick. He thinks he might faint, but then he is mesmerised by the sight of the doctor's grappling, and now he sees a foot. There is a tiny purple foot, in the doctor's hand. Then a leg follows. The baby is appearing, part by part. It looks crazy, to Patrick, as if Brigid has been filmed engulfing her young, and now the tape is being played backwards. It is grotesque, and yet Patrick cannot avert his gaze. His child is almost here, though it looks dead, as the doctor drags it roughly from Brigid's body. It must be dead, thinks Patrick with a sudden sense of panic, it is so listless in the doctor's hands. And he wants to cry out that the baby has died, the blood has drowned the baby, but Brigid says, 'Is it OK?' again and the doctor says, 'Yes the baby is almost out.'

Headless, like a mutilated doll, the baby is half inside and half outside, the cold air on its body, and Patrick feels a sense of pity for this tiny thing, ripped from the womb, the only place it has known. The doctor is delving for the head, and with a last tug, the baby is whole.

Purple and motionless in the doctor's hands.

'It's out,' says Patrick.

The nurse has taken it away, and he hears the first screams, shrill in the sterile room. 'Is it OK?' he says to Dr Gupta. The doctor nods. 'All is fine. You'll have her back in a minute.'

'It's a girl?' says Brigid.

'Yes, a fine girl,' says the doctor.

And suddenly the baby is pushed into Patrick's arms, and he is stunned by how vital she seems, though she looked so fragile before. Now she is like a wild slippery monster, screaming with her mouth wide open and her eyes closed.

'Darling,' says Brigid, looking up at the baby. 'My beautiful darling.'

Patrick cradles the child, says, 'There there, sweetie. There there, it's all OK. Everything will be fine.' He has the child in his arms and now he sees his wife craning her neck upwards. He lowers the baby towards her. 'Can you see?' he says to her.

'Oh, yes, she's wonderful. You're so wonderful, aren't you? Don't cry darling, Mummy and Daddy are here,' says Brigid. And she holds her daughter's hand. The tiny wet hand, covered in blood and vernix. The baby is being wrapped in a towel, but Brigid holds her hand and won't release it.

Worth it and over, what it cost, thinks Brigid. Worth everything. The tugging sensation is over, there is no pain and she hardly remembers the night. She thinks of Calumn and how it was when he was born. She remembers it so vividly now; scenes she had forgotten come pouring into her mind. Her son, she thinks, who she loves beyond measure. And now this girl, this beautiful little girl – Brigid is crying as she holds her daughter's hand, and Patrick sees her crying and thinks, my extraordinary wife, and the children she has created. He is overwhelmed with joy, and relief, that it is all over, that their children are in the world. Safe and with them in the world.

The baby's cries are fading, as Patrick strokes her and kisses her and says, 'There there, everything is OK. I love you and everything is OK.'

'I will always love you,' Brigid whispers to her daughter. 'I will always love you, for ever and ever.'